The Bandalore
Pitch & Sickle
Book One

THE DIABOLUS CHRONICLES

D K GIRL

The Bandalore © 2021 by Danielle K Girl
Cover Art by Deranged Doctor Design

Edited by **Inspired Ink Editing**

ISBN: 978-0-6453274-1-0

CHAPTER 1

S ilas Mercer was dying, and sinking ever deeper into a watery grave. Endless torrents of bitter, cold fluid breached his nostrils, tearing at his throat and making their way deep inside him. The liquid filled him to the very brim, weighing so much as to make it impossible to pull himself upwards, towards that minuscule pinprick of light that taunted him.

Was it the sun that lessened above him? Or was he not so alone as he imagined? Perhaps, by some miracle, a rescuer peered into the oily depths in search of him. Wherever those depths may be. How befuddled his thoughts were, how confused his sense of place. How had he come to be here?

Help me.

His cries bubbled around him. His lungs ached with a ferocity that felt certain to crack his ribs. He kicked and flailed, struggling to raise arms of lead and reach in vain for the fading light. Ever downward he travelled, where the darkness was ripe with unseen horrors. The pressure grew upon him, threatening to shatter his skull. A dull throb cursed him all the while, an ache at his temple he did not dare explore for fear of finding his bone cracked.

The air, what little of it remained, fled his lungs entirely. And the darkness consumed him, pressing his lids tight against the softness of his eyeballs.

A moment, an hour, a day or a year passed by, and at last his eyelids lifted.

He lay upon his back. The darkness had not fled, but the fiendish waters had done so. Silas sucked in a breath of such magnitude he felt as though he might take in all the air in the world. Releasing an anguished, haggard cry, he threw out his arms – and found a fresh enemy. Barely had his arms left his sides and they were halted by a solid barrier.

Dear god, not this.

He kicked his feet, only to find he could barely raise them more than an inch. Fear burrowed beneath his skin and made its prickling way about his body. Blind, Silas pressed at his surrounds and found them all too wanting. He lay in this confounded box yet again, a space that offered only the merest of movement. No matter that he recognised the illusion of the mind that trapped him here, his terror could not be stemmed.

The scream tore its way from his core and dug its claws into his innards, bursting from his mouth with all the force of the terror that had birthed it.

Words tumbled from him. 'Help me! Help me!'

Silas rocked and punched with all the might he could summon, his cries thrust back at him in the confined space, punishing his ears. He was dizzy with panic and desperation. The strangest jangling of a bell came from a distance. What new hell awaited him? The sound was alien to the sharp edges of this old memory. He dared still himself a moment, and was plunged into a silence so deep that he could not bear it. He rocked and punched and kicked anew. But he fought a stalwart enemy. One that did not yield no matter the assault he levelled at it. His energies deserted him, his strength growing as weak as his cries.

Blast this infernal torment, this mindful horror that took him so. When would these memories leave him in peace?

When he at last lay still, sobbing into the darkness, he heard it. A thud above him. Followed by another, and another, so rapid in their succession and clear in their source. Someone dug for him.

A blazing desperation overtook him, and he shouted and punched and cried out: 'I'm here, I'm here, I'm here!' His voice, so terribly overwrought and cracked, could barely form the words at all. 'Here, here. Here!' He sputtered and gasped.

The next thud was right above him, aimed at the barrier that held him from the world. Hot tears pricked at his eyes, burning their way free.

'Fear not, my lad. We'll soon have you upright again.'

How heavenly that voice sounded. Silas's cries hacked at his chest. Blessed salvation had arrived at last to drag him from this nightmare.

The world lightened. The air was cool and caressed his skin like the very feathers of a lover's fan. A silvery light was gentle against him, but his fragile eyes squinted through his tears. Silas sucked in a new breath. The rich, dank scent of turned earth embraced his tortured nostrils.

'Welcome back, dear chap.' Sweeter than honey, the voice was a balm like no other. A face as round as the angelic moon appeared over him. A full-cheeked elderly man of Oriental persuasion, his familiar smile set in place. He had arrived at last to drag Silas free. 'Do take it easy. Death does take a toll on one.'

But Silas would spend not one more moment in these confines. With a raw sob he launched himself out of his grave, clawing at the rise of earth about him, pulling himself ever higher. His fingers found the coarseness of the rope and clung to it. The jangling of the bell returned once more, not a figment of his burdened imagination at all but clear and crisp upon the air.

'Do let go of that rope, dear boy. You'll wake the rest of the dead.'

The amiable man's request was made politely enough, but Silas would no sooner let loose the rope than he would lay back down in his coffin. Along with the frantic ringing of the bell came the animalistic sounds he made as he clambered back into the world, guttural grunts and hisses mixed with rib-snapping sobs. How he loathed this moment most of all, when fear had rendered him more beast than man. His entire body shook so hard that his teeth rattled in his head. He released the rope and threw himself at the only other fixture of substance he could locate. A simple wooden cross, standing tilted at the head of his grave. Not a marking upon it. No name. No note of the date his fate had befallen him.

'Mr Mercer, calm down now.'

This voice was new and foreign and most certainly female. But he cared little for it at the moment. Silas had only one purpose. To be free of his grave. The tingling of the bell grew more chaotic as he scrambled from the earth. His fingers found the hard edge of something above him, curling like raven's claws upon the coolness of metal.

'Silas, Silas, whatever is the problem?'

He threw his elbows up against the woman who sought to stay him. 'Unhand me, I'll not be buried again.'

'Of course not, you foolish dolt.'

He could not see her amusement, his eyes blurred with tears, but he heard it well enough, bubbling her words.

A shape appeared before him, and Silas bared his teeth. He'd be stopped by no one. 'I said unhand me,' he cried. 'Stop her, Mr Ahari. I beg of you.'

Where the blazes had the old man gone? His saviour had left the job undone this time.

'Right, that is quite enough, Mr Mercer.' A sudden blow struck at his cheek. A stinging slap that snapped his head aside.

He blinked, his breath coming in shudders. The world trembled and revealed itself anew. No more did the malodour of the earth fill his scenes, rather it was the richness of jasmine upon the air. Silas found himself on his knees, the softness of the earth replaced by the hardness of a wooden surface. The air was pleasantly warm, not tinged with the chill of the midnight hour as it had been that awful night.

'Mr Mercer?' The woman spoke once more, her voice as soft as a summer breeze. 'Are you quite all right? Can you hear me?'

He nodded, somewhat numbly. His hair was damp, drips glancing off his shoulders. He wiped a hand across his eyes. His face was slick with moisture.

The graveyard was certainly gone. That night's memory chased away once more. But it was not his bed he found himself in as was normally the case, waking in a flood of sweat and twisted sheets.

Instead he knelt in the parlour room of his cottage, the small accommodation he'd come to think of as home these past strange weeks. The fire crackled away cheerfully in the hearth, lit candles adorning the windowsills, his favourite armchair sitting empty and waiting.

'Mr Mercer?'

The woman who had very likely struck him knelt beside him. Her midnight-blue gown, trimmed with black lace, pooled about her with the fabric almost touching his knees. The skirt was marked with dark patches where dampness clung to the material.

'Jane,' he croaked.

The woman nodded, the golden tone of her skin warmed by the glow of the fire, the dancing light catching at the jewels about her slim neck and weighing down the lobes of her ears. Heavy also was the waft of jasmine, for wherever Jane went her perfume dominated.

'Well then,' she said quietly. 'It seems bathing does not sit well with you.'

'Bathing?' He frowned.

She fluttered a hand towards him. 'You can probably release the bath now.'

He turned his head. A copper tub sat alongside him, steam still rising from the waters within, though those waters were indeed rather low. He still clung to the curled lip of the bath, fingers aching, knuckles white. The floorboards about him were drenched, the edge of the rug beneath his favourite armchair saturated.

All at once his jumbled thoughts cleared. 'Oh my goodness.'

His hands flew to his lap, where his manhood lay nestled between his broad thighs, on glaring display. Silas was entirely naked.

'You have gone quite red.' Jane rose to her feet with a coy smile and a rustle of silk. 'But no need to be so abashed. It is hardly anything I've not seen before. I tended you in those first few days after you arrived at Holly Village when you could do little but sleep. And I assure you, you've nothing at all to be ashamed of. In fact if I were you, I'd be showing off that splendid body every moment I could.'

His face burned. He'd not known it was Jane who had nursed him through those first confusing days, and the knowledge did not sit well with him. He scanned the room in desperate search of a covering. A towel was draped over the second of the armchairs in the room, a creaky leather chair that he did not favour.

He coughed. 'Could you please pass me the towel, Miss Handel?'

'Of course.' Jane's gown whispered as she moved, at a pace far too slow for Silas's liking. 'Are you quite recovered? That was a rather bad turn you took. I feared you were going to break a bone, you scrambled so madly from the tub.'

Silas swallowed, recalling it all too well now. Dipping his toes into the water, sinking his body into the depths. Curling his knees up to his chest so he might submerge his head beneath the surface.

The wave of panic that rose up to greet him as the liquid covered his nose and mouth.

'I...I drowned,' he whispered.

'There was no chance of that.' Jane smiled, and what a fine smile it was. 'You could hardly fit that grand body in the tub as it was.'

'No, no. Not here.' Silas stared at the puddle surrounding him. 'I believe it is drowning that sent me to my grave.' He could still feel the burn of the water against the back of his throat, the thunderous beat of his heart, the glimmer of light above that taunted him as he sank ever deeper. 'It came before the other memory this time. I saw my grave, as always, I saw Mr Ahari release me from it. But first I drowned.' He bit at his lips. 'Is it possible I could recall such a thing?'

How he hoped he would never recall it again. Every inch of his being recoiled at the mere thought. If his recollection were indeed a moment of his forgotten life, he prayed it would never haunt him again.

'Anything is likely possible, though Mr Ahari is the only one who would know for certain.' Jane returned to his side and draped the towel gently across his shoulders. He shivered, the heat of his exertions abandoning him. 'It must have been a dreadful recall, you were ever so consumed with fear.' She rubbed at his back, and he leaned into her. Jane was his solitary companion in this place, and since the moment Mr Ahari had introduced them Jane had brought a sense of calm to Silas's chaotic world. Her smile soothed him, and her perfume left him light-headed with ease.

'When do you think I might see him again?' Silas said. His saviour. It was impossible to think of the round-faced gentleman who had dug him from his grave without a peculiar reverence.

'Oh goodness, that is impossible to say I'm afraid. Both he and the Lady Satine work to no-one's schedule.'

'Will he not wish to hear of tonight's business?' Silas clutched the towel to him, not certain he was entirely covered, but too distracted to mind. Tonight he was to leave Holly Village for the very first time since Mr Ahari delivered him here, grave dirt still staining Silas's cheeks.

'He will indeed, but you may not have a chance to present your questions directly. He has many means of keeping abreast of the Order's activities.'

Of that Silas did not doubt. He found himself in a most curious place here in Holly Village. There was nothing conventional about his new home, nor the people in it. Though what Silas's role was to play had yet to be disclosed. *All in good time, dear boy. You've a place here and you'll find it soon enough,* was all Mr Ahari would say on the single occasion he visited Silas at Holly Village in the month since their graveside encounter.

'And you are quite certain nothing is expected of me this evening?' Silas shrugged against the consternation that came with considering the man's words. 'What am I to say when I am asked of my place in the Order?'

'That you are new to its ranks and still in your training days.' Jane set her reassuring smile upon him. 'I assure you nothing but your presence is required at the ball. That will be impressive enough. The ladies, and the gentleman will be quite enamoured by you, believe me.'

'I cannot share your conviction, I'm afraid,' Silas said. 'I'd much rather remain here.'

'Oh don't carry on so,' Jane laughed. 'You'll quite enjoy yourself I'm sure. Besides, it is high time you shared company other than my own.'

'I might agree if it were the company of one other on offer, but this is an entire ballroom of scrutiny.'

The notion of setting foot beyond the safe haven of Holly Village frightened him no end. And yet Mr Ahari had deemed his first outing to be one of such grandeur. Silas was to escort Jane Handel to the Marquess of Ailsa's annual ball.

'True, there might have been subtler ways of introducing you, we are the guests of honour after all. But this is what has been decided, so that is that.'

The invitation to the ball had been extended to Jane to express the Marquess's gratitude for services rendered. She was, as was Mr Ahari, a member of the Order of the Golden Dawn. An organisation whose true purpose remained mostly mystery to Silas. Bothersome, considering the expectation that he should one day present himself as a working member. All he had gleaned so far was that the Order purported to deal with society's more arcane ills and troubles.

'I suppose you are right.' Silas said.

If Mr Ahari wished him to attend the ball then Silas felt no compulsion to protest too loudly. Along with the strange reverence for his saviour came a stranger still sense of confidence in the man. Trust, even.

'Now come.' Jane rose. 'You need to dress quickly. And I promise no more baths for you. You are really far too big for the tub anyway. The washbasin will do just fine.'

'Yes. Yes, it will.' He forced a smile to his lips. 'Most definitely.'

Jane did not exaggerate to call him a giant. When entering the cottage Silas had to lower his head for fear of cracking his skull. And he had been bestowed the width of a body to match—solid, not portly—with a musculature most defined. In comparison, the petite woman who now leaned over him appeared childlike.

He pressed up onto his knees, catching sight of his reflection in the smooth waters within the copper bath. He appeared every bit as unsteady as he felt, a wildness to his brown eyes. The damp waves of his coal-black hair tickled at the lobes of his ears. He peered at the stranger, for that was what he saw: a man with solid shoulders and muscled arms and torso, a broad face and a solid flat nose, and a decidedly thick neck that he did not much admire – nor recognise. Silas remembered nothing beyond that horrendous moment of his death and rebirth. He could recall no family to wonder about, nor a home to consider returning to. Not the slightest inkling of a history that might anchor him more firmly into this life. It was, according to Mr Ahari, completely to be expected in one who had been reanimated. But the cheery grave-digger could offer little more information that may assist, should Silas have harboured a desire to learn more of his life lost. There was no gravestone, only the simple, lop-sided wooden cross Silas recalled. The only other detail of note that Mr Ahari provided was the location of that sad place. And it was far too close for comfort. That empty grave lay in the cemetery right next door to Holly Village. Silas had, the jovial man informed him, lain between the Potter's Field and the magnificence of family mausoleums, in a no-man's land between the forgotten and eternally remembered.

And it was Mr Ahari who had named Silas, for his final resting place did not.

'I shall fetch us some wine, to aid you in soothing your nerves.' Jane brushed at the folds of her gown. She was young, he imagined her to be barely twenty years of age, and quite sublime with her sun-kissed skin. Her chocolate-brown hair was pulled up to sit high on her head, curled in a bun held fast with a floral diamond clasp, and her corset pulled in so tight at her waist he wondered how she took a breath at all. 'How does that sound, Mr Mercer?'

The edge of her corset pushed her breasts high, mounds of soft gold that would sit most perfectly in the palm of Silas's hands. He dropped his head, mortified by the sudden tightness at his groin that followed such a wayward thought.

'Yes, yes, wine,' he said hoarsely, for want of anything better to say.

'I should think the Marquess of Ailsa's ball is exactly what you need right now, despite your apprehension. The marquess has a magnificent collection of champagnes, all rather worth dying for.' Jane pressed her fingers to her lips, the hint of a smile evident. 'Dear me, I do apologise. That was poor taste. But the champagne is not, I assure you. Raise a smile, Mr Mercer. To be a part of the Order is quite the stylish thing at the moment. Society is alight with talk of the arcane, thanks in no small part to those silly Fox sisters in America. You have timed reanimation perfectly. We in the Order no longer need to skulk around in the shadows, for fear of being named witch or devil and stuck upon a dunking chair or onto a flaming pyre. I cannot tell you how many invitations I have received from lords and barons, and even a prince or two, hoping to outshine their fellow nobles with a seance or fortune-telling party that leaves their guests quite dumbstruck. Once we find your place, I'm certain you'll find it most delightful an organisation.'

In truth, it did not sound so delightful to Silas's ears. Seances? Fortune-telling? He could no sooner read a fortune than he could set a decent fire. Fortunately of the latter he had no need to learn, for a marvellously discreet servant tended to all his needs without yet ever having shown sign of themselves. Silas watched Jane sweep from the room, her light feet seeming to float her out of sight. When he was quite sure she was gone, Silas covered himself as best he could with the paltry linen and hurried to his bed chamber upstairs.

He stood before the mirror clad in a crisp, fresh white shirt with onyx buttons and sharply-ironed black trousers. The cut of each was perfect, despite the fact that he had never been fitted for such attire. He had returned earlier today from his post-lunch walk around the grounds to find the suit laid out on his bed. There was no note, nor any sign of the deliverer. Likely it was the same clandestine servant who tended to Silas's fire and food. Each morning a basket of breakfast items appeared on his doorstep, bread still warm with the oven's touch and hard-boiled eggs coddled in a gingham cloth. Another delivery came at midday, another early evening. He had never heard a single footstep, nor ever seen the barest hint of anyone else upon the grounds.

He picked up the blue necktie laid out for him, and frowned. The waft of jasmine announced Jane's always-silent arrival. He had neglected to close his bedroom door, and now she stood in its frame, her full skirts filling the space, two crystal glasses filled with rich red wine in hand. 'My, don't you look rather dashing?' She cocked her head, the long length of her diamond earing touching her shoulder. 'But you do look rather confused by that necktie. Might I assist you?'

Silas nodded, eyeing the glass of wine with no small desire. 'I'd be most grateful.'

'Of course.' Jane rustled into the room. It was the full skirt to blame he was certain, but yet again she moved as though gliding across ice. After setting down her glass, she exchanged Silas's wine for the necktie. Her fingers moved deftly with the tuck and fold of material. 'The Lady Satine spares no expense for clothing for the Order as you can see. Do you not think this attire most wonderful?'

'It is comfortable, to be sure.' He crouched to accommodate her much shorter stature. If Mr Ahari were somewhat mysterious then the Lady Satine was doubly so. He knew from Jane's chatter over their regular evenings of cards and chess that it was the Lady Satine who owned Holly Village, and resided herself in the nearby Holly Lodge which perched upon a hilltop, affording her a prime view down into the village. But Silas was yet to lay eyes upon his benefactor. 'Is her ladyship attending this evening's ball?'

'Oh no, no.' Jane laughed, as though he'd said something most ludicrous. 'She's occupied with far grander things, and probably cares very little about the marquess's trout pond being rid of its supposed evil spirit.'

The heat of the wine reached his stomach. 'I beg your pardon?'

'Well that is why I've secured an invitation. The family were most thankful I sorted out their issue with dying fish. The Marquess was convinced an evil spirit had made its home amongst the waters. He requested the Order investigate the situation. Being as minor an issue as it was, I volunteered myself for the job so as to free up the others for more substantial tasks. Be a dear and lean down a little more for me.'

Silas obliged and Jane resumed the wrangling of his tie.

'And...was there?' He took another generous gulp of the spicy wine.

'What?'

'An evil spirit upsetting the trout?' He offered a half-smile, as though he were a party to the joke. For such things must be folly, surely.

'Oh no, no,' Jane said. 'It was a harmless, but rather ravenous, asrai. Pretty creature, very distantly related to the water nymphs I believe, but far more amiable.' She patted at her handiwork and stood back, hands on corseted hips. 'There. Lovely, don't you think?'

Silas blinked, caring very little about his tie. 'These creatures...they truly exist?'

'They truly do. You'll be astonished at what creatures you have always shared the world with. It is thanks to the Order's endeavours very few humans realise they are not so alone as they might imagine. There is a balance that must be struck, you see, and the Order sees to that.' She reached to trace a finger along the length of his lapel. 'But as you are no longer entirely human Mr Mercer, you shall now be privy to both sides of the scale.'

'Not entirely human?' His tongue was thick in his mouth.

'Come now. Do you know many men who have survived the sweep of death's scythe?'

'I don't...well, I don't recall knowing many men at all. I do not know myself, let alone another. But I suppose you must be right, I am much changed.' He drained the last of his wine. He harboured no burning desire to find himself. Indeed, the notion of exploring his past left him hollow and uneasy, even more so now after the dreadful bathtub experience, but that was not to say he was not prone to bouts of melancholy and loneliness. 'I am not the man I was.'

Jane swept about, gathering up a black velvet coat and top hat that completed Silas's outfit. Her scent drenched the entire room, rich and lush. Perhaps he should be more despairing of his situation but with the heady waft of jasmine it was quite impossible to lament too deeply.

'Well I rather like what you are. I certainly approve of how you appear.' Jane beamed. 'Let us set about building your new life from the ground up. Perhaps this evening we will find someone to warm your bed and smooth away that frown that comes far too easily to you. Come, Mr Mercer. Let us begin simply, and enjoy the dancing and champagne. I can fairly taste the oysters already.'

He slipped his arms into the coat she held and lowered his head so she might press down the top hat to his crown. They were ready.

The gas lamp outside his cottage had been lit. The person responsible for doing so each evening was as elusive as the deliverer of his meals and clothing. By the time night descended, the light burned bright in its glass cage, flames upright and unwavering, a golden soldier standing to attention. Just as it did now. The heat of the wine soothed him and dulled his anxiety well enough that he could almost imagine actually enjoying an evening of frivolity. He strode along, with Jane's hand resting upon his forearm, the gardens ever-silent around them. Holly Village was the oddest of accommodations. Beautiful for certain, the gated community held stunning gardens of which he was most fond of strolling. He favoured especially the pretty brook that meandered through a thicket flourishing within the village's high walls, a divine place at sunset. But of its twelve houses, different styles each, only two of them appeared to have residents living within: Silas's cottage, and Jane's more elaborate residence with its turreted tower and carved gargoyles beneath the eaves.

They strolled along the crushed-stone pathway away from the dark unoccupied cottages to the imposing archway which framed a pair of magnificent wrought-iron gates. At their approach the gates opened, swinging back in utter silence to reveal an awaiting brougham outside. The lower half of the carriage was painted a pale blue, while the rest was gleaming black. A solitary bay stamped its hooves against the cobbles, setting the tracers tinkling.

'Isaac, I do hope we haven't kept you waiting too long,' Jane declared gaily.

Their carriage driver waited in his seat and did not show any sign he had heard her. He was swathed in dark fabric, a wide scarf around his neck hiding the lower part of his face, and his wide-brimmed hat, black also, dipped over his brow. With the man's own dark complexion, Silas felt as though he were gazing up at a shadow. He nodded his head in greeting, touching a finger to his top hat.

'How do you do?' he said, the wine loosening his tongue.

Isaac settled deeper into the folds of his clothing and did not reply.

'Wonderful speaking with you as always, Isaac,' Jane said brightly, managing to board the carriage without having to tug at the generous folds of her gown or accept Silas's waiting hand to balance her. 'Never mind him. Isaac doesn't like anybody; you are not being singled out for special treatment. Now, let us go. We shall be delightfully late. Not so late as to be in bad taste, but enough that the guests will be breathless with anticipation for our arrival. Are you ready, Mr Mercer, to step into the glow of the Order of the Golden Dawn?'

Silas slipped a finger between his starched collar and his neck. Sweat dampened his skin. 'If I were to answer honestly, I would say I am not sure.'

Jane laid her hand upon his. 'Well I shall ask you again once the champagne and music has worked its magic and a fine woman hangs upon your arm.' Her laughter worked upon him like a balm. As light as a wind across a spring meadow.

He returned her smile. 'Very well then.'

Jane called on the driver to be on his way. Isaac whistled at the bay, and Silas's foray into the world commenced with a sudden and not altogether pleasant jolt of the carriage.

CHAPTER 2

The Marquess of Ailsa resided in a stately home in Chelsea with a view of the Thames much admired by other guests but only serving to increase Silas's discomfort. The ballroom was an enormous affair. He was quite certain that it could have accommodated his parlour a dozen times over. On a raised platform at the head of the room a quartet of musicians sat amongst potted palms, teasing beautiful music from their violins and cellos. Above, three embellished chandeliers dripped with sparkling crystal and shone with flames. The waft of wax mixed with the eau de parfums of the lavishly-clothed men and women mingling around the edges of a polished dance floor, and Silas's head fairly spun.

A surly, thin-haired footman escorted them through the throng, with Silas all too aware of the murmur their arrival garnered. He hunched his shoulders in a pathetic attempt to diminish himself, as much from prying eyes as from the noise and bustle. He'd not realised until this moment just how quiet Holly Village was. Silas's heart thudded so hard he felt its pulse in the depths of his throat. He could not help but feel like a freak in a travelling show, on display for all to see.

The footman bowed in a sharp movement. 'I hope the Order enjoys their invitation to His Lordship's entertainments this evening,' he said.

Despite being well below Silas's towering stature, the man somehow managed to gaze upon him down the length of his nose. If Silas were not mistaken, there was a harshness to the man's welcome, a note of derision evident upon his pronunciation of the word Order. Jane gave no sign that she had noticed the slight, her pink-lipped smile firmly in place.

'I have no doubt we will be wondrously entertained,' she said.

The moment the footman departed, a waiter pressed forward a silver tray brimming with champagne-filled crystal glasses. Silas abandoned all pretence of decorum and selected one. He drew a pinch-faced look from the waiter, whose dull grey eyes moved between Silas and Jane.

'Oh, I'm sorry.' He offered Jane the glass he'd already touched his lips to. Her eyes alight with amusement, she shook her head and selected her own glass from the tray. The waiter gave her a brief bow and moved to attend to other guests.

'Take a deep breath, Mr Mercer. You are doing well,' Jane said behind the cover of her raised glass.

She was far too kind. He hovered on the edge of panic. 'There are so many eyes upon us.'

'Of course. Have you taken a look at yourself? You are quite the impressive figure, even without the Order's reputation upon you. Now, finish your drink. We are here to impress the dear marquess's guests, drink his liquors, and dance. Will you dance with me?'

Before he could refuse, Jane stole his glass and set it down with her own empty one, pulling him onto the dance floor as the opening notes of a waltz filled the air. She took his hands, placing them in position, pressing one to the curve of her back where the firmness of her corset was evident. A fresh terror struck him.

'I'm not sure I can dance.'

'I disagree, Mr Mercer.' Jane laughed, leaning into him. 'Now do relax, we don't want you to give that newly beating heart an attack, do we?'

For a length of time too long and arduous to be anything but unpleasant, Silas stumbled his way around the dance floor. Admittedly, he managed far better than he could have imagined. Just as he would despair of what placement his feet should take next, he found himself stepping happily in the correct direction or whirling Jane around in a passable twirl, as though his limbs knew the music and movement while his brain did not. Pleased as he was, there was something undeniably odd about his movement, and he had not the faintest sense that he'd danced this way before.

As the quartet launched into a vibrant new tune, Silas was struck by an idea. One that would have been ludicrous at any other time, he was sure.

'Jane, is this your doing?' He glanced down at his feet, which were hidden beneath the reaching folds of her gown. 'I have not been so assured on my feet since I awoke.'

'Whatever do you mean?' She batted her lashes.

All at once, Silas's left foot tangled in her skirt's multitude of cotton and satin layers, and he uttered a sharp cry, certain he would bring them both crashing to the floor.

'Do stand up.' Jane laughed and righted him as though he were no heavier than the fan that dangled from a lady's wrist, and not a towering bulk of muscle and bone. Such strength should be impossible for a woman of her stature, were she all she seemed. 'And yes, Mr Mercer, I may be responsible for your aptitude for dance. Which is just as well, as I dare say in your last life you were not one for such efforts.'

He was saved from defending himself by a rough tap to his arm. Standing there was a portly gentleman smelling strongly of gin and dressed in a suit of the deepest forest green.

'Might I step in?' He rather slurred his question, and if Silas were not so eager to depart the dance floor, he might have harboured misgivings about leaving Jane in the man's company. He was relieved when Jane gave a delighted cry of recognition.

'My Lord Scarborough.' She dropped into a short curtsy. 'How wonderful to see you again.'

'And you, Miss Handel.' The man's moustache was an elaborate swirl of oiled black, an oil that Silas suspected had also been used upon the man's eyebrows. 'I suspect we have not crossed paths since the hunt last autumn. Lady Scarbrough still speaks of your prowess for cartomancy, though she refuses to indulge me with the questions she sought from your cards.'

'And nor shall I, my lord.' Jane dipped her shoulder, leaning ever so briefly into the man, in a rather unsubtle flirtation. 'I should never desire to betray your wife's confidences.'

He laughed, a deep rumble of sound. 'Fair play. I wonder though if I might take you into my confidence and a dance or two as we discuss some business that the Order may see fit to attend to?'

'Of course, of course.' Her smile was flawless. 'But I am being ever so rude. Might I introduce you to the newest member of the Order, Your Lordship. This is Mr Silas Mercer. Mr Mercer, this is the Earl of Scarbrough, quite a regular utiliser of the Order's services.'

For a brief moment Silas imagined a wry grin twisted her lips, but it vanished before he could fully discern it.

He bobbed his head. 'Your Lordship.'

'Well, one could hardly miss you, Mr Mercer.' The earl's cheeks were bright with the vigour of dancing and drink. 'Good god, I see now where my payments to the Order might go. Towards this giant of a man's tailor and baker, no doubt.' He laughed far louder and heartier than the jest warranted, drawing the glances of those who were not already observing the trio. If the polished wooden floor had split apart and Silas were swallowed whole, he would not have minded.

'What are you then, man?' The earl swayed as he spoke, nudging against Jane, who appeared not to notice. 'What special talent do you own?'

Silas's lips opened but he could not find a word to release. This was his first conversation with someone beyond the walls of Holly Village, and he was at an utter loss.

Jane took up Silas's cause. 'Mr Mercer is our newest spiritualist, Your Lordship. And this is his first foray in public as one of our members. So do be kind, my lord, won't you?'

There, it was said. His identity made solid and real. A pity Silas had no clue what being a spiritualist might entail.

Feigning shock with eyes widened, the earl chortled. 'Am I ever anything but kind, my dear?'

'The fox upon the hunt may not think so.'

A dark glint came to the earl's hazel-flecked eyes. 'But I do so love a good chase, Miss Handel.'

His words crawled upon Silas's skin, but Jane merely lifted her fan to cover her mouth, her eyes never leaving the man's face. Silas frowned, when had Jane obtained a fan?

'I've seen evidence of your love for the hunt quite clearly, my lord,' Jane said. 'Now, the dance begins. Am I to be partnered or left floundering?'

'Of course, of course.' The earl offered his plump arm. 'It has been a pleasure, Mr Mercer.' His eyes ran the full length of Silas's body, perhaps still wondering at the lengths of fabric a tailor might require. Whatever the reason, it caused Silas great discomfort. 'Perhaps I'll have need of a spiritualist soon, and we shall meet again.'

Mouth parchment dry, Silas couldn't work a word free before the Earl of Scarbrough whisked Jane deep into the dance floor.

Silas hurried through a forest of couples but failed to vacate the dance floor before they once again launched into an energetic dance. He sidestepped frantically to avoid collision, but succeeded only in ensuring he was forced to offer endless apologies for toes stepped upon and dresses caught beneath his heels.

'Pardon me, pardon me.'

If he'd harboured hopes of slipping into obscurity at the ball and finding a quiet balcony on which to perch himself until Jane was tired of the festivities, those hopes were quite destroyed now. Ladies tittered behind gloved hands, watching his clumsy exit, and gentlemen exhibited smirks that told of great amusement at Silas's expense. He damned the superfluous use of brightly-lit chandeliers, which highlighted his every move.

Gloved fingers touched his arm. 'Mr Mercer, is it?'

He turned to find a well-built gentleman at his side. The man looked to be in his thirties, though his manicured beard was greying around his temples and along his jawline. He wore a suit of rich black, which complimented his short dark hair and emphasised his light complexion. On his chest were pinned several medals, suggesting a military rank of some kind. The man's smile was pleasant, his light grey eyes kind.

'Yes. I'm sorry, did I disturb you?' Silas glanced at the floor, horrified that he might have knocked the man's glass from his hands.

'No, no. Not at all.' His voice was light and higher than Silas might have accounted for. He had a confidence about him, a straightness to his shoulders and tilt to his chin, but there was no air of superiority. 'Shall I lead you somewhere you might catch your breath? If you don't mind me saying so, it appears you require a drink and some fresh air.'

Reddening at the honest appraisal, Silas inclined his head. 'Thank you.'

'This way. There is a reading room I believe will be suitable.'

Silas hesitated, uncertain whether he should accept such an invitation. But Jane was nowhere to be seen, and he certainly was not braving the dance floor again to ask her advice. He'd endured death and reanimation, surely he could handle a conversation with a stranger over a glass of something strong? He followed his host, passing through the double doors that allowed them to escape from the ballroom and into a richly-wooded hallway, one half as wide as Silas's entire cottage. The man he followed was greeted by many of the passersby.

'Lieutenant.' A nod from a gentleman here, a tilt of the head from a lady there. 'Lieutenant.'

Evidently, Silas's summation that the man was military was correct, but it was not just his companion who drew attention as they walked. Silas himself was causing quite the mortifying disturbance. Dainty rose-coloured lips parted, heavy eyebrows rose, and monocled eyes widened as guests passed them by. All stared up at Silas as though they were beholding something quite unexpected. Which he well he might be. Most of the men he happened upon were either slight of build or portly of stomach, none were quite so solidly built and tall in stature as he. Good gracious, had he endured such scrutiny in life? It was rather appalling.

By the time they reached the end of a lengthy hallway decorated with a barrage of palms in lushly detailed ceramic pots, Silas had learnt that the man's name was Edward. The discovery of such a detail had come through rather uncomfortable means, however. Just a minute earlier Silas's escort had been accosted by an unsteady fellow who had practically thrown himself at the poor man.

'Edward, my dear. You're here.'

Clearly inebriated, the smartly tailored gentleman's hands had settled upon the Lieutenant's backside as he leaned in close to whisper words Silas reddened to hear. Edward hurried himself free of the encounter, striding on as though nothing untoward had happened. But Silas had heard enough. He glanced back down the length of the corridor, the music now a distant murmur, wincing at the knowledge that his agreement to join the man in a drink may have been miscalculated. Silas might not recall the man he was, but he was quite sure he did not share the drunken man's need to put his mouth upon Edward's cock and suck him dry. Silas's moment for polite withdrawal escaped him though as Edward stopped at a carved oak door.

'Here we are,' he said. 'I must apologise for the lengthy walk.'

He opened the door and led them into a sumptuous library. Silas was much relieved to note that the room was not theirs alone. Two older gentlemen were seated at a bay window, deep in conversation with thick cigars and cognac snifters in hand. They glanced at the door as Silas and Edward entered.

'Lieutenant Charters.' The more rotund of the two men nodded. 'Pleasant evening?'

'Quite, Sir Reginald, but we rather fancied a moment to allow our feet to recover.'

Sir Reginald made a harrumphing sound that might have been laughter and returned to his conversation.

'Brandy? Or cognac?' Edward gestured at the array of decanters on the drinks cart.

Silas had awoken at Holly Village with no clue what type of alcohol he preferred, but he'd quickly discovered his preference. 'Brandy, if you would please.'

'Good choice, my personal favourite as well.' Edward smiled, genuine enough, but rather lack-lustre. As though all the dancing had quite worn him out. He poured their drinks. 'I say, that fire is rather warm. I'm frightened it might melt this dastardly medal. Do you mind if we sit on the couch?'

Silas had just started towards the two armchairs by the fire but smiled. 'Of course.'

He settled himself into the deep brown leather studded with gold buttons. The material creaked with his weight. Edward handed him the brandy in a snifter of such fine glass that Silas dreaded the responsibility of nursing it.

'Thank you,' he said. 'I appreciate your offer of respite from the dance. As you can see, I am not a natural upon the floor.' The brandy hit his tongue and slid with fiery abandon down his throat. It was all he could do not to sigh.

'Not at all.' Edward settled into the couch, crossing his legs. His weight did not elicit a groan from the leather as Silas's had done. 'You saved me rather. My friend, the Baron Feversham, took it upon himself to see me out and about and insisted I attend this evening. He does not take no for an answer kindly.' He smiled, his oval face tinged ever so slightly orange by the firelight. 'I would suggest you understand entirely. Miss Handel is behind your attendance here, is she not?'

With the brandy sinking into his belly, Silas returned his smile. 'She is, yes.' He wiped his hand against his trouser leg, hoping against hope that Edward did not notice the uncouth move before he offered that same palm in greeting. 'I don't believe we have done the formal introductions. I'm Silas –'

'Mercer. Yes. The place was quite awash with talk of you and Miss Handel.' He took Silas's hand, his grip firm but not too much so. 'I'm Lieutenant Edward Charters, with the Northumberland Fusiliers, First Battalion. At least I...'

He paused and withdrew from the handshake, chewing at his lip. Silas waited, certain that he was going to say more, but the lieutenant gazed back towards the fire, and the silence stretched to uncomfortable lengths.

'I must say this brandy is rather impressive.' Silas intended to touch a finger lightly to the delicate glass. Instead, he managed to rap his nail so hard against the surface that he feared a crack was certain. 'Oh my.' He peered at the glass, searching for signs of damage.

Edward's focus returned, along with his bright smile. 'Fear not. Should you break the glass, there are another dozen to take its place.' He tugged at the high collar of his shirt. 'Forgive me, I believe I grew rather distracted for a moment there. I must be honest with you, Mr Mercer, as pleasant as your company has turned out to be, I originally sought you out for other reasons.'

Silas held still, preparing a polite refusal. 'Oh really?'

'Yes, would you mind terribly if I asked you a few questions about the Order of the Golden Dawn?'

Silas took an indelicately large sip of brandy. He would have preferred a gesture of flirtation after all. The liquid burned its passage down his throat, seeping into his senses with haste. He had overindulged only once since his reanimation and regretted it with much fervour the day after, but this may be an occasion where the unpleasantness was worth revisiting.

'I'm not sure that I am the one best suited to your needs,' he said. 'I have only just joined the ranks of the Order.'

And had not the slightest clue what that meant for him.

'But by association I am to understand you are a believer in the supernatural,' the man pressed.

'Well, I...I suppose that...well, yes. Though perhaps I would say instead I believe in the strange and unusual.'

How much more comfortably that definition sat with Silas rather than talk of the arcane and supernatural. Perhaps it was a foolish state of denial he rested in but he embraced it wholeheartedly.

'Then that is all I need.' Edward shifted his seat, leaning in closer towards Silas, casting a furtive glance at the men by the window. How nicely his grey eyes caught the firelight. 'You see, I must be honest with you. I have long been a sceptic of...the...fantastical things that the Order is said to assist with. I no more believe in ghosts than I believe we will walk on the moon. I don't mean to insult you or Miss Handel, but I have always felt that it is a mere trick of the mind that a fortune-teller uses, an intimate observance of human nature. I've been no friend of the spiritualists, either, I can assure you. All salubrious nonsense.' He grimaced. 'Mr Mercer, I apologise –'

'No, no, not necessary.' Silas rose, gesturing with his now-empty glass. 'Would you care for another?' Denial required deeper inebriation. He'd quite regained his taste for brandy, and it was a fine one at that.

'Yes, that's most kind.'

Silas poured them both far too generous servings and resettled on the couch. Their companions, the older gentlemen, chose that moment to leave, the heady scent of their cigars lingering. They stepped into the hall, and Silas shifted his attention back to the conversation. A movement by the closing door caught his eye. For a moment he thought someone else had entered the room. But the deception must have been caused by the shudder of fire and gaslight, for there was no one to be seen but Edward and Silas himself.

Edward swirled his brandy in silence, studying the liquid as though it were the crystal ball he so derided. Perhaps another trick of the light was cast against his face, for in that moment the man appeared terribly tired. The rings beneath his eyes were notable for their darkness, a feature Silas had not noticed before. After another mouthful, Silas decided to offer his thoughts.

'I can understand, Lieutenant –'

'Edward, please. I really shouldn't be using the...I'm afraid that...well, never mind. Just Edward, please.'

'Fine, Edward, of course.' Silas paused, considering his words. 'I can certainly understand your hesitancy to accept the strangeness of the world around us.' Silas himself was guilty of just such a thing. He had played at blissful ignorance for many a week at Holly Village, happy to accept his return to the world but stubbornly refusing to consider too deeply what might follow. And what lurked in the shadows of his past. 'But if I tell you nothing else, I will say that we know less about the truth of things than we could ever imagine. I have had some...experiences...that have given me cause to question not only what I might know but what I am to learn.' He shook his head. 'I am making no sense I'm sure.'

'No, no, Mr Mercer. You make far more sense than you might know.' The Lieutenant's earnestness wiped the fatigue from his face. He had brightened and it suited him well.

'Well, that is a good thing. For most days nothing at all makes reasonable sense to me.' Silas offered up an unsteady smile. 'And I dare say this brandy isn't helping things at all. I believe I can see two of you right now.'

The Lieutenant burst into a gale of laughter, a sound so delightfully contagious Silas could not help but join him. How wonderful it was that the laughter did not come at Silas's expense for once.

'Thank you, Mr Mercer.' Silas did not flinch when Edward laid his fingers briefly on his knee. 'You are most amusing, and I did so need some lifting of spirits this evening.'

'Do call me Silas, will you?'

Edward gave him a shy smile and nodded.

They sat in surprisingly comfortable silence. There was an absence of airs and graces about the man that was most appealing. A dart of movement by the window stirred Silas from his contemplations. A lost guest perhaps, or footmen moving about. By the time he'd turned to note its cause, the scene beyond the window was undisturbed. An oak tree swayed in the distance, nothing more.

'It makes no sense at all to consider oneself possessed, does it?' Edward lifted his glass and sighed. 'I fear I have not had near enough food this evening for all this drink.'

'Possessed, Edward? What do you mean?'

The lieutenant glanced up at him from beneath lowered lashes. 'Forgive me my ramblings now, Silas, for I fear you shall believe me more than drunk once I am done.' He focused once more on his glass. 'I have...well, you see, I've not been myself for quite some time. I have been placed on medical leave from the Fusiliers, a fact that is yet to become common knowledge. The doctors deemed me unfit for duty, on account of my unexplained absences and...delusions.' He sipped, taking his time. 'When we talk of the strangeness of things, I think perhaps it is I who am the strangest of all. I'm sure they believe my mind is failing me, and well they may be right, as here I am, sitting with you, entertaining the idea that perhaps I am not mad but possessed. What better sign that a man has gone mad?' He stared absently into his now empty glass, and Silas decided against interrupting. It was a long while before the man spoke again. 'I am so dreadfully tired, you see, on account of the ferocity of my dreams.'

'Ferocity?'

'Intensity, perhaps is a better word. They are so filled with...I'm not sure how to describe it...light, I suppose. A brightness that blinds the mind, rather than the eye. I am lost in these dreams. When I wake, I'm never certain I have done so. It takes some time to realise the dreams were not actually my reality. A language is spoken too, more lyrical than French, more passionate than Italian. Foreign to me, and yet not. I never see who is speaking, even though it feels at times he is so close he is within me. His voice is always the same. So glorious it pains me.' He closed his eyes, and was silent so long Silas wondered if he'd actually gone to sleep. 'He is beauty, I feel it, Silas. Utter and complete perfection. But how he frightens me at times.' A shiver ran the length of Silas's arms. 'He overwhelms me. I cannot breathe for it but I do not want it to end.

Even when I wake, when I know for certain I am back in the real world, I feel his touch.' He pressed his hand to his throat, and ran his fingers down its length. 'I do not know where he starts, and I begin. Perhaps I have brought this madness on myself, for the things I am guilty of. The sinful things I crave. For it is always worst after I have laid with - ' The fire cracked and hissed, and Edward fell silent, his teeth digging into his lower lip.

Neither he nor Silas moved. Not an inch. Silas held his breath, waiting. A sudden burst of laughter from beyond the closed doors shattered the moment.

Edward shook himself, his face reddening. 'Oh my, I am so dreadfully sorry. I have forgotten myself, Mr Mercer. I truly must apologise. See, they are right, are they not? Truly I am a man on the edge of sanity to take such flights of fancy. You must think me revolting. Please forgive me.'

'There is nothing to forgive.' Silas took his glass and rose hurriedly, his pulse thumping with the intimacy of the moment. 'And if the only words of any comfort I can offer are these, then hear me clearly. I do not think you revolting.' Far from it. He poured them fresh glasses with trembling hands. To Silas's personal horror his trousers pressed uncomfortably tight at his groin. Good god, surely he was not a man of such leanings? Why, only two nights hence in his dreams he had mounted a sprightly, breathless lass. He could not recall her face but certainly recalled her legs wrapped firm about him, his cock sunk deep into her wetness, and his imagined pleasure soiling his sheets. 'But I fear I am not to be of assistance in this matter. I am neither doctor of the mind, nor experienced member of the Order. Perhaps if you were to share your story with Miss Handel - '

'No,' Edward said, panic evident in his widened eyes. 'Please I must insist that you forget all the repulsive nonsense I've uttered.' Edward rose from the couch and accepted the glass Silas offered, taking a generous gulp before he continued. 'Forgive me, I don't know what came over me. You are far too easy to speak with, Mr Mercer, I fear. When I first invited you to join me for a drink, I did not intend to embarrass myself and interrogate you. I am sleep deprived, and quite delusional for it. Nothing more than that.' His laugh was so diminished as to barely exist at all. 'Can we speak of other things? I wondered if I might request an appointment. Not for myself, of course.' He did not take a breath from one sentence to another. 'My acquaintance, the Baron Feversham, has long insisted that his London residence is frequented by a ghost. He carries on about it so. It makes card nights quite draining. Would you attend and set his mind at ease?' He grinned, too wide, and the brandy rippled in his glass. 'It's his birthday this month and he will hold a party. A visit from the Order would make the celebrations rather unique. I wonder if you would indulge me such a request, Mr Mercer?'

His eyes held a desperation that Silas could not look upon without some sympathy. This was a man haunted by many things, of that there was no doubt. To his great surprise, and no doubt thanks in part to the brandy, Silas found himself agreeing.

'Of course. I'll speak with Miss Handel,' he said. 'To see what might be arranged. Where might you be reached?' Dear god, he had taken full leave of his senses. Silas stifled a belch, regretting the last glass.

Edward fumbled at his pocket, withdrawing a slender silver card case. 'Here is my card.' He thrust a milky white calling card at Silas. He had grown dangerously pale. 'I hope you will forgive my strange utterances, Mr Mercer. You've been most kind, but I fear I must make my apologies now and leave you.' He touched his fingers to his lips. 'Thank you once again.'

Silas moved to ask if he required assistance, for it was clear the man was unwell, when a peculiar tingling set off in his fingertips. The lieutenant rushed out the door, leaving it open in his haste. In the depths of the shadows between wall and door, something shifted, edging just clear enough that its shape was discernible. Silas squinted, uncertain if he should believe his bleary eyes. It appeared vaguely human, blurred as though glimpsed through a mist. There were no eyes to speak off, just a haze of indecipherable features, yet he was certain the figure's attention was fixed on him. All the while his fingertips rang with a strange vibration under the skin, as though the blood struggled to make its way beneath his nails.

For long minutes there was no movement, from either Silas or the apparition. He wished, so fervently, that he too might blame lack of sleep for what he saw. But his stomach sank at the truth of it.

*All in good time, dear boy. You've a place here and you'll find it soon
enough.*

Mr Ahari's words returned to him, crystalline in their clarity. Silas's
new life could not be without purpose, no matter how he might desire
it so, and he could not shift the inkling that he may well be on the cusp
of his purpose's discovery right now.

The chill in the room grew ever more intense, quite enough to raise
gooseflesh across his skin. The clatter of people passing by in the hallway
shattered the strange standoff, and all at once the figure elongated, sliding
up the walls, stretching out until there was nothing vaguely human to
speak of at all. The shadow traced all the way to the roof, slithering across
the ceiling until it reached the ornate rose, and disappeared, leaving Silas
alone. If his purpose was to stare aghast at shadows come to life then he
had accomplished his task well, but he was not so foolish, nor drunk, as to
imagine that was to be his lot. Silas's attention shifted to Edward's calling
card, now crumpled in his overly-tight grasp. His comfortable, blissful
state of denial was being eroded. Silas shoved the card into his trouser
pocket, set down his glass, and hurried off to find Jane.

CHAPTER 3

T he spill of sunshine and the rattling caw of a crow woke Silas. He
jerked from sleep, blinking madly against the light. He was not in
his bed, as he should be, but in his parlour, seated in one of the deep
leather high-back chairs by the fireside. Angry muscles tensed in his neck.
Though the chair had ample stuffing and soft leather, spending the entire
evening in its embrace was not to be recommended. He squinted at the
clock on the mantel, a simple device of walnut and glass. Its thin metal
arms declared it was near on half past ten. The fire had burned out long
ago, leaving not even a coal or two in existence, but the room still held
some warmth.

Stretching his arms overhead, Silas caught sight of his discarded coat,
vest, and dreaded necktie, piled just in front of the couch, as though he'd
intended to throw the items onto it but failed dismally. Little wonder.
The decanter of whisky that sat on the table at the back of the room was
notably lacking much whisky at all. His mouth was parched dry and his
chin sticky with dribble. The room seemed to wobble if he moved too
quickly.

After his intense conversation with the lieutenant, and the highly
unusual encounter with the shadow creature, Silas had fairly burst from
the library to seek out Jane. But to his great consternation, he had been
unable to locate her. After all her talk of being at his side, she was
nowhere of the sort. Silas was bombarded by requests for a dance, most
of which he managed to weasel his way out of, but he was unable to

avoid much casual conversation with an untold number of people. They ranged from those who were enamoured with the Order's reputation to those who were clearly bemused by and rather unflattering of his employer.

'Show us your parlour tricks then, man.'

'It is said that the Fox sisters have never had any special skills, that it is all an elaborate hoax. I hear tell that the one called Margaretta is far too fond of the drink. What say you, Mr Mercer? Is the Order of the Golden Dawn having an amusement with us all?'

Silas had little to say. To begin with he knew next to nothing of the American Fox sisters, save for the brief mention Jane had made of them. And he was hardly going to launch into talk of his own unique situation. *Here stands a dead man raised.* Dare he even speak of such things? Jane had given no instruction on casual intercourse, let alone anything else. Silas had never been so grateful for a request to dance, accepting Mrs Claudette's invitation to join her in the polka with so much enthusiasm he fairly spat his reply.

By the time the unpleasant footman appeared once more at Silas's side and informed him that Miss Handel had departed the festivities, leaving word she had left Isaac the coachman at Silas's disposal, it was well after midnight. Silas was quite ill with all the social interaction. His cheeks had never blushed for so long, his tongue never been so notable in its ability to trip over itself as he tried to appear as something he was not. Namely, a conversationalist. He could not even locate the lieutenant, whose familiarity would at least offer some respite, and had been advised by an overfriendly young woman that he'd taken ill and left for the evening. The moment the footman had finished relaying Jane's message, Silas made short work of gathering his coat and rushing to find Isaac. He struggled to keep from breaking into a run in front of other slowly-departing guests.

'Do you know where I might find Miss Handel?' he'd asked of the sombre coachman. 'Has she returned to Holly Village?'

'Far too early for that. And she won't want you bothering her. Get in.' Isaac had replied gruffly and set the bay into a brisk trot. He delivered Silas to the Village with not another word passing between them. Too highly strung to sleep immediately, Silas had nursed the whisky into the early hours.

Brandy and whisky did not good bedfellows make. He'd woken with stomach churning and head pounding.

Rising now from his chair, he arched his back, aiming to return the flow of blood to his cramped body. He wriggled his fingers, recalling the odd tingling that had consumed them in the library. Had he truly noted a figure in those shadows? Or had the brandy played tricks upon his eyes? This morning, with his head so clouded and mouth so bone dry, he was no longer certain. Silas moved to the window, with its view out over the green.

The Village's twelve buildings were each elaborately different in style, and all were unusual in design. His own, one of only two detached houses, had contrasting patterns within the brickwork, four ornate chimneys on the peaked slate roof, and carved teak wood hanging from the eaves. Jane's residence, the most fanciful of the twelve, sat across the green from Silas's cottage. He could not quite see the front door, as the building's imposing turret jutted out and hid the entrance in its shadow. But in the early hours of this morning, in his inebriated state, Silas had stood at this very window for some time, his gaze fixed on the dark pebbled pathway Jane would have to travel to reach her home. He had waited until his eyelids would no longer remain open and his feet began to ache before finally moving to the chair. Though there were gas lamps outside each dwelling, there were precious few elsewhere, so there was every chance she had arrived and he'd failed to notice her in the darkness that held sway over the pathway. The lavishness of the Village would suggest the Lady Satine was a woman of some means, but apparently she saw no reason to illuminate the walkways for her tenants. Silas pressed his forehead to the glass, its coolness welcome against the alcohol-fuelled warmth of his skin. He supposed there was little need for extravagance when there were so few residents. Who were the houses meant for? Was this some kind of halfway house for the newly risen?

He exhaled, fogging the glass with his warm breath. His list of questions grew ever longer, and the answers so few. Damn it, he would have an answer for at least one of his questions today. He would seek Jane out this instant, and demand to know why she had abandoned him last evening.

With a determined, though wobbly, stride he set off. Quite possibly he should change, or at least redress himself in his vest for propriety, but he was too irritated to truly mind that he wore only his trousers and an undershirt. And with no one else in the Village to see him, what did it matter? If Jane disapproved, then fine, so be it. Silas disapproved most heartily of being abandoned at his first venture into society.

He flung open the door and almost placed a boot on the large wicker basket that sat on the mat. His breakfast had arrived, served once more by the Village's phantom, with not even the crunch of a pebble to betray their presence. He was hit by the scent of fresh bread and kippers, and his stomach growled with mortifying alacrity. A moment later though, it roiled as Silas considered the act of eating. Hungry as he may be, the brandy and whisky were not sitting well together.

He lifted the basket and thrust it with little delicacy into the hall, uncaring whether anyone noted the gesture and disapproved of the carelessness. He left the door ajar and strode across the green. As usual, his eye was drawn to the meticulous cut and uniformity of colour of the lawn. Quite why such detail appealed to him, Silas couldn't say, but stepping out into the grounds of Holly Village always brought with it a restfulness that he could not deny.

The morning was surprisingly mild, and the sun upon his face was pleasant, although far too bright for tired eyes. As soon as he was done with his conversation with Jane, he would make his way back to the warmth of his bed and sleep off the heady weight of his evening.

Silas lifted the solid lead ring that hung beneath a rather ugly leaden goblin face on Jane's front door and pounded it against the blackwood. He was startled to find the door unlatched, easing open at his pressure. He cast a glance over his shoulder. Perhaps he should seek out help? With a hiss of annoyance, Silas remonstrated himself. Help from whom? Besides, he was hardly a feeble man. The sight of him alone may well frighten off any intruder, and Jane was clearly a capable woman.

He pushed the door open, wincing at the betraying whine of hinges. The weight of the wood was substantial, and he had to lean into it to ensure it opened wide enough for him to enter. If he'd not seen evidence of Jane's preternatural strength last night, he might have wondered how she managed.

The scent of wood smoke hit him first, a chimney not drawing well and needing attendance. If his mood weren't so foul, he might have taken care of it himself, but Silas intended a short, brisk visit. Mingling with the heaviness of the smoke was the lighter, airy scent of winter jasmine. Jane's signature. She'd been mildly surprised that he could pinpoint the exact variety, as had Silas himself, leading him to wonder if gardens had been at all a part of his lost life.

'Jane?' The foyer was a tiled space and sparsely furnished. His voice echoed down its length. A staircase, made of a wood so dark it appeared black, rose at the end of the hallway, leading the way to the upper floors. The foyer was dim, with only a meagre amount of light making it through the narrow panels of yellow stained glass set in the front door. Three unlit candles sat in puddles of wax that anchored them upon a silver tray on the hall table. Jane was frugal with her candles. More than once they'd conversed with the light of only one paltry flame in her parlour. There was little chance they would be flaming now, with midday approaching.

A sound reached him, drifting down the stairs, but too sudden to decipher.

'Jane, are you there?'

He pressed a finger to his temple. His headache was making itself well known. Perhaps rest was in order before a confrontation. Silas turned to leave when the sound reached him again. Clearer this time. A woman's cry, somewhat muffled, as though she were being smothered. Taking the stairs two at a time, he raced towards the sound. He reached the landing and hesitated. He'd never been privy to Jane's upper levels, far more expansive than his own. There were at least four separate rooms available to choose from.

There. The sound came again. More desperate this time. And clearer as to its origins. He hurried along the hallway, towards the door he marked as the source. It was ajar, and he strode into the room before thinking better of it.

'Jane, are you alright?'

He saw too quickly what caused the sounds. Not distress at all. Not the kind that required rescue at least. Jane was in her four-poster bed, astride the prostrate body of a man, her loosened brown hair spilling down her bare back, her voluptuous bottom on full display. His arrival did not disturb her, and her hips swayed side to side as she ground down against the man beneath her.

'Oh, my word.' Silas spun on his heels, his already-delicate stomach threatening to dislodge its contents entirely.

'Good god man, what do you think you're doing?' the man roared, his face hidden by Jane's body. And just as well. Silas suspected he'd see murder in the insulted gentleman's gaze.

He rushed from the room, mortified beyond all belief.

'Good morning, Silas.' Jane called after him, laughter in her voice. 'There, there, Freddie, no need to work yourself up any further. Don't you remember Silas from last night?'

He did not hear the man's reply, dashing headlong for the stairs. Taking them down at a faster pace than he'd moved up. Silas's heel slipped upon the third-to-last step, and he crashed onto the wood, thumping down the remainder on his backside.

'Silas, leaving so soon?'

It hardly seemed possible that she had moved from her delicate position so fast, but Jane was making her way down the stairs behind him, a purple satin-embellished robe thrown around her naked body. Barefoot, she once again seemed to float towards him, reaching the bottom step just as he found his feet.

'I am profoundly sorry, Miss Handel.' His tailbone ached, and his throat burned with bile.

'Miss Handel? I thought you hit your arse not your head when you fell, Silas.' The waft of jasmine toyed with his nostrils as she took a step closer. 'No need for the formality. What you saw was a perfectly natural act. Or do you not recall?' She cocked her head to one side, her tousled hair covering one eye. 'Would you care to join us?'

It was a question too far. Silas slapped a hand to his mouth, his stomach spasming. The front door was indomitably far away. He was set to regurgitate his evening upon her tiles. Jane dodged around his flimsy one-armed barrier, pushing onto her toes and placing a hand to the back of his head. Her grip was not altogether gentle, and he found himself with no alternative but to bow his head. The scent of jasmine increased, engulfing him, filling his nostrils and making its way into his throat and deep into his lungs.

Instinctively, he drew in a deep breath and found the air crisp and clean and wonderfully fresh. At once his gut settled, his muscles relaxed. The headache seemed no longer intent on splitting his skull apart. He exhaled, a slow and steady breath. Jane released him, but he continued to stare down at the floor, not yet ready to lift his head. Jane wiggled her bare toes. As with the rest of her they were petite, and immaculately groomed with nails cut and trimmed into perfect crescents. But there was something odd about her feet that Silas couldn't put a finger upon.

'I'm sorry. I shouldn't have goaded you, it was clear you were decidedly unwell. Do you feel better now?' Jane asked.

'I do. Thank you.' He frowned. 'How did you –'

'You can thank Mr Ahari for the banishing of the headache, pressure points. He taught me something of the ways of the Orient. But nothing quite clears the mind like fresh air, the very freshest, and for that I take full credit. It's rather my speciality.'

Though he was unreservedly better, there was something out of place about their encounter that nagged at Silas. He raised his head. Jane's robe had slipped, and her breasts were barely covered, curves of flesh the same rich golden hue as the rest of her body. A body of which Silas had seen far too much for one day.

He lowered his eyes. 'Jane, you…you might want to…cover…'

'Well, I learn more of you each day, dear Silas. And I must admit, I did not mark you for a prude.'

'Jane?' her deserted bedfellow called. 'If he is not to join us, then be done with him. I have a gift for you I believe you shall quite enjoy.'

'I am certain of that, my lord. I'll be up momentarily.' Jane laughed softly. 'You are very pale, Silas. Come, sit with me in the parlour. I sense you have something you wish to speak to me about. Isaac told me you were quite agitated when you left the ball. Did you not enjoy yourself?'

Glancing up the staircase, Silas shook his head. 'We can speak another time.'

34

'Why ever for? Do you worry for the earl? He'll quite enjoy the respite, I can assure you.'

'The Earl of Scarbrough?' Silas sputtered. 'The one with a –' He caught himself.

'With a wife?' Jane's brown eyes seemed to shimmer. 'Yes, the very one. But don't worry for her. The Lady Scarbrough's maid tends very well to all her mistress's needs. Here, let me soothe your sensibilities.' She held a hand beneath her lips, palm up, whispering words he could not discern, before curling her lips and blowing softly.

'There,' she declared. 'He sleeps, and will do so until we have had our discussion.'

Silas frowned. 'Jane, I really don't –'

'Listen.' Jane cupped a hand to her ear. A rumbling snore drifted down from above. 'There we are, fast asleep. He won't bother us until I wish him to. Come, come. Pretend he is not here at all.'

Shifting his gaze between Jane and the staircase, Silas stood with mouth agape, trying to find one element of sanity in his morning. 'How did you do that?'

'Another talent of mine.'

She turned on her bare heels and entered the parlour, which lay just to their right. The sun's rays had found their way into the room, spilling through the patterned glass and drenching the interior. And it was then, as Jane stepped into the brightness, that Silas realised what had given him consternation earlier. She was utterly devoid of a shadow.

CHAPTER 4

'I s there something wrong?' Jane asked. 'Are you feeling ill again?'
Silas gave a brief shake of his head and joined her in the parlour.
In keeping with the starkness of the decor in Jane's home, this room
too was furnished only with the basics: a couch that looked to be long
beyond its best years with tears in the patchwork fabric suggesting a
cat or two had taken an extreme dislike to it; and a low wooden table
that an apprentice might make in their formative years. The mantel
held two stubby off-white candles at each end, the melted wax puddling
around them. Lying between them was an assortment of sticks and dying
wildflowers. He studied Jane again. There was no doubt about it. Her
form cast no shadow despite the items around her doing so.

'You're behaving rather strangely.' Jane seated herself at one end of the
couch, patting the space beside her. 'What ails you, aside from liquor,
Silas? I believe you were a raging success last evening. I felt quite assured
of leaving you on your own, though I probably should have told you of
my intentions.'

'Yes, you bloody well should have,' he blurted, startling himself but
soldiering on. 'What ails me, you ask? Where do I begin with such a list?
There is the small issue of finding myself raised from the dead, without
a dash of memory of the life I must have lived, and no clue as to why I
stand here once more. Then you abandoned me last night to frolic with
your paramour –'

'If I'd known you so wished to join in –'

'I certainly did not wish to join your tryst, Miss Handel.' Silas glowered. 'I required your assistance last night and you were not there.' He raised a hand to her protests. 'Allow me to finish.' Quite where this righteous indignation was coming from, he didn't know. Remnants of the brandy perhaps. Whatever it was, it powered him. 'Last night I believe I saw an apparition, a barely human thing. It found me in the library, where I spoke with a man who believes himself possessed, or mad. He is leaning towards the latter. Which perhaps describes my state as well, for the duress my mind is under. It is but one month ago since I climbed screaming from my grave.' His voice was rising to an unpleasant level. 'Now I find myself a part of an Order I have no clue about, and promising a poor deranged man I will attend the home of his friend to see to their ghost issue. I have no clue what that entails, and I fear that no one seems interested enough to educate me, least of all you.' His chaotic thoughts jumped from one troubling thing to another, pouring from him in a nonsensical fashion. 'You, Miss Handel, are asking me to believe that an entire world of supernaturals exist right under my very nose and seem quite astonished that it has unsettled me. And now you brandish skills for conjuring the breeze, and ministering a sleeping draught from a distance whilst you stand there with no shadow upon your person. It is not I who is behaving strangely at all, Miss Handel, but it is I who fear I will be driven to drink forevermore before long.' He snapped his mouth closed. His voice had risen until he all but shouted at her.

Jane suddenly stood up on the couch, and darted at him, planting a kiss upon his cheek before Silas could blink. 'Silas Mercer, this is wonderful. Your eyes are opening. That ball was worth every dull moment.' She glanced at the ceiling. 'Give or take a few moments of delight. Mr Ahari and Lady Satine were right, of course, that if left to your own devices your true nature would emerge.'

'True nature?' Silas regretted not eating at least one slice of the bread in the basket on his doorstep. 'Would someone be so kind as to share such knowledge with me?'

'They may do, but that someone is not me, dear Silas, for I know about as much of it as you do.' She laughed, and sprang away from him, though she did not leave the couch. The leather protested her dancing about. Her hair was dishevelled, her cheeks dark. 'Now, let us trace back to that which is of greatest import, just to be sure. Look at me, truly look. Tell me what you see.'

Silas was not quick to answer.

'Come, come,' she urged. 'Look closely, what do you see?'

Perhaps he was as prudish as Jane summised, for what came to mind would never cross his lips. With her tousled hair and sheer clothing, she appeared as a woman who had just cried out beneath the bedclothes as she summited her pleasure. Silas lifted his shoulders with a disconsolate shrug. Jane gestured at the candles on the mantel, and they lit at once with flames far larger than such slender candles should demand. He drew in a quick breath, uncertain if he should laugh hysterically or sob into his hands. How many more preternatural skills did she possess?

'Tell me what you see, Silas.' she repeated.

It was unnerving enough to stare at a woman in a state of undress, even more so when that woman was studying him with ferocious intent, a viper about to pounce on his reply. He cleared his throat.

'I...it is what I don't see. Your shadow does not exist, as though the light doesn't notice you. Perhaps my eyes are failing me?' He touched his face. 'Is there a chance that I am...unwell...physically, I mean? Mr Ahari did say something of the possibility that I might, ah...dissolve...or...leak after reanimation.'

She clapped her hands together, dancing in a quick step upon the cushioned seat. 'You are an adorable giant oaf. No, you are not falling apart, if that's what concerns you. I do believe you are safe from that worry now. Enough time has passed that Mr Ahari no longer considered it a possibility, and I'm certain once we relay the news that you now have the sight he will be quite certain all is well. You are steadfast in your skin.'

'I suppose that is reassuring.'

'Not everyone is suitable for reanimation, of course. It is quite an undertaking, as you can imagine.'

He preferred not to imagine. Moving along swiftly, Silas asked, 'Then it is as it appears? You cast no shadow?'

'Indeed. Nor do any of the supernatural persuasion, whether they are born into it like me, or created, like you, Silas. But our lack of shadow is evident only to others of our kind. Those of the ordinary world see nothing untoward.'

Silas sank onto the couch. 'So I am truly no longer of the ordinary world.' A small part of him still harboured hopes that all the strangeness was but a dream.

She rested on her knees beside him, the robe threatening to expose far more than her thighs. The scent of jasmine was softer but still evident. 'I'm afraid not, Silas. That time has long ended.'

His voice was very small when he spoke. 'You said I was created. For what? By whom? When do you think I might learn what is expected of me? For I do not think I can bare the suspense much longer.'

'Even if I knew those answers I doubt I'd be at liberty to say, I'm afraid. I simply do as I'm told.' Her smile suggested she did not mind so much. 'But your sight has emerged, and that can only be a positive sign. I will inform Lady Satine immediately.' A coy smile played at her lips. 'Well, as soon as I have seen to the earl, which I will do as soon as you tell me more of the apparition.'

'I may have been mistaken.' A sense of dread came over him, sweeping with it the sense that last night marked the start of a great change, one he was not sure he was prepared for. He ran his hands through his hair, wishing, quite ludicrously that he had declined the lieutenant's invitation to converse. As though the poor delusional man had something to do with all this.

'You know you were not mistaken.' Jane watched him closely. The room's silence blanketed them, the candles still burning bright. 'Tell me.'

Silas brushed his fingertips against the fabric of his trousers. 'I first noted a few odd movements in the library while I spoke with Lieutenant Charters –'

'And he is the man you believe mad?'

He grimaced. 'I am not fit to diagnose him, obviously, but he believed himself unwell. That he was...possessed. Certainly his nerves were frayed, and he seemed terribly tired. It is why he sought out my company, to call on my supposed expertise as a member of the Order. The poor man could not have made a poorer choice.'

'I'm sure you were delightful. I don't believe I know of the lieutenant.'

Silas remembered the calling card Edward had pressed into his hands.

'I have his card.' He dug into his trouser pocket, pulling out the crumpled card. 'He wished to see me again.'

'Naked, I presume?' Jane took the card from him, her smile ripe with suggestion. 'Well done, Silas. A vigorous seeing-to might alleviate your stress.'

'Must you be so vulgar?'

Jane held the card so it caught the brunt of the candlelight, reading its inscription. 'Must you be wound so tight?'

Clearly she had not listened to a word of his earlier diatribe. Silas sighed. 'The Lieutenant wishes to arrange an appointment.'

'I'm quite sure he does.' She fanned her face with the tiny card. 'I shall be certain to organise that.'

'It is not for him though. His friend, the Baron Feversham, believes there is some issue in his London residence, and Lieutenant Charters would like to offer the Order's services as a birthday gift.'

Jane rolled her eyes. 'I do so love it when the Order is treated like an exotic fruit bought from Harrods. An indulgence to be enjoyed with wine. They are oblivious, most of them, to what it is that we do, and it can be ever so frustrating at times, the lack of true gratitude.'

'I'm afraid I'm as in the dark as the next man.' Silas was conscious of the dryness of his mouth and suspected his breath was less pleasing than it should be. 'You spoke of a balance that must be struck. How so? Most of those I spoke with at the ball were suggesting that...well...that there is a certain...theatrical element...to the Order's proceedings.'

'Theatrical element?' Jane laughed. There was always a tinkling quality to the sound, as though crystals brushed against one another. 'Why, Mr Mercer, if I were a different sort of person, I might be insulted by your suggestion that we are little more than charlatans. In truth, I wish it were so, but the supernatural are no different to humans. Some are good, some are decidedly not.' She staved off his next question before he'd opened his mouth to speak it. 'I promise you, you will learn more of all that soon enough. But for now let's return to your evening. Tell me of the apparition.'

Silas shifted his weight to the edge of the couch, turning so he did not have such a deliberate view of Jane's cleavage. 'It was certainly human in shape, but I couldn't make out any features. I am certain that it watched me though.' He looked down at his fingers. 'There was a strange tingling in my fingers, a coldness in the room that belied the enormous fire there. A ridiculous size really.'

She nodded. 'The apparition?'

'The fire.'

'Tell me of the apparition, Silas.'

'I've done so. We gazed at one another, wordlessly, then it slid up the walls and vanished. I'm not certain it wasn't the copious amount of brandy –'

'It was not the brandy.' Jane gestured at the candles, and the blaze of light was snuffed out, descending the room back into its original gloomy depths. 'Allow yourself to believe.'

They sat in silence a while before Silas gathered himself enough to speak.

'May I ask...how...how you can do such things? The candles, the adeptness at carrying my weight upon a dance floor.' He glanced at the ceiling. 'The sedating of your companion...'

She gave him a gentle smile. 'I'm certain even the Lady Satine would be agreeable to me speaking of myself with you now. I am a sylph, an elemental of the air. In fact the humans name my kind as air spirits, and I suppose they are not far wrong. I am borne of the breeze and wind, the element made flesh. I'm rather old, would you believe? You would certainly never guess upon my age, I have endured the years astonishingly well.' She framed her face with her hands, batting her eyelids. 'Silas? You'd do well to agree.'

Silas stumbled over himself to reply. 'You look...very well.'

A woman in her prime, her skin supple, desirable. Inhuman. Silas bit at his tongue.

'Good gods, man,' Jane declared, rising to her feet. 'If that is the best of your compliments I rather imagine you were a virgin when you died.'

Silas's jaw tightened. He'd had enough of conversing for one day. He stood, dwarfing Jane in stature but feeling immensely small alongside her. 'I think perhaps I will take my leave.'

'I have upset you.' Jane finally adjusted her robe, covering her sylph self more entirely. 'I'm sure you rutted to your heart's content, dear Silas. Your life was no doubt filled with eager bedfellows, I'm sure. Pay me no mind.'

41

An ache stretched across his chest as he considered a reply. 'I remember nothing of my life at all. Save for its end.'

Jane rubbed his arm, causing him to flinch. 'I'm sorry, Silas. It must be difficult for you, to not know who you were, but it is all behind you now anyway. You are doing very well, just as you are.'

Was it difficult, not knowing who he was? Silas pondered her words, searching for a hint of longing for such memories, and finding none. Rather there came an odd stirring of discontent. He recoiled from the idea of finding himself, rather than hungered for it. The waters of his drowning were fresh in his mind.

'Keep your spirits up.' Jane rose as she uttered her cheerful advice. 'Lady Satine will be most pleased with our conversation.'

'You will tell me before Her Ladyship returns, will you not?'

'Are you anxious about your meeting?'

He toyed with his undershirt, embarrassment mingling with his unease. 'I'll say that I am, yes.'

'Well, I shall ensure I am with you.' She did not, he noted, tell him his concerns were unwarranted. 'And I'll most certainly inform you as soon as I too am aware of her return. Her Ladyship is not much one for communication or deadlines, I'm afraid.' The sleeve of her nightgown slid free of her shoulder as she turned to leave. 'Now go and relax, Silas. I'll send word to Mr Ahari of your advancement, and have him arrange the particulars of the appointment with Baron Feversham. He'll be delighted I'm sure.'

Jane departed on light feet to return to her slumbering earl. Silas took his leave and stepped out into the sunshine, a welcome brightness after the confines of Jane's abode. The scent of jasmine disappeared the moment he set foot beyond her main door. Outside, the gentler waft of cut grass mingled with the richness of nearby pines. It was as though an age had passed since he'd stormed out of his cottage to demand an audience with Jane. He rubbed his face and set off back across the green, far more drained than when he'd set out. His boots crunched up the gravel pathway towards his door, his mind jumbled with all the things he'd learnt. So distracted was he that Silas almost collided with the impossibly short man who stood on the front steps. He wore a peaked cap and held a small parcel in his hands.

Startled, Silas stumbled back. 'Excuse me. Can I help you?'

'Well, that's about bloomin' time then. You've finally got the sight.' The man thrust the parcel upwards. He barely reached Silas's waist. 'I'm to give you this. Her Ladyship's orders. Consider it a welcome gift.'

'Thank you.' Silas worked hard not to stare. The diminutive chap was robust, with pale hair cut in a somewhat unrefined side part and eyes set deep in his skull. He was also the first living soul Silas had seen in the Village in three weeks, aside from Jane...and her companion.

Silas's gaze shifted to the gravel at the small man's feet. Though he stood in the full sun, there was no shadow. 'You say Lady Satine sent this for me?'

'Done already said it, ain't sayin' it again. You're a bit slow, ain't ya?' he said gruffly.

'No, I am not - '

'Yeah, you are. Been delivering your food every day for three weeks, and you was too blind to see. Almost stood on me a week ago, and you ain't exactly a slender fellow.'

'You're the one preparing the food?'

'Now, don't look so bloody shocked at the idea.' The man sniffed. 'Cooked it and delivered it. And without a word of thanks, might I say.'

Silas toyed with the string wrapped around the plain brown parcel. 'I'm sorry. Thank you. I wasn't aware that...well you see, I wasn't entirely sure –'

'You couldn't bloody see me. I know. But you do now, so a thanks will be expected in the future.' He touched a finger to his cap. 'Good day to you, Mr Mercer.'

The man trundled off, his short legs slightly bowed and his gait swaying his entire body side to side.

'What is your name?' Silas called. 'So I...might...thank you properly.'

'Gilmore,' the man replied before disappearing in behind the trestle of rose bushes that grew along the east side of Silas's cottage.

Silas stood still for several breaths, considering the oddness of his day so far, before he reentered his cottage. The air inside was actually cooler than outdoors. He would need to stoke the fire, but first, he determined to discover the contents of the mysterious package. Direct from Lady Satine herself. He entered the diminutive study situated across the hall from the parlour. The room had been furnished with all he might require, were he a man in need of a writing desk, bookshelves, and a window seat on which to contemplate his studies. At this time of day it took in the full sun, which highlighted the dust lying atop everything.

He laid the package on the empty desktop and tore into the brown paper wrapping. A crudely-made pine box lay within. He noted a brownish stain upon the lid as he removed it. Its insides were stuffed with straw. There was something mildly familiar about the box, though it had no label or markings to differentiate it from any other. Digging into the depths, Silas found the contents of the box readily. A rounded lump of wood. He pulled it from the straw, though the strands insisted on clinging, ensuring that the desktop became awash with lengths of pale gold. Silas surveyed his gift with a twist of his lips.

'What am I to do with this?' He peered at the rounded disc carved from boxwood with a fine swirl of grain at its heart. A thin length of string was wound into the deep groove around the edge of the disc. A bandalore. A frivolous device meant for amusement, the intended goal being to release the disc down the length of string and pull it back to one's hand with a perfectly-timed flick of the wrist. He knew with certainty what it was, but whether or not he could utilise it was beyond him. With some amusement, Silas poked his finger through the rounded loop at the end of the string and set the bandalore free. He fully expected it to clatter to the ground with his ineptitude, but he was set for a surprise. His motion was perfect, his tilt of wrist just so, and the disc fled down the length of string at great speed.

Without consideration he adjusted his hand once more, and just as the disc looked certain to strike the floorboards, he reversed its motion. The wood rushed into his grasp with a slap against his skin.

'Well then. I suppose I might have done this before.' He brought the bandalore closer to his face as though fine inspection might stir some memory. He sighed at the blankness that came. Really, anyone might have toyed with such a device. It was hardly remarkable. This was likely just a thoughtful, though odd, gesture from the Lady Satine to provide him with some distraction.

Setting the bandalore back into its nest of straw, Silas paid heed to the demands of his empty stomach and determined to make the most of the fresh bread and kippers that the newly-revealed chef Gilmore had delivered.

CHAPTER 5

F ive days passed somewhat pleasantly, with no word about when Silas might be expected to attend Baron Feversham. Which suited Silas just fine. But also with no hint from Mr Ahari, or Lady Satine, that his sighting of the apparition was significant. With such silence, he assumed perhaps it was not as wonderful as Jane had claimed, and he was not sure if that made him feel better about the whole incident, or rather worse.

At times, with so little to occupy his days, he amused himself with pretending he lived as a nobleman, free of responsibility, albeit one without any social commitments. Silas filled his time with taking walks in the grounds, his most enjoyed of pastimes. Spending time in the gardens never grew dull, and he'd begun to indulge in a spot of birdwatching. Jane had offered him a canvas and brush and oils, and Silas had tried his hand at painting the starlings that flitted by his cottage. He'd discovered that he was as terrible at it as he was reading, and the abandoned canvas was now hidden beneath his bed.

To his great relief he had not been requested to join Jane again at any dastardly balls, nor was he invited to accompany her on her appointments. She was regularly absent from the Village, her services in much demand apparently. This morning, with the sun alone in a cloudless sky and just strong enough to chase back some of the October chill, Silas set off on his midmorning walk. He slipped the bandalore into the pocket of a superbly-comfortable coat he'd found in the cupboard beneath the stairs. Royal blue in colour, with a black lapel, it reached down to his knees and had a fetching short cape that draped about his shoulders. He was quite sure it was called an Inverness coat, and wondered, as he did with most things familiar, if he had owned such an item once.

He grasped the door handle, catching sight of a grey bruise upon his knuckle. Luckily, he seemed to heal rather rapidly, for some of his more extravagant flourishes of the bandalore did not always proceed according to plan, and more than once the wood had wrapped sharply at his fingers as the disc fairly flew through the air. But he was quite mesmerised by the hum of the string as it moved, and the challenge of mastering it was a pleasant distraction.

Silas passed by Jane's residence. He was all but certain he'd heard her leaving sometime in the early hours. Sure enough the curtains were drawn on all the downstairs rooms, a habit of hers that denoted her absence. He was mildly disappointed. He'd admit he found her company pleasant enough, and was quite entranced by her manipulation of the air. Yesterday they'd enjoyed the pull of the wind tugging a pair of kites high into the air. The wind did not touch upon the row of aspen just beyond the back wall of Holly Village, or ruffle the climbing-roses surrounding Silas's cottage, it spared itself only for the kites they held upon the Village green, the strong breeze summoned with a whisper from Jane. It was a rather marvellous new pastime that Silas was eager to repeat.

He continued to stroll in an easterly direction, as he was so often drawn to do. Even with his intentions set elsewhere, Silas often found himself meandering towards the eastern wall of the Village boundary. Certainly the area was pleasing to the eye, with its cluster of willows huddled around a small pond and a grand layout of rose hedges, with some oddly late blooms evident, snow white petals stunning in their brightness, all set against the backdrop of a curious stone wall, the only section of the Village's exterior wall that was constructed of rocks rather than red brick. But in this part of the garden, at least, it was not nature that lured him.

When he reached the wall, Silas walked some distance along the boundary before he came across the intricate gate of iron set within the rocks. It was near buried beneath the heavy overhang of ivy that blanketed most of this section of wall and it had taken him several visits before he at last noticed the metal beneath the foliage. He held the slender vines aside, gazing out beyond the boundary of Holly Village. A wide expanse of meadow lay before him, with long grass and wildflowers bobbing in a gentle breeze. A beautiful sight indeed, but it was not what drew Silas's eye.

Beyond the open expanse he could just make out the jut of stonework rising from the ground. Slabs of chiselled stone that marked a graveyard.

His graveyard.

Silas breathed in, drawing in the earthy scent of turned soil. Relishing it far more than he would admit to anyone who wondered why he stood here with his nose tilted to the sky and eyelids heavy with contentment. For that was what came over him here. Contentment. Only when he laid eyes upon the graveyard did Silas long to breach the safety of the Village. Vulgar, really, to be drawn so to the place where his body had lain ready for the mealworms. He had ignored the strange compulsion for some time, blaming his rattled nerves for such an odd desire. But since his encounter with the spirit in the library the compulsion had grown ever steadily less deniable. He rattled the gate's latch, but it was locked fast as always. He curled his hands around the bars, surly with disappointment. It was not the coldness of iron he wished to feel, and nor was it his own grave he longed to visit. Silas winced. No, he had no desire to set eyes upon that empty place again. Truthfully, he was not certain what compelled him, only that something did indeed tug at him. Urged him to wander about those final resting places.

'Oh to be where death's shadow falls,' he whispered.

He pressed his face to the bars, and at once the sharp cold of the metal snapped him free of the strange melancholy overwhelming him. He pulled away, frowning at fingers that were as cold as ice. He shoved them into his pockets, where his right hand landed upon the bandalore. His hands must have been colder than he imagined, for it seemed to him that the wood itself was warm.

He nudged the gate once more with his foot. There would be no passing through without a key. Perhaps that was just as well. What had come over him? Whispering of death's shadow like some madman. Shrugging his shoulders to ward off the briskness of the air, Silas turned his back on the gate, deciding that his need for fresh air had expired. He continued on along the perimeter of the Village boundary until he found himself once more returned to the comfort of the cottage. His lunch basket sat awaiting him and he took it up readily, suddenly ravenous. He had just settled at the table to enjoy the beef broth when a knock came at the door.

'Gilmore.' Silas smiled down at the grim-faced man. 'This is an unexpected pleasure. The broth is quite wondrous.'

The man dismissed Silas's attempt at pleasantries with a grunt. 'Don't have time for natter. I'm instructed to tell you that you will be attending the Baron Feversham's residence this evening at eight, for the purpose of holding a seance. You're to be ready for collection at seven. Wait outside the gates and Isaac will collect you.'

Silas stared at him. 'I beg your pardon?'

'Ain't your ears working?'

'Well, yes, of course.'

'What's the problem then?'

'No problem as such,' Silas returned. 'It's just this seems very short notice. And I haven't the slightest clue about holding a seance.'

'Nothing to it. You sit round a table holding hands and talking utter rot.' Gilmore sniffed. 'Shall I tell Mr Ahari you are refusing?'

'I'm not refusing –'

'Sounds like it to me.'

'Well, you are hearing wrongly.' Silas fought to keep from slamming the door in the impertinent man's face. 'When is Miss Handel due back? She'll be attending with me, I presume.'

'And now you presume wrongly, Mr Mercer.' Gilmore's smirk told of a man who was rather enjoying himself. 'She's busy.'

Wide-eyed, Silas struggled to find a response. 'Is that so? Who is to attend with me?'

'No one.'

'I beg your pardon?' A twirl of temper played at his gut.

Gilmore's nose lifted as though Silas had expelled gas. 'That all you can say?'

'Gilmore, are you certain I'm to go alone?'

'What's wrong? You scared?'

Certainly, but he'd admit no such thing to this man. 'Uncomfortable, I should say.'

'Well, best you get comfortable with it, because that's what's happening. But don't worry your oversized head over it too much,' Gilmore said. 'Isaac will be about.'

'The man who has barely said three words to me since I arrived?'

'That one. Me point is, you ain't alone. And there ain't no big deal in what you'll be doing. Pandering to a bunch of dandies who've drunk themselves stupid and jump at their own shadows most likely. Like I said, get 'em to hold hands while you talk all mysterious like, maybe roll your eyes back in your 'ead a bit. They'll lap it up. You still fall over your own feet. Not likely Mr Ahari will give you a proper job to do just yet. Now, repeat the orders back to me.'

Gilmore was not, Silas decided, a fine communicator. But rather numbed with shock, he repeated as instructed, 'Be ready outside the gate at seven for collection. Appointment is at Baron Feversham's at eight.' He frowned. 'That's a fair journey, where does the baron reside?'

'Grosvenor Square. Make sure you dress fine. Don't give 'em reason to look down their bloody noses at you.' And with that sound advice, he trundled off.

'Right then.' Silas wrung his hands. 'I have been abandoned again. How bloody wonderful.'

By the time he stood outside the main gates just before seven, on a road that never seemed to have any traffic upon it, he was quite ill with worry. No drink to blame this time though. Nerves alone were making him a shuddering mess. And he'd run out of possible adjustments he could make to his Inverness coat, which he'd chosen to wear as a sort of self-appointed good luck charm. He had kept watch on Jane's home, jumping at every sound that might have been the gates allowing her entry. But no one came, and no one went. As was usually the case, he was alone in the Village, and never had he felt it more keenly.

At precisely seven, with a church clock chiming the hour in the distance, Isaac drew the bay to a halt before the gates. This time the steed pulled a dark brown brougham, his driver perched at the fore of the carriage in his usual layers of dark fabric. With the night descending quickly, and the lack of gas lamps even here on the main road, Isaac might as well have been a storm cloud perched in the driver's seat.

'Is there any word from Miss Handel?' Silas enquired. The short cape of his coat lifted with a breeze that had quickened considerably since his walk through the grounds. He set aside thoughts of the odd moment at the gate. Now was not the time to think of such things.

'What word were you expecting?' Isaac seemed to use his voice so rarely that his vocal cords were quite rusted.

'Information about how I am supposed to conduct myself this evening. I know nothing of what a spiritualist does.'

'You'll know it soon enough, if that's the way it's to be.'

Silas's grip on the leather seat tightened. 'What is that supposed to mean?' Could no one in this new life give him a straight answer? 'I have no idea what the Order wants me to do. Surely there should be someone there to watch me?'

Isaac laughed, short and sharp and hard. 'Who says there's not? Calm yourself, and follow your instinct, if you have one. If not, enjoy the wine. Now, I'd ask you to get in the carriage, Mr Mercer. The Order doesn't take kindly to their members being late to an appointment.'

And that was all he'd say on the matter, leaving Silas no option but to settle into his seat and be led to his own private nightmare. An entire night as the centre of attention. And with not a clue as to how to conduct himself.

Chapter 6

Grosvenor Square was a good distance away, leading them deep into the looming, bustling London boroughs that quite overwhelmed Silas's senses. Had he ever laid eyes on such a number of carriages or clutter of houses? If he had lived in this city once, he recalled nothing of it and quite suspected he would have disliked it immensely. The noise alone would drive a man insane. People shouted upon the street for any number of reasons. Coachmen sharply rebuked those who impeded their journey, hawkers forced their wares upon unsuspecting strollers, and at one point a fair gaggle of children, all clad in tattered rags, screeched and hollered their way across the road. They caught the sharp edge of Isaac's tongue, crossing dangerously close to the carriage. Silas spied more than one rag-and-bone man lugging an enormous sack upon his back, the material stained dark with what lurked within. Gas lamps threw their light against the infringing darkness, several being attended to by men on tall ladders, the passing crowd sweeping around them like a flock of birds avoiding the turrets of a chimney.

The traffic came from all directions, and Silas sank deeper into his coat, trying to edge back from the frantic nature of the world around him. It was only when they travelled alongside a great sweeping expanse of open space, a wondrously large garden whose name might have been revealed by one of the many signs passing him by, that Silas could regather any semblance of calm. He resolved to speak to Jane of the location, for he much desired to stroll the paths that wound through that peaceful haven.

After an interminably long time, though perhaps barely half an hour, Isaac drew up the brougham with a jolt so violent that Silas was thrust against his seat. The baron's residence was a magnificent townhouse, reaching up three levels, with Corinthian pillars standing to attention on either side of the rich mahogany door. Chandeliers were visible through the front windows, and candlelight illuminated an interior with a deep burgundy and gold wallpaper. The room on the right was occupied by an alarming number of people. Silas perched at his own small window, worrying at his dry bottom lip, reticent to step down from the carriage. Isaac offered no alternative when he pulled open the carriage door.

'Go on then,' he mumbled.

With no enthusiasm, Silas stepped out, eyeing the street. After all the business of the journey, this street was empty of foot traffic, putting a fast end to his notion of vanishing into the crowd.

'How do I send for you when this is done?' he asked.

'You don't. I'll be back when I'm needed.' Isaac pulled himself back onto his seat, clucking at the bay and jiggling the reins. He set off as rapidly as he had arrived.

Silas wrapped his arms about himself, staring after the carriage, so very close to hollering for the driver to return. Even Isaac's miserable company would be preferable to this evening.

A swathe of light blanketed him, and the muttering of voices grew loud as the front door opened. A stern voice ruined fledgling plans for escape.

'Mr Mercer, this way please. They are waiting on you.'

The man's clipped tone suggested lateness, but Silas doubted very much that Isaac had been anything but exactly on time.

'Yes, of course.'

The baron's butler was a severe man in both tone and appearance, with his ruddy hair thin on the crown and slicked back sharply at the sides. His nose veered towards beakish, and his dull brown eyes considered Silas with caustic disapproval. His mood sinking further still, Silas followed the butler inside. Despite a desperate attempt to appear suave, his feet betrayed him, toes clipping the thick wood at the base of the doorway, and he nearly fell into the foyer. The space at least was comfortably warm and bright, the floor laid with rich cherrywood.

'Your coat, Mr Mercer.'

'Oh, yes. I'm sorry.' Silas hurried to undress, cursing his thick fingers for their inability to negotiate the buttons. He was quite sure he heard the man utter a sigh.

At last undone, he handed over the coat. The air was thick with the scent of candle wax despite the gaslighting in the corridor, and the waft of cigars mingled with a floral perfume far headier than the jasmine Jane wore. Silas's apprehension rose anew at the thought of his absent companion. Her abandonment at this crucial moment was really quite distressing.

The butler announced Silas, the words apparently bitter on his tongue. The surly man stepped back to allow him entry. Silas must have taken too long to move, because the man's scowl deepened. Quick-stepping into the room, Silas drew in a breath. Apparently the baron was a popular man, for the parlour was filled to bursting with an array of brightly-clothed patrons. Two couples lounged upon a large blood-red chaise, while a trio of men conversed at the window with the street lighting silhouetting them. Another tickled the ivories of an astonishing Erard grand piano, ebony veneered with elaborate ivory marquetry. Leaning on the exquisite instrument was a voluptuous woman, whose layers of sky-blue silk spilled across the plum-coloured rug like some enchanting waterfall.

The scene was made all the more ethereal by the overuse of candles. There was barely a flat surface that did not provide a home to pillars of wax. Gaslights dotted the walls, both here and in the entry foyer – an obtrusive nod to the baron's wealth – but the glass cages in this room were dark.

It took all of a heartbeat for the eyes of the room to fall upon him, and Silas could barely breathe for the wave of panic it set rising within him. If he had been a self-assured man in life, capable of entertaining such a crowd, he felt no inkling of it now.

'We are so excited to have you here, Mr Mercer. I am Baron Feversham.' The baron rushed up to him, a full glass of champagne on offer, bushy eyebrows lifted. 'And aren't you just delightful? What a mammoth of a man. I don't suppose any spirit would dare tarry with you.'

The baron's love of indulgence was evident. His cheeks were full, his belly protruded ever so slightly beneath his vest of bottle green, but his light brown eyes were welcoming, and his smile was wide upon thick lips.

'Thank you, Your Lordship.' Silas accepted the champagne most readily. 'I am honoured to be of service.' The lie would need the champagne to wash it down.

'My dearest ladies and gentlemen.' The baron raised his own glass to the room. 'As promised, our guest of honour has arrived, a thoughtful gift from that most impish Lieutenant Charters. My friend seeks to assist me in gaining a full night's rest at long last. He believes the Order can settle the nefarious spirit that plagues my beautiful home. Sadly, the dear lieutenant is unwell and cannot attend.' There was a suitable amount of sympathetic muttering.

'Poor chap is unwell again?' someone asked.

'He has suffered for some months now, has he not?' came another concerned call.

'Regretfully, yes.' The baron frowned his concern. 'Though he hopes to join us at the Savoy later in the week as planned. Now, Mr Silas Mercer here is a spiritualist and a most esteemed member of the Order of the Golden Dawn. Please make him feel welcome.'

The room erupted in unexpected applause, rather more gregarious than decorum might dictate. Thanks in part to the chilled bottles of champagne dotted about the room.

'Please, please.' Silas held up broad hands, which were far more roughened than any of those around him. 'Thank you, but His Lordship does flatter me far too much. It is I who is honoured to be in such esteemed company.' Before the ball, Jane had offered a smidgen of advice, flatter the bloody hell out of them. Her own words.

There was a titter of approval, a raise of one or two fans and eyebrows. The woman by the piano had eyes to match her dress, a stunning shade of blue, and they were fixed on him. Silas tugged at his bothersome cravat, conscious that they were far from the only eyes upon him. The baron gestured to the oval blackwood table set in front of a fireplace low with embers.

'Shall we be seated?' he enquired. 'Will this suffice for you? Is there a direction you should be facing?' He patted the chair that sat with its back to the fire.

In truth, Silas would have preferred his direction to have been towards the door, marching right through it preferably.

He offered the bright-eyed baron a smile. 'This will be quite perfect.' He took a long sip of the champagne. What had Mr Ahari been thinking? Silas was sure to erode the Order's reputation in one fell swoop here.

'Wonderful.' The baron touched his arm and giggled in a most childish way. 'I don't know if I am excited or terrified.'

'There is nothing to fear, Your Lordship.' Except perhaps disappointment.

Silas took his seat, thankful the fire had not been stoked higher. He had no desire to drip with sweat any more than he already was. At the moment the dampness lay trapped beneath his undershirt, though how long before unsightly stains appeared, he could not say. His chair was moderately comfortable, a wood frame with a cushion inlaid in the seat of the same plum colour as the rug, but it was too small by the barest fraction, and the arms pressed into his hips. Silas studied the table as the guests studied him. He viewed its contents with some dismay. At the centre of the table, a Ouija board had been laid, a tiny crystal glass set upside down at its centre. At the ready to relay messages from the deceased. He was afforded a solitary moment of amusement when he thought on the irony of it. A dead man sat at the head of their table, and they were none the wiser.

Those in the room with him, ten in all, hurried in a rustle of silk and adjusting of coats to take their seats. He found himself watching each for signs of their shadows, and was pleased to note that all were as they should be, dark silhouettes at their backs and heels, moving in unison with the human who cast them. The baron took a seat to Silas's left, and when all other guests had settled, there remained two empty chairs at the far end of the dining table.

'Are there more guests to come?' he enquired of his host.

Baron Feversham rolled his eyes, laughing. 'Well yes, but honestly it is anyone's guess when Tobias might grace us with his presence, occupied as he is.' He gestured to the butler, who stood at the ready by the door. 'Geraldton, see that Mr Astaroth joins us. I don't care if he is cock deep.'

The room rippled with titters and laughter, the guests nonplussed by the baron's vulgar instructions. Silas managed to push a wry smile to his lips, lest they believe him the prude Jane declared he was.

The butler exited on silent feet, and the baron patted the slender hand of the red-haired woman at his side. She bit at her lip, shaking her bosom in an exaggerated shiver. Her silver gown was cinched tight at her waist but could not disguise her rather wide girth.

'I'm so excited, Albert.' She spoke to the baron, but Silas felt her gaze upon him. 'And yet, I do believe I'm quite afraid.'

'But, oh my Clare, isn't it delicious?' He shrugged his shoulders with shared excitement. 'A good night's sleep awaits me, I can feel it. Mr Mercer shall rid this house of its hauntings, I have no doubt. He is quite formidable, don't you think?' The baron lifted her hand, pressing it to his lips, and they huddled against one another, the two of them as giddy as children.

'Such a pity that Edward could not make it,' the woman, Clare, whispered, though not low enough to offer any real privacy. 'Is it another of his turns?'

'I fear so, my love.' The baron's excitement faltered. 'He sent his apologies only a few hours ago but would not elaborate why. I fear the latest treatments are not successful. Poor dear.'

'Does it hurt?'

Silas had not taken notice of the bespectacled man to his left, until now. 'Pardon me?' he asked him.

'This.' The man fluttered his fingers. 'Removing spirits, I mean. For that is what you intend to do, is it not? Exorcise those dastardly fiends from this world. How elaborate shall your show be then? I've witnessed a medium fairly expel her eyeballs from her head, such was the violence of her efforts. Shall we see such a performance today, my dear chap?'

His smirk was more bemused than ill-meaning, but it was plain he wished Silas to know he was a cynic of today's gathering. His shrewd eyes were an intense amber and locked upon Silas's own. This man assumed him a charlatan, and in this instance he was likely correct. Silas rubbed his chin, turning his gaze to a solitary candle beside the Ouija board. It sat, unlit, in a silver holder, which had been carved to resemble a tulip. He was not certain what was intended for it, but it was certainly not for illumination, as the room abounded with already flickering wicks.

'I hold no concern for the retention of my eyeballs. I can assure you.' Silas eyed his half-empty glass of champagne. 'And I am not here as a showman. I am to investigate the haunting that plagues His Lordship.'

To his great surprise, the man burst into vigorous laughter and slapped a hand to his back. 'Of course you are.' He lifted his spectacles to wipe at a jovial tear. 'I understand the Order has a remarkable reputation, but despite the fact you are a bloody great giant of a man, I'd wager that if a real ghost were to show itself, you would quite soil your trousers. If you don't mind me saying so, you look as though you are quite terrified. How many of these have you done, exactly?'

Silas's cheeks flushed warm, but he was thankfully saved from giving any answer at all by the clatter of heels upon the staircase and the high-pitched squeal of a woman. It was not a sound of ill-contentedness, rather a trill of excitement. Goosebumps rose along Silas's arms, and a most peculiar sensation came across him, as though feathers brushed at his hands. He shifted, startled by the sudden prickle of skin. But not even the inquisitive man took any note. All eyes were on the doorway. Several of the men began to clap, while the women suppressed coy smiles.

A ruddy-cheeked man spoke around his cigar. 'About bloody time, Tobias.'

'Mr Astaroth, for heaven's sake,' the baron called out. 'Do button up your trousers faster, we'd like to begin.'

A woman stepped through the doorway first, adjusting loosened strands of black hair back into her chignon. Her cheeks were touched with smudges of rouge and her lips were a pronounced shade of red. Those lips held a coquettish smile, the woman not abashed in the least with their welcome. Lines about her eyes suggested she was not young, but her age suited her well.

'Calm down, calm down.' She held a throaty voice for a woman, and it was filled with amusement. 'Mr Astaroth wished me to read him his tarot, it can't be rushed.'

Her response drew a round of laughter, but Silas did not join them. The peculiar sensation in his hands was quite distracting, as though he were dipping the tips against a bed of pins.

'Victoria was very thorough, both I, and my cock, can assure you. Good grief, why have you not begun?' A rather pretty gentleman, sharp featured, pale and fine, stepped into the room with a flourish of raised hands. His tousled light brown hair was wild about his shoulders, and his eyes so green it was as though emeralds had been pressed into the sockets. 'Let the amusements begin...or should I say...continue.'

His velvet coat, a red almost as bold as the woman's lips, was unbuttoned, revealing a black shirt with a silver brocade of Chinese dragons upon it. An elaborate ruffling of silk tumbled from the collar and covered a good portion of his chest. His choice of trousers was equally curious, a rather outdated fall-front style in black silk.

The baron groaned, but his smile was ever-present. 'Good god, man, we thought you two would never be done.'

'Perfection takes time, does it not?'

'Take your seat, you rascal, and stop your showmanship, at least just for a moment.'

Silas scratched his right palm absently, attempting to stymie the prickle. Like many things about himself he wasn't certain of his age, his late twenties was likely, much the same as the man who had just swept into the room.

Mr Astaroth tilted his head, pursing lips that held a near-perfect Cupid's bow. 'Am I to stand aside so another showman can perform?'

'Exactly,' the baron declared.

As Mr Astaroth made his way to his seat with his companion, he had a notable effect on those in attendance. The ladies all at once seemed incapable of deciding how they should adjust their gowns upon their seats, and the men were equally as fidgety. All of them were fixated on Mr Astaroth's procession across the room. The man had not spared Silas a glance yet, even when he was deriding him, and Silas had no issue with that at all. He was not sure he'd enjoy the pierce of those green eyes upon him. But he could not deny there was indeed something mesmerising about the lad, the sway of his hips, the coiled tension in his body that gave the impression he might suddenly leap unannounced in any direction.

Mr Astaroth stopped to take a glass of champagne from the tray offered by a somewhat flustered young footman. The liquid wobbled in its crystal confines, and the boy's eyes darted so quickly between the floor and the man before him, it was as though he'd lost control of his eyeballs.

'Thank you, kind sir. What a wonderful job you do.' Mr Astaroth's smile was discomfortingly suggestive, his whispered appreciation of the boy's offering far too intimate, and the serving boy nearly stumbled over his own feet to move away.

Mr Astaroth was slender, not remarkable in height, and the angles of his face were delicate to the point of being feminine, but he held a presence that quite overwhelmed the room. Silas's gaze moved down the length of the man's body to his feet. He wore heeled boots, which meant he was shorter than first impressions allowed. The glean of polished leather distracted Silas from what became startlingly obvious a moment later. He tensed and closed his eyes a second, as though that might change things. But alas it was not to be.

The ground at Tobias Astaroth's feet held no shadow.

Whoever this man was, he was not, for all intents and purposes, human. Silas took hold of the arms of the chair, filled with the sudden desire to depart. No one had thought to instruct him on an encounter such as this.

'Stop frightening the help and get your arse on a chair,' declared the bespectacled man at Silas's left. 'We know how you hate to have attention diverted from you, so do try and behave, Pitch old boy.'

Evidently the group knew the man well enough to have endowed him with a nickname. Silas could only imagine its origins.

'Oh Brenton,' Victoria, Mr Astaroth's companion, said. 'As far as I'm concerned, Tobias has been on his best behaviour all evening.' She had taken her seat and leaned her elbows upon the table, utterly at ease.

'Thank you, my dear,' Mr Astaroth said. 'You are as sensible as you are extremely talented in the art of, what were we calling it? Tarot reading.' He tilted his glass towards her before turning to Silas. The air quite vanished from Silas's lungs beneath the daggers of his emerald stare. 'How very nice to make your acquaintance, Mr Mercer. I do hope we are in for a wonderful show.'

It took an enormous effort just to inhale. 'Th...thank...thank...'

Pitch raised fine eyebrows, and not a wrinkle formed upon his brow. 'Are you quite all right?'

'I think you've got him rather riled up,' the bespectacled man, Brenton, determined.

'Oh dear, that does seem to keep happening. How absolutely dreadful of me.' Dirty undertones lurked in Mr Astaroth's reply.

The sharp tingle in Silas's fingertips grew more intense, and his face was aflame. All told, he really felt quite unwell. With the distraction of his painful hands combining with Mr Astaroth's unsettling presence, Silas considered a hasty departure, perhaps citing ill health. How was he to know he was not in danger, that the pinpricks upon his fingers were not a warning of some kind? Maybe that's what had happened to him in the library, his senses alerting him there to the presence of the apparition. The disconcerting supernatural watched him from the far end of the table. Silas's underarms were slick with sweat, his upper lip damp. The sanctity of Holly Village seemed a world away, and he was terribly far from its gated shelter. He cursed Jane. She'd been more concerned with having him join her and her paramour in bed than instructing Silas on more valuable lessons that might give him ease when a man like Tobias Astaroth appeared. Just as Silas braced to rise from his seat, Tobias's attention shifted, and his radiant gaze fell upon the baron.

'The lieutenant, wasn't he to attend this evening?' A blankness fell upon Mr Astaroth's features as he spoke, the bemused smirk leaving his lips. 'I thought you said this whole affair was his doing?'

The baron waved off the question. 'It was. But the silly sod took his leave of us. I only got word a short time ago, while you were indisposed.'

'Did he say why he could not attend?' Mr Astaroth lifted his glass and ran a slow finger around the rim.

The baron's laughter came from his belly, but Silas noted that Clare was not so amused, placing a hand upon her partner's arm as though in warning. One the baron ignored. 'He's escaped your clutches, has he? Surely you've bedded the man before now. I thought it a done deal long ago.'

Mr Astaroth slammed his champagne upon the table, spilling the liquid across the blackwood. There were several gasps, quickly stifled.

The only movement in the room came from the fire, which had birthed flames at the most inopportune time.

'I asked a simple question, dear Baron,' Tobias fairly growled, head lowered so that his hair covered his features.

The baron took a notable breath before answering. 'The lieutenant was unwell. He has struggled with ill health for quite some time now, as you know.'

Tobias's fingers splayed against the wetness on the table, and he nodded. 'Indeed I do. Does he suffer?'

The baron leaned towards his companion, perhaps regretting not heeding her warning. 'I don't believe so. Fatigue mostly, he does not sleep well.'

The group was rigid, soldiers to attention. No one daring to so much as blink.

Tobias lifted his head, his hair falling back to reveal the smile crawling up his cheeks. 'Look at you all.' He laughed, sharpness evident in the sound. 'So very easily rattled. As though I care an iota what state the lieutenant is in. Baron, if I wanted him beneath me, there would be no stopping it. Mr Mercer, you shall have no problem unsettling this merry bunch. They are frightened of their own shadows.'

The look he sent Silas's way could have pinned a butterfly upon a display board. And he was in no doubt that Tobias Astaroth saw him for what he was.

'Pitch, you really are a bastard,' the baron declared, and the room exhaled.

Victoria collapsed against Mr Astaroth, giggling with barely-concealed nerves. The man to his left slapped the table and remarked on how terrifically terrifying the ruse had been. The host leapt from his chair, snapping his fingers to summon a footman who arrived inordinately fast with a fresh bottle of champagne, one the baron now took from him, hurrying to fill Tobias's half-empty glass.

'Would you expect any less, dear Albert?' Mr Astaroth licked the spilled drink from his fingers.

'I'd be worried about you if you weren't being a cad.' The baron left the bottle with Tobias and returned to his seat. 'Let us begin then, Mr

Mercer. Take no notice of our exuberant friend here. Mr Astaroth enjoys a drama. His acting does rather keep us on our toes.'

Silas was not so sure what he'd just witnessed was mere histrionics, but he held his tongue.

'I've simply warmed up your audience for you, Mr Mercer.' Tobias's emeralds found Silas once again. 'My apologies for the delay. Won't you let the show, that is to say, the seance, begin?'

Begin, and end, Silas thought. The sooner he was back in the silent company of Isaac and on his way home, the sooner he would be at ease.

'No apology necessary, sir.' Silas coughed, adjusting a cravat that sat perfectly well. All he could rely on now was that Gilmore's rough instructions on conducting a seance were not about to make him the laughing stock of the baron's party. 'Now, I will ask you all to join hands. And we shall see what truly disturbs the baron.'

He declined the baron's outstretched hand, not eager to have anyone touch his irritated skin. 'I will need to remain untouched.'

The baron nodded firmly and reached right across the table so he might take Brenton's hand. The two men had to lean against the table to make contact. It hardly appeared the most comfortable of positions, but it would have to do.

'We will begin.'

Silas swallowed a last gulp of champagne before he closed his eyes, took a breath, and allowed words of utter nonsense to fall from his lips.

CHAPTER 7

A fter a short while, he ran out of nonsensical utterances, never mind feeling the greatest of fools. Silas sat in the whisper-quiet room with his hands spread upon the table, his gaze lowered, and at an utter loss as to what might come next.

'I...I call upon any spirit that may be in residence.'

A sound came, but it was not remotely ghostly. He eased one eye open, peering through his own lashes. Tobias held hands with no one, sitting back with his legs crossed, regarding his fingernails. Silas would wager the sound he heard was Mr Astaroth scoffing. With a scowl, he regathered himself and began again, all at once quite irritated by the man's brazen disregard for manners.

'Spirits that surround us, show yourself.' He raised his voice, shoulders back. 'I command you. Speak to me and show reason for the trouble you bring upon those who live in this home.'

He was rewarded with a shiver from several of the guests, a dour-faced woman glancing nervously about the room, and the spindly gentleman with a monocle swallowing so hard his Adam's apple did a jig. Gilmore was right in that at least. They were indeed lapping it up.

The tingling in his fingers sharpened and Silas winced. Rather than fading with time, it seemed the affliction grew worse. At the far end of the table Mr Astaroth appeared not the least bit interested in proceedings. He tugged insistently at the lace adorning Victoria's gown, earning him dainty, half-hearted slaps to desist, which he duly ignored. Truly the man was more child than adult.

Silas closed his eyes and hastened the end of the show. 'I call on you once more. Show yourselves. Face me.'

The heat of the fire at his back rose sharply, and small cries came from his audience. Silas opened his eyes to behold a most curious sight. The candle at the centre of the table, previously unlit, now sported a strong, steady flame. The fire at his back let out a sharp crack. Brenton jumped, thumping his knee beneath the table and releasing the baron's hand. He was quick to chuckle off his fright and reach for his glass. Silas held back from doing the exact same thing, if only to try to numb the bothersome pain in his fingers. It was as though tiny mites burrowed beneath the skin, seeking to escape.

'Please, do not release your grasp,' Silas warned.

'Is the spirit with us?' The baron, and his companion, were quite breathless and pale.

'I believe so.' Silas eyed the still-distracted Mr Astaroth. Surely this was his doing. He could not say how the man had lit the candle, but Tobias was supernatural, was he not? Jane had shown a propensity for just such a talent. Perhaps it was shared amongst the arcane.

The man in question stifled a yawn behind slender fingers and rose from his seat.

'Don't mind me, Mr Mercer,' he whispered in a voice that could hardly be ignored. 'I have somewhere to be.'

'You're leaving?' Victoria pouted.

'I very much am. We'll speak soon.' Tobias gave her a light peck on the check, and the baron a nod. 'A pleasure as always, Bertie.'

'Off you trot then, Pitch.' The baron appeared nonplussed with the interruption. Tobias Astaroth bid them all good night with an extravagant bow and sauntered from the room, glass still in hand.

Silas stared at the departing man's back, flummoxed by his utter disregard for those around him, but more than a little relieved at his departure. At least now no one would toy with him. Surely only a few more minutes were required and he could be done. The air was certainly lighter without Tobias Astaroth.

'A pound says he's at the lieutenant's residence in an hour,' the piano player of earlier remarked.

'I'd not bet against you,' the baron returned.

Silas was still staring at the now-empty doorway when Brenton nudged him. 'Never mind Pitch. The silly fop isn't happy unless he's the centre of attention. I dare say you stole his limelight and he's none too pleased. This won't be the first time he's abandoned us for another pleasure.'

'Yes, do go on, Mr Mercer.' Victoria still remained, wide-eyed with fright. 'Has it frightened off our visitor? Can you still see the spirit?'

Gathering himself, Silas lay his hands on the table with his palms facing the ceiling. The flame still stood bright and unwavering in its ornate silver holder, and his audience clutched at one another's hands with evident fervour.

'Thankfully, the spirit is still present. The flame tells us so.' Right on cue the fire expelled another sharp crack, making Silas's back blaze with its heat. 'This moment is of the utmost importance, so I beseech you, whatever occurs, do not let go of your neighbour's hand.'

The blatant falsehoods flowed from him rather too easily, and he had to admit there was something to be enjoyed in the theatrics. The audience too appeared thrilled, rustling with whispered excitement.

'Come hither, show yourself,' Silas said. 'Come hither, show yourself. Come hither, show yourself.' Repetition had a dramatic effect, he decided. 'Come hither, show yourself.'

The fire at his back grew ever stronger, now barely tolerable where he sat. Was someone feeding it without his notice? Perspiration gathered at his temples. 'Come hither, show yourself.' He was devoid of a notion as to how long this should continue. 'Come hither, show yourself.' Should he attempt to lift the table with a clandestine raise of his knee? Perhaps he should have given more thought to his decision to plant his hands so visibly upon the table, giving him no chance to rap at its underside. 'Come hither, show –'

The petite glass on the Ouija board toppled onto its side and rolled across the table. Straight towards Silas. At the same moment the candlestick wobbled dangerously, wax dripping onto the wood. Cries of alarm went up from the group. Silas almost joined them, catching himself only barely.

'We are not alone,' he declared, and hoped they did not hear the waver in his voice. 'Reveal yourself to...'

Silas jerked at a sudden warmth at the top of his thigh, as though someone pressed a warm stone there.

'What is it?' the baron hissed. 'Are we in peril?'

'No, no,' he replied absently. He reached into his pocket, and his tingling fingers met with a familiar solidness. The curve of boxwood. The bandalore rested in his trouser pocket. 'How is that possible?' he muttered.

Alarm tightened his throat. He knew with certainty he had not removed the trinket from where he'd last left it. On the bedside table in his cottage. What purpose would he have for an amusement such as this at a seance?

The shocking heat of the fire extinguished so suddenly it was as though the flames had been doused all at once. Silas swivelled in his seat. The flames still swayed and licked in the hearth, the blaze well and truly alight. He returned to the bandalore, quite at a loss regarding its sudden appearance.

'What is it?' Brenton demanded. The disbeliever was quite perturbed now. 'Mr Mercer, you look most alarmed. Are we in danger?'

Silas pulled his attention from the bandalore and lifted his head to a far more astonishing sight. A gasp escaped him. There, by the grand piano, an apparition drifted as easily as the kite he had flown with Jane so recently.

'What is it, man?' Brenton demanded.

Silas could no sooner force a word clear than he could tear his eyes from the apparition. The spirit held only the barest of definition, but considerably more than the one that had shown itself at the library. Here there was a flow of darkness around the head that had him imagining long flowing locks of hair. And the smudge of grey suggested a frock of some kind, a simple dress that did not reveal anything of the figure beneath. Of the face there was nothing to speak of save a deep darkness where it should have existed. Silas struggled to remain even remotely composed. The fire snapped and cracked behind him, but not a lick of its warmth reached his skin. Silas had moved from desperately hot to shiver-inducing cold in the merest of moments. Everywhere except for the hand that held the bandalore, that was. It was as warm as a cake fresh out of the oven.

'Mr Mercer?' The baron spoke in a loud whisper. 'I must insist you speak.'

Silas was not certain that was possible. His throat had quite dried up at the understanding that none of those around him saw what he did. The spirit was revealed to him alone.

'What is wrong with him?' someone whispered.

'Is he possessed?' came another anxious question.

Silas enclosed the bandalore in shaking hands. The prickling in his fingertips was quite dreadful. 'Stand fast. The spirit is indeed amongst us.'

Simply hovering there. Like a ghostly piece of clothing upon a line.

'What happens next, Mr Mercer? Will we be able to bear it?' Brenton laughed shortly, a tremor in his voice. He was affected by the fire's great heat, a sheen of sweat upon his face. Silas envied him that now. For him the room might as well have been situated in the North Pole.

'Now, I shall rid us of this entity, sir. As I have promised.' Silas's underclothes were soaked with cooling sweat, and he was racked with strengthening shivers. His heart was thundering in his chest. He'd succeeded in frightening everyone, but none more so than himself. And what *did* happen now? Gilmore had not spoken of this.

The spirit hung still, the blur of its feet just above the rug, the faint outline of the piano visible through its form. Silas had no more idea of how to exorcise an unwelcome spirit than he did to conduct a seance.

Clare pressed in tight against her baron, her chest rising in heavy shudders. A bearded gentleman further down the table looked set to burst into tears.

'What does it look like?' The baron threw a fear-soaked glance towards the piano.

'She,' Silas replied. 'It is a woman, I believe.'

Barely. Her essence leaked into the world around her, a painting caught in an invisible downpour. The spirit moved with sudden purpose – towards the gathered guests. Silas pressed back into his chair.

The baron threw off Clare's grasp to reach for Silas's hand. 'Does it come for me?'

Ankou, release me. The apparition's words ground like stones against one another, but no one at the table started at the sound. The words were for Silas alone.

'No, no. It does not come for you, sir.' Silas shook off the panicked baron's hold. The bandalore remained warm and secure in his grasp, the only weapon at his disposal should the spirit draw any nearer. What strange word had the creature uttered? Ankou?

Silas swallowed against his desperately tight throat. 'What name do you cast upon me?'

Release me.

The candle's flame fluttered, and at once a new sensation descended upon Silas. A hum of sound, a vibrancy throughout his body as though he stood too close to a cathedral's organ as its notes vibrated the air. It was not entirely unpleasant.

'Release you?' Silas stood but did not leave the table. The sharpness abandoned his fingertips, a gentle tingling replacing it.

'She speaks to you?' The baron's voice was hoarse, a wildness in his gaze. 'Tell me where she stands. Why does she plague me so? I demand an answer.'

Release me.

The apparition drifted to the opposite end of the table and passed right through Victoria, eliciting a ferocious shiver from the woman.

'Oh by the devil, I feel her!' she exclaimed, sending her fingers into a maddened sign of the cross across her chest. 'Banish it, Mr Mercer. Banish it!'

But he wished to do no such thing. The spirit, delicate as gossamer, drew herself through the table, headed for him. All the while the melodious, distant hum pulsed through Silas. A note which murmured beneath his skull, as miraculous as it was strange. The apparition's lower half was hidden beneath the wood of the table, her movement fluid and near-on graceful, taking her to where the candle stood. The flame reacted to her passing, jumping madly against the tethering wick. Startled cries flew from those at the table.

'Why does she haunt me?' The baron rose to his feet, once again clutching Clare's hand. The poor woman appeared ready to faint, her face pale as the mist that formed the apparition itself.

Not I.

The flame upon the candle at the centre of the table whooshed out. The women, and no few of the men, screamed, several pushing back in their chairs. The monocled chap whimpered, 'We must leave.'

All the calamity came from a distance, the vibration that had taken hold of Silas far louder than the frightened men and women in their fine silks and beautifully cut suits.

'Stay where you are, hold fast,' Silas cried. To change any aspect may well see this spirit disappear from his sight, and that he could not bear. Her presence and her song were as exquisite as they were perplexing. In his hand, the bandalore remained warm as a cup of freshly-poured tea.

'Hold your nerve,' he declared, as much to himself as the restless audience.

The baron abandoned any pretence of enjoying the spectacle. The man was shuddering with terror. 'Be gone, foul spirit. I've battled you this long, I'll not be subdued this day. Let me sleep, sicken me no more.'

Not I. Know this. Come so you might release me.

The spirit rushed at Silas, and the vibrating melody grew hard and fast, shaking the very teeth in his head. Her course altered at the last instant, and the apparition dashed against the wall, disappearing. Silas pushed back his seat with such vigour that it tipped entirely, crashing close to where the flames roared within the hearth. But he'd halt for nothing.

'Stay where you are,' he shouted, having no care whether his directions were followed or not.

He rushed into the corridor, eliciting a startled cry from a maid and the stern scowl of the ever-present butler.

'Can I assist you, sir?'

Silas had no time for an answer, spotting the apparition where she hovered halfway up the stairs. Waiting on him. He brushed past the servants wordlessly, following behind the spirit, who moved like a soft cloud towards the second floor. He took two of the wide stairs at a time, tripping on the very top, barely preventing himself from colliding with a potted plant that stood there in a gleaming brass pot. The bandalore's temperature shifted from soothing to rather less so. And if Silas were not so single-minded about maintaining contact with the spirit, he might have cast it back into his pocket. But he'd grown rather intoxicated by the sensation that filled him and dared not risk unhanding the bandalore, lest the marvellous song that drenched him end. His hands tingled, entirely alive with a strange but alluring energy.

The spirit swept into a room further along another luxuriously-appointed hall. Gaslights perched in etched glass coverings along the wall made his progress trouble-free. Silas's heavy footfalls echoed off the wood panelling, the hall runner too thin to muffle his weight. He reached the room where the spirit had withdrawn and found himself inside a bedroom.

Startling gold wallpaper embellished with a mesh of grape vines and autumn leaves covered the walls, the light catching against reflective specks within the paper. A grand bed stood between two French windows, its canopy a deep crimson, its coverings patterned yellows and reds, all expertly fitted and not a cushion out of place. The room smelled faintly of tobacco smoke. The baron's room perhaps? A small fire had been lit in a white marble fireplace, spreading warmth through the room. But the spirit had not lingered in this main room. Silas moved with caution towards the water closet, its oak door ajar. That she waited for him in there, Silas had no doubt. She was a musical note in his body's song, and he simply followed the tune. But should he? What if this were not a spirit at all but some kind of evildoer? A daemon perhaps?

The bandalore shifted in his grasp, a sudden enough jolt that Silas uttered a startled cry. The sound of footsteps reached him. His audience had not heeded his instruction. Soon, he would not be alone. He took a purposeful step forward, but before he could reach for the water closet's door, it swung open on creaky hinges.

Silas stared in wonder. The spirit stood before him, far more defined than before. There was no doubt now of her sex, and he'd been correct about what he suspected was the flow of long hair. She bore a slender neck and a petite face, whose features were still a little blurred. Not a woman but a girl.

A distant sadness tugged at him.

She lifted her arms, letting them drift towards the walls around her. Here the wallpaper was even more elaborate, swirls of blue and white at floor level, meant to mimic the curl of waves. Birds with long pink legs and flouncy white feathers stood amongst them, their elongated necks reaching for the dangling brilliance of the green plants that consumed most of the pattern. The vibrant colour brought to mind Tobias's emerald eyes.

Here is his ghost.

'I don't understand.' For Silas did not.

Release me.

Her longing distorted their song, changing it into something mournful and devastating. Silas hunched beneath the weight of it, a half-formed sob escaping him. His innards ached, his belly unsettled by something untoward. He must release her. It was as certain as the sun. The tune changed its chord, reaching higher. More urgent. The bandalore stung his palm, such was its heat. Silas clenched his teeth, holding fast, and the song rose higher still. Louder. Drowning all but itself. He must release this poor soul. He would rather burn than fail at the task. At once the string unwound from the wooden disc and found his finger. Anchoring there.

Silas drew back his hand, and with the song soaring to a crescendo, he struck forward. The disc flew from his grasp, unfurling down the length of the dirty string. Reaching, reaching, for the spirit that awaited it. She flung her arms wide, unafraid.

The disc struck right at her core, piercing through her ethereal form. But she did not cry out. She did not recoil.

And in that instant she was stunning in her clarity. Silas stared into the soft brown eyes of a young girl. Her face was gaunt, eyes sunken, speaking of the troubles of her life, but she smiled at him.

And vanished.

The song stopped. A sudden silence that shuddered through his bones.

The disc reached as far as it could travel along its anchoring string and whipped back into Silas's grasp, slamming into his waiting palm. His hands were steady, unbothered by the tingling, all pain removed. He stood there, breathing in short gasps. Seeking to absorb what had just happened.

'What have I done?' he whispered.

From a far corner of the room came a soft sound. A shuffle of feet. Silas whirled around to find the room fairly crammed with people. Even the butler had followed, and stood peering around the edge of the doorway. Everyone was adorned with various expressions of wonderment. The baron crossed his arms tight across his chest, his face pale, while Clare huddled behind him, her dress betraying her hiding spot.

'It is done, isn't it? What you did, just there –' Baron Feversham flicked his fingers at the bandalore in Silas's grasp. 'You disposed of that thing, didn't you?'

Silas scowled at the man's choice of words. 'She was a girl, not a thing. And she had lived a harsh life.' He paused, struck by the depth of emptiness that filled him. 'And yes. She has been moved on. And will trouble you no more.'

'Quite the show, dear boy.' A portly man removed a cigar from his vest pocket with trembling hands. 'Quite the show. Who needs a whisky?'

There was a mumble of agreement, but Brenton frowned and moved closer to the water closet, keeping some distance between himself and Silas. He peered into the smaller room.

'Bloody hell, Bertie.' He shook his head. 'Haven't you heard about this blasted wallpaper? You need to rid yourself of it.'

The baron didn't answer, his eyes fixed on Silas.

'Bertie does so adore that print.' Clare touched the back of her hand to the distracted baron's cheek. 'What harm can mere colours cause?'

Silas recalled the spirit's outstretched arms. *Here is his ghost.*

'All the harm in the world,' Brenton declared. 'Scheele's green, your wallpaper is filled with it. William Morris is poisoning us all with his damned arsenic so he can keep his bloody mines going. If you don't believe me, ask the Swedes. They've banned it over there, they have. Get rid of it, Bertie, for god's sake.' He pursed his lips, turning on Silas. 'You knew of this, didn't you? There's no haunting here at all. Baron Feversham is simply suffering the effects of this dastardly wallpaper. The Swedes say it brings on hallucinations, fever, stomach upsets. Blast it, man, I believe you've hoodwinked us all. The Order must have had a spy at one of your parties, Bertie.' He adjusted his spectacles and sniffed. 'Granted, it was a fine display you put on there, Mr Mercer. Had us all quite abuzz. I'll admit I was taken. I suppose that makes it worth the fee. Shall we move to the parlour for a celebratory drink?'

Silas was far too exhausted to contradict the man, and what did it matter anyway? She was at rest. He was not sure he'd ever felt so contented.

'Thank you, but no.' Silas slid the bandalore into his pocket. 'I'll be taking my leave. My work here is done.'

Brenton inclined his head and then left the room at some pace.

The baron stared into the water closet, lost in thought. Clare tugged at his sleeve, urging him back to the parlour, but the man shook his head.

'Was there truly nothing, Mr Mercer? I felt so certain...that I was not alone here. But is Brenton right?'

Silas considered his answer. Brenton's reasoning made sense and seemed far more likely than a lost soul seeking to help the living. But Silas did not enjoy the idea of leaving the girl's act of generosity unknown. The echo of her notes still played through him at a distance, not yet faded as she was.

'I would take the advice you are given, if I were you, and see to it that you remove that wallpaper. I believe you will find your slumber is most restful once it is done, and you'll be haunted no more. But I can assure you unreservedly that the spirit was not of your imagination. She led me here, she showed me what was responsible for your tortured night hours and it is just as your gentleman friend suggests. I do believe you owe the spirit a debt of gratitude for what amounts to your rescue. Now, I am quite done here and I shall bid you good evening, sir. Good evening, my lady.'

And without waiting for a reply from the dazed baron, Silas took his leave with far more buoyancy than he had arrived.

74

CHAPTER 8

Isaac drew the bay to a halt, in his sudden and uncomfortable way. The rough calamity of motion nudged Silas from contemplation of the device he held. A toy, essentially. A trinket. And yet, the bandalore could not be further from either of these things. Silas noted the tremble still evident in his hands. The tingling had ceased the moment the ghostly young woman met his bandalore, but the echo of that most marvellous song still filled him. The breathy notes as much a part of him as his own ribs. Even now, Silas could barely catch his breath at the memory of it. He longed to hear it again, as one might wish to listen once more to the notes of a lover's melody.

The bay shifted, the animal restless in its harness, drawing Silas fully to the world. Beyond the smudged glass of the carriage window lay an unfamiliar sight. Not the Holly Village gates, as he'd expected, but somewhere rather different. Their destination appeared to be a public house. Above the wide wooden door hung a sign painted sunflower yellow. Black writing was scrawled across the face. The letters no doubt declared the name of the place but to Silas's uneducated eye it might as well have been chicken scratchings.

The pub's exterior was painted a charming claret. Great hanging baskets, green foliage spilling from their thick weaves, jutted out over latticed windows, charming with their quarrelled panes. The establishment sat snugly in a row of nearly identical buildings, each three levels high. Silas craned his neck to peer skyward. Ivy covered the upper walls extensively, reaching almost to the very top of the building. As he took it all in, he found himself wondering if he might be required to use the bandalore here once more. And the idea rather gave him a delicious shiver of anticipation. Oh to hear that tune again. He opened his hand, the bandalore resting against his palm. But the trinket showed no sign of stirring, warmed by his own skin and nothing more. The air was filled with little more than the rattle of passing carriages.

'Are you going to get out?' Isaac was quite suddenly and very unexpectedly at the carriage door. Silas started, and the bandalore fell from his hand, hitting the cabin floor with a light thud, and rolling into the darkness beneath his seat.

'Blast.' He edged his broad frame off the seat and moved with a decided lack of grace onto his knees in the cramped quarters. 'Yes, yes of course. One moment.'

Isaac did not open the carriage door nor move to assist Silas. He just stood there, the wrap of his muffler covering his mouth entirely, his eyes dark coals. The solitary gaslight nearby was weak and did little to illuminate him.

'Hurry it up. Mr Ahari is waiting on you.'

Silas sat back on his heels. 'I'm...I'm sorry, did you say Mr Ahari? He is here?'

Isaac surprised Silas with a chuckle, a not altogether unpleasant sound. 'Course he's here, he lives here a good part of the time. I thought it best you relay your night's experience to the man direct.'

'My experience?' Silas stared at him, perplexed.

The coachman heaved a sigh. 'Yes, Mr Mercer. Or did nothing of the evening strike you as unusual? You go about reaping lost souls on a regular basis, do you?'

'No. No, I do not. But how on earth did you –'

'Don't you worry your head about that. Best you get inside and tell the boss how it all went.'

'I must find the bandalore first.' To Silas's mind it was quite impossible that he could consider stepping foot out of the carriage without it. The very thought of leaving it behind caused an odd tightness to come to his stomach. 'I really must find it.' He really must. He might have no clue where it had come from to begin with, or from whom, but Silas now readied himself for argument, prepared to remain where he was no matter what the coachman might threaten. But Isaac simply shrugged.

'I think you'll find that trinket of yours quite hard to lose, Mr Mercer.' He turned on his heels and stepped away. Silas stared at the empty space beyond the window. The carriage wobbled as the driver took his seat up front.

'Must everyone speak in riddles?' Silas muttered to himself.

He puffed his cheeks, and lowered himself so he might peer beneath the fabric which draped to conceal the cavity beneath the seat. His hair brushed the floor. There was an unpleasant odour down low, horse dung, and another, fouler smell Silas did not wish to contemplate, but no sign of the bandalore. A trill of nerves struck him, a thin sheen of sweat appearing upon his palms. He simply must find the bandalore.

He shifted and his buttocks met the carriage door, causing it to rattle in its lock. 'For mercy's sake,' he hissed through gritted teeth, unsettled by his cramped quarters but growing ever more fervent in his efforts to reunite with the bandalore.

He grasped about in the shadows. What light came from the gaslight was too weak to infiltrate the darkness of the carriage. He patted at the floor, wincing as his hand came into contact with clumps of soft dampness. Clumps he hoped were no more than dirt. He pressed his lips tight. His heart had taken up quite the tempo, far greater than such efforts required. The thought of another moment's separation from the bandalore left him quite breathless. Shaken, even. He simply must have it upon his person again. Silas focused his attentions through the threatening wave of panic. He was being quite ludicrous. The device was but a reach away, and with some level-headed control, he'd retrieve it and soon be enjoying an ale, thinking himself the fool for such desperation. He closed his eyes, sinking into a deeper darkness, attempting to ignore how his thighs burned.

'Come on now,' he whispered. He'd lost leave of his senses. He was speaking to a piece of wood as though it were a house cat. 'Come back to me, now.' But it felt the utterly right thing to do.

A light touch brushed his seeking fingers. He held perfectly still, and his shoulders protested at the sudden strange angle. Another brush of something light, soft caressed his middle finger. Silas's smile shoved at his cheeks. There came a gentle scraping sound, and a tap of wood against his fingertips. He opened his hand, and the bandalore slipped into his palm. He released a triumphant cry, and the terrible tension that gripped him slid away. He laughed, somewhat giddy with it all.

'Wonderful!' Silas held the device aloft, admiring it as though it were the most perfect diamond. 'That is much better.' It was astounding, and strange, and entirely as it should be, that he held the bandalore once more. A piece of him no longer missing.

'Bloody marvellous,' came a raspy voice thick with the drawl of the Irish. 'You found your toy.'

A stocky woman with a mass of tangled red hair and pale skin covered with light brown freckles stood alongside the carriage. The swell of her chest left no doubt of her sex, but she wore trousers and a shirt that appeared a size too big and clearly intended for a man of the country fields. She had a rather wide mouth in contrast to small, close-set eyes that watched him carefully.

With a clearing of his throat, Silas shoved the bandalore into his pocket and pushed up from his knees. The cab rocked, and the woman released a sharp laugh through flared nostrils.

'Careful there, Mr Mercer. You'll topple your fine carriage right over.'

'I'm sorry, have we met?' He frowned.

'I 'aven't 'ad the pleasure, sweetness.' She smiled wide. 'Been visiting 'olyhead these past few weeks on account of my work, but there's lots of talk about the new lad. Not much luck involved in working out you're the one they spoke of. You're quite 'ard to mistake, being the strapping lad you are.'

'Are you...from the Order?' Silas remained in the safety of the carriage but was sure a growl to depart would soon come from Isaac.

'The 'ermetic Order of the Golden Dawn.' The woman planted her hands upon her hips and nodded with great enthusiasm. 'You bet your firm chin I am. You're in the company of the Order's premier soothsayer, the Hag of Beara, though I'll let ya call me Tyvain. That's me name.'

He saw now that she had rather brilliant amber-coloured eyes and remarkably good teeth too, considering her title of hag and her dishevelled appearance. Silas was quite certain a tiny bird's feather jutted from her hair at her left temple.

'You coming from a job?' she asked.

He nodded slowly.

'Same for me. Let me tell you, I was not the bearer of good news for that bloated old fool I saw. Man'll eat 'imself to death before the year's out, and I didn't need me bones to tell me that. Death is waiting for 'im , plain as day.' She paused, staring up at Silas. The brightness of her eyes dulled. 'Plain as day,' she muttered, before dislodging a lump of sputum upon the cobblestones. 'But he sure didn't like being told death was coming for 'im sooner rather than later.'

'Indeed,' Silas said, for he could think of nothing more substantial. She peered at him in a most discomforting way.

'Come on, man, are you just gonna 'uddle there like a giant bloody lump? Or shall we go and get ourselves nice and tanked on some so-so ale?' The woman shrugged at her shirt where the wide collar had slipped over a shoulder awash with freckling. 'Don't get me wrong, I love Mr Ahari with all me 'art. He's a good enough boss, I'll admit, but 'is stout doesn't hold up to the one at the Black Lion. Been down Chelsea way?'

'No, I'm afraid I can't say I have,' Silas said. 'So, Mr Ahari runs this establishment?'

'Smart one, ain't ya? He not only runs The Atlas, 'e owns it and preens over it like a mother 'en with a bloated chick.'

Talk of ale reminded Silas of how parched and hungry he was. He adjusted his coat, brushed dirt from his knees, and clambered from the carriage. Barely had he closed the door behind him before Isaac flicked the bay into action and trotted away without a word. The air had chilled considerably, catching at the back of Silas's neck. He followed Tyvain towards the double doors that would give them entry. She walked with a limp, favouring her right leg. He wondered how the woman stood the cold with such thin layers upon her.

'So what they got you doing then? They should 'ave you as a debt collector.' Tyvain laughed, or rather cackled, like some strange bird. 'I'd piss in me pantaloons if you turned up on my doorstep, my friend.'

'I am not a debt collector, no.' Silas wrinkled his nose at her declaration. 'I am a spiritualist, at least that is what I'm told.'

She did not seem the right person at all to divulge what the ghost had called him.

Tyvain snorted. 'Nay, you ain't. No such bloody thing. If you don't wanna tell me your true nature, I won't pry. It don't matter none to me. What matters is ale and food. Come on then, let's see if they 'ave enough of either to fill your britches. Gods man, see you don't step on me. You're a damned big, tall one, reckon ya'd snap me in two.'

There was no arguing her blunt observation of his form. The top of her head barely met his chest, but he doubted Tyvain was half as vulnerable as she sought to sound, for the Hag of Beara had no shadow at her feet.

Silas's stomach growled with some ferocity, and Tyvain's eyes widened.

'By the chaplain's balls, you're fair starvin' then. Best get you fed before you decide on an appetite for red-'eaded hags .'

She pushed the doors open, and the warmth of the interior battled valiantly against the external cold. Silas hurried into the heat, eager to be out of the elements, and was met by the heady scent of ale and the pleasing waft of a kitchen.

'Fish and chips good enough for ya?' Tyvain called as she limped towards the bar.

'Oh, yes. Thank you.' He was not about to argue, quite ravenous now. Eager as he was to speak with Mr Ahari, past experience had shown him that answers were so rarely forthcoming from anyone in authority that a rush hardly seemed warranted. And it would be far wiser, surely, to face the man on a full stomach.

The large mahogany-clad room was warmly lit by an array of etched-glass gas lamps set against diamond-shaped mirrors upon the walls. An enormous fire roared at the centre of a black marble mantelpiece. The two armchairs set before it were occupied by two gentlemen, who halted their conversation to stare at him. By the flickering, dancing light of the fire Silas could make out their shadows with little effort. To his surprise, the men were human. As were the three women seated at a raised table further back in the room, all of which were being none too subtle with their stares and whispers. They were friendly enough, he supposed, one of them offering a bold wave, which he returned with a polite nod of his head. Tyvain called on him to hurry up in no uncertain terms, and Silas abandoned his observance of the greater part of the room to join her at the bar.

A sole patron was seated there already, a reedy man with a mop of blond curls, who stared at Silas over the rim of his golden-liquid-filled glass. He took a slow sip, which Silas could hear from where he stood. The only one who did not pay him much mind was the bartender, occupied as he was with Tyvain's order. He was a full-faced bald man, who appeared to be of similar Oriental extraction as Mr Ahari himself. This man, though, suffered unfortunate pockmarks decorating his cheeks. He pressed a pint glass beneath a tap, pouring a rich dark ale. Silas's mouth fairly watered at the sight.

'I'll 'ave me usual, and make sure you fill it to the rim this time, won't ya?' Tyvain didn't bother waiting for a reply, and the bartender didn't offer one. 'What'll you 'ave , Mercer?'

He hesitated, conscious of the lack of money upon his person. He'd had no need of it these past few weeks and had forgotten about it entirely. His face warmed and he pressed in close to her side, so not all in the room might hear him. 'I'm sorry,' he said at a whisper. 'But I do not have any money with which to pay for a meal or drink.'

'Guess he's going 'ungry and thirsty then, eh, Benedict?'

She nudged the loudly-sipping patron seated at her other side. He lowered his glass, considering Silas. Benedict was a bony man, his cheekbones intent on piercing the skin, and his shoulders hunched forward even when he lifted his elbows from the bar to sit up straight. His skin was touched by the sun, suggesting he might have travelled in the recent past, though Silas struggled to imagine the man upon an adventure.

'That one will send the Order broke before long,' Benedict finally said, with an accent that suggested some breeding. 'Both with feeding and clothing. I pity your tailor, boy. Does he need a stepladder to reach your crotch and do his measurements?'

The bartender scowled down at the pint glass as it filled. 'Leave him be, Benedict.'

'It is but an innocent inquiry.'

'Certainly not, what a strange thing to suggest.' Silas touched at the collar of his coat, which he had not been inclined to remove. He'd seen neither tailor, nor stepladder, but was not about to indulge the man with the full story of the coat's discovery and perfect fit.

'Look at 'is face.' Tyvain laughed. 'You've gone and insulted our precious giant, Benedict.'

Both of them appeared to find Silas's discomfort highly entertaining. He was quickly coming to resent Isaac's unrequested decision to bring him here. By now Silas could have been seated before his own fire in his dressing gown with his favoured brandy warming his belly, taking a full and deep appreciation of the evening's most startling events in peaceful contemplation. He wished to be done with this place as soon as possible, his appetite could wait.

'Excuse me, sir.' Silas leaned down to avoid the jugs and glasses hanging from hooks above the bar. 'Might I ask if Mr Ahari is available to speak with now?'

The bartender set down the fresh-poured stout, brown as syrup with a creamy froth, in front of Silas. 'I'll enquire for you, of course. Allow me to introduce myself, my name is Kaneko. Welcome to The Atlas, Mr Mercer. Enjoy your ale, and anything else you desire, whilst you wait and do not worry about the cost, for members of the Order do not pay for anything here. These two are sporting with you. The hag likes her drink and the djinn just enjoys irritating us all.'

'Where the 'ell is mine?' Tyvain thumped the bar. 'The man didn't even bloody order a drink and he gets served. You trying to kill me, Kaneko?'

If looks alone could do so, Kaneko was certainly giving it his all. He gave Silas a more congenial nod. 'I'll let Mr Ahari know you'd like a word.'

And with that, the bartender vanished. Neither here, nor there. Not walking away but popping out of view as though he'd never stood there at all.

'Wonderful job, hag. You've pissed him off,' Benedict sighed, cradling his half-drunk pint. 'As if Kaneko needs to inform Ahari of anything that goes on in this place. I'll guarantee you that bloody tsukumogami has folded back into his umbrella right now and won't be coming out anytime soon. No telling when our next drink'll be.'

'Bastard,' Tyvain declared.

Silas peered over the wooden countertop, as though the man might have simply crouched down to remove himself from sight. It was empty behind the bar save for dirty boot prints marking the once-white tiles. So, there were supernaturals who could just vanish on a whim. Astonishing.

'What did you just call him?' Silas asked. 'The bartender, you called him a tuku...'

'Tsukumogami,' Tyvain said, scowling. ''Cause that's what 'e is. Anything gets old enough, there's a chance it'll find some life. I'm being treated right miserably by a bloody umbrella.'

Silas's face must have shown his confusion, for Tyvain huffed. 'Yeah, you 'eard me right. Everybody is something 'ere, Mr Mercer, and none of it human.'

'But...how could that man be an umbrella?'

'You mean 'ow can an umbrella become a man. By living a bloody long time and being around the right people to begin with. Spend over a hundred years being used by someone like Mr Ahari, and things can 'appen. The lifeless get life. Ain't that what happened to you, Mr Mercer? Only difference was you were a man to begin with, not a parasol.' Her laughter erupted and dissolved into a snort. 'Likely you were as oblivious as those two there.' She gestured to the men by the fire. 'Purebred human. Not a speck of special about ya, and totally blind to what's going on around ya.'

She was not kind with the word *purebred*, licking at it like it was the sourest of lemons. Silas watched the conversing men. An uncomfortable emptiness came with considering his past and he spent little time considering it. 'How is it that they are able to enter here? I mean to say, if they are not of the Order, and not of...well, any particular talents?'

'Through the bloody door like anyone else,' Benedict sniffed. 'The Atlas is many things but it is not exclusive. Anyone can enter, even the pures. But they don't know a bloody thing about the truth of the place or the people they are sharing a pint with. It's convenient anyways, to have them in here. Some of us naturals, that's what most of us like to call ourselves, you see, have a strong urge to indulge in humankind every now and then.' He spread his arm to take in the room. 'The Atlas is a silver platter, so far as some are concerned.'

He and Tyvain shared a dark laugh, and Silas did not enjoy the sound of it at all. But he had no chance to question them further. A swinging door behind the bar, one whose lack of handle had hidden it before now, opened wide, and the beaming visage of Mr Ahari filled the space. The Oriental gentleman was exactly as Silas recalled from their solitary meeting. Plump of face, rosy of cheeks, and thick of lips. His smile never seemed to waver, as though the curves to his lips were permanent. His deeply hooded, narrow eyes were dark but warm. His wrinkles suggested his youth was far behind him, but they suited his face so well it was hard to imagine him without their charms.

'Tyvain, now what have we said about abusing poor Kaneko?' Mr Ahari said. 'He really does a marvellous job running the place, and you know it.'

'Wasn't saying any different.' Tyvain sniffed. 'I was just thirsty, is all.'

Mr Ahari wrapped thick fingers around the middle of three wooden beer taps. 'Dark ale, that's your preference I believe, Tyvain?'

She nodded, the spark at once returning to her eyes. Her tongue ran across her bottom lip. 'And we ordered fish and chips, one for me, one for our giant friend 'ere .'

Mr Ahari's laughter was melodious and oddly soothing. Silas found himself smiling as he took a long sip of the stout. 'I see you've been introduced to our soothsayer, Mr Mercer.' He'd not yet looked Silas's way.

'Yes, I've had the pleasure,' Silas replied.

Mr Ahari's eyes, so rich brown they appeared black, narrowed further as his smile lifted.

'Premier soothsayer.' Tyvain tapped her fingers against the wood, her impatience for the ale unconstrained. 'Old Bess needs to quit shoutin' about bein' your number one. A lot of rot that is.'

Mr Ahari placed the pint in front of Tyvain with a flourish. 'There. Now how about I see if I can encourage Kaneko to attend to kitchen duties.' His dark eyes found Silas at last. 'And you and I are in need of a conversation, are we not, Mr Mercer?'

Without waiting on Silas's answer, the old man left the way he had come, humming to himself. Silas frowned at the closing door.

'What the devil you waiting for?' Benedict said.

'Oh, am I to follow him?' Silas said.

Tyvain wrinkled her face, hands tight around her pint. 'You're pretty, but you ain't bright, are you, Mr Mercer? Get along with you. It wouldn't do to keep 'im waiting. But hurry yourself back. I'm mighty partial to chips and can't say yours will be waiting for ya if you take too long.'

Throwing back his stout, the thick drink hitting his stomach with heat and heaviness, Silas jumped from his stool and hurried to follow after Mr Ahari. He made his way in behind the bar and had just pushed through the swinging door when Benedict called out.

'Good luck with them stairs.'

CHAPTER 9

S ilas made his way along the dimly-lit corridor with great caution, his head filled with the conversation that had just taken place. As if the events of his evening were not befuddling enough, he'd now been in the company of a soothsayer and a djinn, whatever that might be, and they would have him believe that the bartender had once been an umbrella, and that humans were an indulgence of sorts to some supernaturals. Naturals, as Benedict liked to call them. Did Silas even wish to know what sort of indulgence was being discussed? He touched his pocket, reassuring himself that the bandalore still lay there.

The corridor held the odour of stale ale and dampness, and he thought he spied a mouse scuttle ahead in the shadows. Not exactly the sort of place he'd imagined Mr Ahari might reside. Silas reached the end of the corridor. Here lay the staircase Benedict had wished him luck with. They appeared normal enough, rather on the steep side he supposed, with one side holding a balustrade and the other touching the wall. The first step creaked loudly beneath his weight and the sound seemed to echo up the entire staircase. Silas gripped the balustrade, a dark wood smoothed by years of handling. He could see no sign of any landing in the gloom above.

He paused, touching at his temple where an ache bothered him. He'd swallowed that stout far too quickly for sure. Overindulgence was becoming a feature of his new life, and he was none too pleased at himself.

Setting his shoulders, Silas continued on. And on. And on. The number of stairs was astonishing. From the carriage it had appeared The Atlas rose three levels, no more, yet Silas's legs fairly trembled with the work. He puffed and panted his way ever upward.

'Mr Ahari?' he called. He saw no sign of gaslights or candles up ahead. Mr Ahari's cheerful reply floated down to him. 'Yes, yes. Come on up.'

With a grimace, Silas set on. The width of the steps narrowed as he rose higher, and before long it was inadequate for the length of his feet. His heel dangled over the edge with each step. His coat brushed against the faded wallpaper, an elaborate garden print with delicate hummingbirds dipping long beaks into faded pink lilies. It was a print more suited to a fine parlour, rather than here where the steeply angled staircase would have suited the servant's quarters more ably. With his attention focused on what lay ahead, Silas's booted toe caught the edge of the next step. He threw out his hands, slapping one against the wood, the other against the wall.

'Everything all right out there?' Ahari's voice was closer now, but there was still no sign of a landing.

'Fine. Thank you.'

'Not much further now. You've done well.'

Buoyed by the prospect of finishing his climb, Silas quickened his pace. And there, as though out of thin air, appeared a landing. It was lit by a single wall sconce, cut in the shape of a shell, a candle dancing behind its clouded glass. Silas stared in astonishment at the three corridors that stretched before him, each vastly longer than the width of the building might suggest. In fact, he could not see to the ends of any of them, darkness swallowing what lay there. A multitude of doors stretched along each corridor, and all of them were closed with no sign of Mr Ahari. The staircase doubled back on itself, reaching ever further upwards. Considering how high Silas had already laboured, a further ascent seemed impossible. He might well touch the moon at this rate.

'Mr Ahari? Where might I find you?' He doubted his legs would handle a further climb. Movement came from the corridor at his right, and he turned with much relief.

'There you are, Mr Mercer.' Mr Ahari leaned out of a room several doorways down. 'Do come in. I've a warm brandy awaiting, I believe that is your preference. Yes? Come, come. There's a cheerful fire too.'

'Cheerful' was rather the understatement. 'Roaring' was a far better description, and it was quite unpleasant after the heat of the climb. The fire was so bright that no other lighting existed in the room at all. Candles perched on the mantel unlit, pointless in the glare. The fire's flames danced madly in a deep hearth, framed by grey-streaked white marble. An odd assortment of items lined the mantel. At the centre was a twin candelabra shaped like the horns of a stag and made from what he guessed to be ivory. On either side of it lay several skulls Silas recognised as those of birds, crows likely, though how he was so certain was yet another mystery. Tilted against the wall sat a framed display of startlingly-coloured butterflies, who all appeared to be attempting to take flight thanks to the flicker of the fire. Last but not least was a curious mask. A fox's face, with sharp pointed ears and a long slender snout, painted in a rich orange shade that held glittering fragments within.

Mr Ahari must have reached the room in impressive haste, while Silas laboured up the endless stairs, as he had changed his clothing. He wore a black smoking jacket with wide quilted cuffs and collar, and black silk trousers, which made him appear as though prepared for bed rather than a visitor.

'Did you locate the room easily enough?' Mr Ahari poured a generous serving of brandy into green crystal glasses. Silas considered declining. His last experience with the drink had not ended well, but to refuse seemed ill-advised.

'I'd not say easily.' Or in a regular way, he mused. 'I'll not lie, the stairs seemed rather endless. I thought I was going to end up in the heavens.'

'And I can assure you, you do not want that.' Mr Ahari held the bottle high above the glasses, allowing a long stream of honey-brown liquid to cascade with remarkable accuracy. 'But you are right to note the peculiarity of the staircase. And were you the wrong type of visitor, they would indeed prove to be as you feared. Endless.'

'Whatever do you mean?' Silas was far too sweat-caked and tired for great decorum. Besides, Mr Ahari had a rather easy manner about him, no air of superiority that set Silas on edge. The man turned, glasses in hand, his ever-present beaming smile in place. 'Exactly what I said. The Atlas is very discerning about her guests. And rather protective of myself.' He handed Silas his glass.

'The building is protective?' Silas removed his coat, for the heat was truly stifling. The room itself was cluttered, every inch of space covered. The walls were thick with paintings: from enormous gilt-framed landscapes to portraits of speckled hunting hounds barely larger than a snuffbox.

'Yes. But you are here, access has been granted. Here's to you, Mr Mercer. I feel that great progress has been made this evening.' He clinked his glass against Silas's before seating himself in an armchair that rested so close to the roaring fire that it was a wonder its wooden frame did not combust. 'Wonderful news of your success.'

'So you have heard?' Silas said, oddly disappointed that news had already reached Mr Ahari.

'Of course. I'd not be much of a head of the Order if I had not.' Mr Ahari laughed, kicking off the slippers he wore and stretching his short legs so his bare feet were closer to the fire. 'Tell me, how do you feel?'

Silas took a long sip of sweet, burning liquid before he spoke. He was rather queasy in truth, but well aware that was not what the man spoke of. 'Confused, of course, but...content, somehow.' He rubbed his thumb against the glass, recalling the vibration of the song. 'As though something lost...' He frowned in thought. 'Has been found. Is this what Jane spoke of? My true nature I mean, has it shown itself? I am to banish spirits. An exorcist, as it were.'

To imagine himself saying such a thing with so little consternation just a few days ago would have been impossible.

'Banish, Mr Mercer? Goodness me, no. That is not what you do at all. It is far more honourable than that. You restore lost souls to their rightful path, dear boy. Here, sit, sit. Join me.'

Invitation to seat himself closer to the fire was not appealing, but Silas did as he was bid. Once seated, he took another sip, conscious of Mr Ahari's eyes upon him. 'I'm not certain I understand my purpose any better, my apologies, Mr Ahari –'

'Oh, pish posh, don't apologise for something that is perfectly understandable. You've been kept in the dark, I know, and it is I who should apologise for that. But we have found, myself and the Lady Satine, that it is always best to allow a true nature to find its own course. You did wonderfully this evening, by all accounts, but I would so love to hear of it in your own words. Tell me every detail as you remember it, from the moment Isaac delivered you.'

'Every detail?'

'Yes, please.'

Silas glanced at where his coat hung from a hook behind the door, the bandalore buried in the depths of one of the pockets. He wished he held it now, the smoothness of wood between his fingers. There was a large vase to one side of the door, its print a royal blue not far removed from the material of Silas's coat. Mr Ahari's walking cane rested within, the carved ivory fox head jutting over its rim. The way it faced Silas, it was as though the animal kept its wide white eyes upon him.

Silas began his tale, beginning with the surly butler. As he spoke, his gaze drifted over the cluttered room so as to avoid the penetrating stare of Mr Ahari, who appeared intent on every word relayed. The floorboards were covered with an assortment of rugs, utterly mismatched. A rag rug lay beneath a card table, colourful strips of material all woven together and meant for a working family's cottage. Beneath a leather lounge, which was in truth far too big for the room, lay a Persian carpet woven in stunning hues of ochre and russet.

'Tobias Astaroth was there?' Mr Ahari interrupted.

Silas nodded.

Pursing his lips, Mr Ahari finally released Silas from his gaze and considered the fire. 'Asking for trouble there, my lady. At least give him something to do to occupy his time.'

'I'm sorry?'

Mr Ahari waved off the question with a grin. 'Do go on, don't mind me.' He sipped at his brandy.

After many more diversions and questions from Mr Ahari, Silas finally arrived at the moment when he brandished the bandalore at the spirit.

'Might I see it?' Mr Ahari said.

'It is in my coat.' Silas moved to rise.

'No. Sit down, sit down.' Mr Ahari tutted. 'There is no need for you to move. Bring the bandalore to you, Mr Mercer.'

'I beg your pardon?'

Mr Ahari gave him a sly grin. 'Come now, you have done such a thing before. Just now, in the carriage.'

Silas blinked, his thoughts slippery with the warmth of brandy and ale. Tyvain must have informed the old man of the incident. Or Isaac. Silas must endeavour to remember there was little privacy in this new world. 'That may be so, but I do not understand how I managed it.'

'Why must you understand? Just simply do it. Call the bandalore to you, Mr Mercer. Wish it so, and you'll find it is so.' He settled back into his chair, awaiting the performance.

Certainly Silas had drawn the bandalore to him, but earlier it had been a sense of desperation that drove him, an anxiousness that came with the removal of the bandalore from his person. That was not the case now. He was at ease, his mind lazy with drink, his muscles fatigued by the climb, and fully aware that the wooden trinket was close by and within reach. Mr Ahari folded his hands over the top of his empty glass, seemingly ready to wait as long as necessary. Silas shifted to the edge of his chair. He set down his glass and wiped his hands against his trouser legs.

'Focus an image of it in your mind, then imagine it with you. At hand.'

Mr Ahari's voice was low and gentle. Utterly soothing. Silas's trepidation fell beneath it, and he closed his eyes. He pictured the disc of boxwood, with its stark white string resting in its box of straw. A strange, anonymous gift. His body felt light, relaxed. A smile found his lips. Silas opened his palms, as though offering up prayers to an invisible god. But it was no deity he sought, it was something far more important.

'That's it.' Mr Ahari's words lulled him deeper into a composed state. 'Well done, Mr Mercer. Well done.'

The knock of something against his right hand saw his eyes fly open. The bandalore lay in his palm. Silas had achieved the impossible not once but twice now.

'I did that.' Not a question but a statement. 'I did that.' He laughed, turning the disc this way and that. Mr Ahari had not moved from his seat, Silas was sure. This was no trickery. Silas's very own thoughts had brought the bandalore to him.

'You certainly did.' Now Mr Ahari rose. He padded barefoot to the decanter, pouring himself another. 'And the spirit named you for what you are.'

'When she called me ankou?' Silas had not dared interrupt his storytelling to bother Mr Ahari with a question about the meaning of the word, but he did so now with fervour. 'But what does it mean? What am I?'

'An ankou is a servant of death, Mr Mercer. An honour granted to any human who dies upon the last stroke of midnight, on the very last evening of the year. You are one such person, amongst many others.'

'A servant of death?' Silas knew not to expect a reasonable explanation for his existence, but this took his breath away. 'I'm a Grim Reaper?'

'A reaper? No, no. You are no such thing because no such thing as a Grim Reaper exists.' Mr Ahari returned to stand by the fire, stretching a short arm to lean against the mantel. Despite the intense heat, the man had not raised a sweat. 'The humans do so love a good story, don't they? As though death could reside in one form, striding about, cutting down a single soul at a time. Terribly impractical way to do it, if ever there was one. Like that Santa Claus fellow. It's as likely that he climbs down each chimney as the Grim Reaper escorts each soul to the afterlife.' He chuckled gently. 'Izanami does not work herself upon this world in such a way. The goddess of death touches down upon the living like a massive ocean wave, a storm-ridden wind that no man can outrun, and she strikes without care or countenance. Which makes for quite a mess really. And that's where you come in. The ankou are not so dissimilar to street cleaners, sweeping up the debris after an event. In this case the debris are human souls. The only part of the humans' Grim Reaper story that rings true is the instrument of death you wield when you work in the goddess's name. A scythe. And yours, Mr Mercer, lies in your hand now. With your bandalore you will ingather the lost souls, all those who have been left behind in the goddess's wake for one reason or another, and send them on their true way. For one year, you shall bear the title of ankou, until it is time for you too to pass on. Rather more permanently this time.'

'One year?' Silas's stomach churned a little. 'That is all?'

Ahari gazed into the flames. 'Did you assume immortality?' He chuckled. 'I'm afraid not, my friend. Izanami has touched you, so there is no escaping it. Death will claim you, but for now she has another purpose. Relish the time. Would you like another?'

It took a moment to realise Mr Ahari referred to the brandy and not another life.

'No. Thank you. This is a lot to comprehend.' Which was putting it mildly. A servant of death? It was too much to consider, what with the heat of the room and the wrench of his gut. It was far easier to focus instead on another bit of information gleaned. A glimpse of his former life. He had died on New Year's Eve. Silas took an absent-minded sip. The knowledge set his pulse thumping and the ache at his temple bothered him once more. Harsher this time.

'You must be quite overwhelmed,' Mr Ahari said. 'But you seem a reasonable chap and have handled everything very admirably so far. The Lady Satine would never say it out loud, but I believe she is quite impressed. Whatever doubts she may have, I believe you are allaying them. Which is just as well, for she is watching you inordinately closely.'

'She watches me?' Silas sat up straighter in his chair, his hand going self-consciously to his jacket to adjust the fit. 'I was of the understanding Her Ladyship has not been in the country since I arrived.'

'Since the day after you arrived, to be more precise.' Mr Ahari turned his back to the fire and lifted the hem of his jacket as though he wished to warm even further. 'She is so rarely in one place long, I'm afraid. There is little rest for one such as her. I may appear to toil hard, Mr Mercer, but I can assure you, none work as hard at ensuring the balance is maintained in this world as Her Ladyship.' Mr Ahari swept a hand towards the fire. The flames rose higher, brilliant oranges and reds that split into sections resembling a peacock's fanned tail. 'Wouldn't you agree, Isaac?'

The fire cracked loudly, and behind Silas the window panes rattled with the vibration.

'Oh don't worry, dear boy. Isaac may not be one for conversation, but he rather enjoys theatrics,' Mr Ahari said. 'A fire elemental does have a temper, as you can imagine. Now settle down, Isaac. I'll be done with Mr Mercer soon enough, and then you can be on your way.' He waggled a finger at the fire.

Silas glanced between the hearth and the man. 'A fire elemental?'

'Yes, though he does prefer the more salubrious title of Salamander, as you can imagine. Isaac is a grand manipulator of the flame. Fire is as much a part of him as the bandalore is now a part of you.'

First the bartender was an umbrella, now the coachman was a reptile who could manipulate flame?

Silas spoke slowly. 'Are you suggesting Isaac is a lizard,' he glanced at the fire. 'One that is capable of producing flame?'

Surely the man was not suggesting that dragons too were real.

'Good gods, man, no.' Mr Ahari made a show of wincing. 'You are set for a rough journey home with talk like that. Compare Isaac to a dragon at your peril, you might as well compare Queen Victoria to a sewer rat, I'm afraid. Dragons are messy, uncouth and rather pungent. No, no, there is no comparison to salamanders, even if Isaac was one, which he is not. The fire elementals use the Salamander title as an honorific only, reserved for the strongest amongst them. It's something to do with an incident long ago, I'm not entirely sure of specifics. But apparently a salamander, the beady-eyed kind, rescued one of the earth's original fire elementals from a rather excruciating predicament. Don't press me for details for I cannot recall, I'm rather old you see with too much to commit to memory. But the fire elementals took the name to honour that occasion, that I do remember. Isaac might find it in himself to advise you of the details some time.' Mr Ahari laughed. 'Can you imagine the fuss Mr Mercer, if your carriage were actually being driven by a web-footed, pink-tongued amphibian?' He laughed as though Silas had been quite hilarious. All at once his gaze darted to the fire. 'I'm sorry Isaac but you're wrong, it would be terribly amusing.' He wiped at his eyes. 'Gracious, Isaac, would it pain you to be mirthful once in a while?'

He sighed at whatever answer came from the flames.

'You are speaking with him...now?' Silas rubbed at his cheek. Had Mr Ahari truly just spoken so flippantly of the existence of dragons?

'Yes. And he in turn will inform the Lady Satine of our conversation.' Mr Ahari bent to rub his hands closer to the flames.

Silas eyed the fire with some trepidation. His cottage contained a fireplace. Isaac might have spied upon him in his most personal moments. His skin warmed at the thought.

Mr Ahari continued. 'You see four elementals were placed in Lady Satine's employ when her time here began. Suffice to say, it has been a long, long servitude for them all but elementals are ever so handy to have about. Especially old Isaac here. With Satine so often away, it does rather make communications easier, for there is rarely a place in the British Isles that is bereft of fire in some shape or form. I dare say I'm in some amount of trouble myself, reprimanding her about Tobias Astaroth.' His bubbly laugh did not speak of concern for such indiscretion. 'But why she burdens herself with that creature, I do not know, and she will not say.'

Silas shuddered at the mention of Tobias. 'He too is in the Order?'

Mr Ahari wrinkled his nose. 'No. That walking calamity is Her Ladyship's personal ward. Best to keep your distance, Mr Mercer. Tobias Astaroth tends to leave injured parties in his wake.'

That was one thing out of Mr Ahari's mouth that Silas had no trouble believing. 'I must say I do not wish to come across him again anytime soon.'

'Good, good.' He leaned towards the flames. 'Isaac, will you allow Mr Mercer some supper? I do believe Kaneko has it ready for him.'

The fans of flame lowered, sinking until they were barely more than glowing orange embers before bursting once more into a spray of flame. Mr Ahari waved off whatever the reply might have been. 'Ignore him. I asked out of politeness only, which really is a waste of time when it comes to Isaac. Come, Mr Mercer, you have more than earned this meal. I have some things to attend to, but spend as long as you may like in the bar, drink and eat to your heart's content. And welcome, officially, to the Order of the Golden Dawn. I do hope this will be a long and fruitful association.'

Long? Hadn't the man just told Silas an ankou existed for but a year? Perhaps that was considered long for a second life.

'Thank you, sir. I do have a great many questions –'

Mr Ahari pointed a finger towards the door, and it swung open on silent hinges. 'Of course, of course. And Jane is there for just that purpose, dear boy.' He picked up Silas's glass and set it back on the serving trolley. The meeting was clearly at an end. 'Do feel free to speak with her whenever you need. And she will advise you of your next appointment as soon as it becomes apparent. Good evening, Mr Mercer.'

And with that he settled into the vacant armchair by the fire. A book appeared in his lap, leather-bound with tattered edges upon the pages, and spectacles found their place on the bridge of his nose.

'This way, Mr Mercer.' Silas fairly yelped with surprise, whirling around to find Kaneko in the doorway. The pockmarked man waved him out of the room. 'I've set up one of our private rooms for you to dine. I thought perhaps you might need some time alone with your thoughts.'

Silas doubted three lifetimes alone with his thoughts would make any of this more comprehensible. 'Very kind, thank you.'

He grabbed his coat and followed the bartender into the hall, studying the man as they went. Of course there was no sign of anything remotely umbrella-like about his person. Silas was definitely in need of a decent meal, something to clear his head.

At the top of the landing, he paused to look back. The hallway was dim, the door to Mr Ahari's room having closed without a sound behind them. Silas continued down the stairs after Kaneko, and this time, thankfully, the journey was a swift one. In less than half the time it had taken him to climb them, he descended the stairs, returning to the narrow corridor with its dank odours, his life stranger now than when he had last set foot here. His stomach growled with hunger, and it was oddly comforting.

One thing, at least, had not changed.

A servant of death could grow as famished as any other man.

CHAPTER 10

Silas might well blame the fish curry for his sleepless night. Exquisite as the meal Kaneko had prepared was, the level of spice had been eye-watering, and Silas downed many a glass of milk in order to extinguish the burn. But he doubted even that assault on his stomach was behind his inability to fall into a deep sleep. Far more likely it was the gamut of thoughts that plagued him. The encounter with the ghost and the remarkable bandalore for one, The Atlas for another, with its endless staircase and curious owner, and the carriage driver who watched him through the flames. When Silas returned home last evening, sometime after three in the morning, he did not set his fire. As a consequence his toes were now ice and his body shook despite the layers of bedcovers he'd hauled from a chest at the foot of his bed. But he did not regret the cold hearth. The idea that Isaac might watch him slumber was enough to give anyone insomnia.

Silas groaned and pulled the covers over his head, succeeding in baring his toes to the room's brisk ambiance. The bed might be sufficient for his height and width, but the blankets were made for a smaller body than his.

In truth there was but one thing that kept him awake. The revelation of his true nature. He was an ankou. The name itself was strange and did not ring with any familiarity. But servant of death was clear enough. Silas's reason for rebirth had been set by the goddess of death herself.

Izanami. There, and there alone, lay the reason he could not calm himself into slumber despite the lateness of the night.

Silas pulled his toes back into the meagre warmth offered by the blankets. He'd yearned to know more of his renewed existence, certainly, but could never have imagined such a tale. He closed his eyes, desiring to remember the extraordinary tune of the bandalore. It escaped him now, the particular notes, but just to think upon it brought him calm. The melody was the beat of his heart, the pump of blood, the rush of air in his lungs. The very finest particles that made up his body held the tune within them. As though the song were not *part* of him but in fact *was* him.

He shoved the covers free of his head, wishing to lay eyes upon the bandalore. He had placed it upon the bedside table, laying it on a linen kerchief embellished with his initials, *S. M.* He'd located the embroidered linen in the chest of drawers, neatly pressed and folded.

There could be no denying the sense of completeness the bandalore's tune had imbued in him. He'd no sooner discard the wretched thing than he would sever his own arm. But why had Mr Ahari and Lady Satine been so clandestine about his true nature when they knew it all along? Lady Satine had harboured doubts about Silas, Mr Ahari said, but doubts about what? And what were the consequences if he had failed at a task he knew so little of? The delirium of a sleepless night must have been upon him, for he resolved to march himself to her residence, Holly Lodge, and await her return. Whenever it might be.

'She avoids me, I'm sure of it,' Silas muttered to his bedclothes. 'Well, I shall refuse to brandish the bandalore until we speak, that is all there is to it.'

Even as he spoke the childish words aloud, they crumbled. If the bandalore called on him, he'd answer. The very thought of once again tending to a lost soul sent a shiver of excitement along his spine. But he was not keen on Isaac as his chaperon. Perhaps he could request a horse of his own?

It occurred to Silas that since the day he'd woken in this bed, he had not made one attempt to walk out the gates and vanish into the chaos of London. Was it possible an enchantment of some kind squashed such thoughts? Even now, with the idea dangling before him, there was no urge to rise and at the very least attempt to stroll out onto the main road. Rather it quite frightened him. More so than anything that had come before. Beyond the walls of Holly Village, Silas knew nothing of his place in the world. He might have been a vagabond, a pauper, or a prisoner. There may be those who wished to settle some dispute with him, in a gruesome way, or he might have laboured in a trade he despised. Certainly, the opposite might be true. Silas may have been a man of means, or engaged in a most pleasing relationship. He might have been in love. A father.

Silas threw off the covers, the blast of early morning air prickling the hairs on his legs. The simple wooden clock upon the mantel declared it to be just beyond seven. He made his way to the window, pushing open the heavy fabric with its motif of falling autumn leaves. The print did not please him, too fussy and gregarious. He knew simple things such as this, what he enjoyed to eat, what colours he preferred, but nothing of true substance.

The white blush of morning was upon the air. The lights in the turret of Jane's home were on. As he watched, a shadow passed between light and window in one of the upstairs rooms, a man's figure he was certain. It seemed she entertained company yet again. He eyed the gate once more, one corner just visible from where he stood. He imagined striding out through the wrought iron, making his way up the hill towards Lady Satine's grand home. Demanding an audience.

The twitter of birds reached him from the garden, the creatures slowly awakening.

'Good god, man,' he admonished his weak reflection. 'You'd no sooner do that than choose to dine with Mr Astaroth.'

There could be no denying the fact that the mere mention of the lady made him quite uneasy. They'd never met, of course, but he sensed in the way she was spoken of that it would be an encounter to remember. The thought of standing before her made his belly churn.

All at once his room brightened with light, as though someone had entered with a candle held aloft. He turned to find the room quite empty, but the culprit quite clear. There upon the bedside table the bandalore gleamed as though the sun's rays lay upon it. Silas made his way to the bedside table, a short journey of just a few steps, but by the time he arrived the string had unwound from its place around the disc's edge, rising into the air like a viper. The bandalore too had lost its glow, his attention now gained. The string snaked its way towards him, a sliver of white that twisted and turned. Silas remained where he was, unafraid. He held out his hand. This time the string did not wind around his middle finger as it had done at the baron's. It simply furled in upon itself at the centre of his palm. Silas noted that his fingers did not tingle as they had at the baron's either. The entire situation felt vastly different. More personal. The furled string tugged the wooden disc with it, until the bandalore rested in Silas's hand. At once the wood vibrated against his skin, and several exquisite notes rose against the air. Faint, so as to be almost indiscernible, but Silas heard the lyrical message loud and very clear nonetheless.

Take care, he was told. *Take care.*

There was a lack of urgency to the melody. Whatever he was warned of was not an imminent danger, just a call to pay attention. Be cautious. Silas decided there was a definitive need for trousers and hoped the bandalore would not take offence to being set down so that he might dress. He lay the bandalore on his pillow, and its remaining glow subsided, its song falling silent. Silas hurried himself into his trousers, the same pair from last night, smelling of wood smoke and curry. He took up the bandalore as he might a baby bird and held it with a gentle firmness. He was about to move to the door when a distant sound caught his attention. A shout, though of humour or temper he could not say. From where he stood he could see well enough out the window, but the noise appeared to be coming from the far side of his house, beyond his scope of vision.

'Do you wish me to investigate?' Silas peered at the bandalore. He shook himself. 'What are you doing, you fool?' The trinket was hardly about to grow a face and answer him. Was it?

He set off, catching sight of himself in a mirror by his door. His hair was dishevelled after being stuffed beneath a pillow most of the night. There was every chance his appearance alone would frighten off whoever was causing the disturbance. He hurried down the stairs and strode across the foyer, not entirely certain what he intended to do once he set foot outside the door, or if that was even what the bandalore required of him. He threw open the front door lest he reconsider. A scream erupted from the figure bent at his door mat.

'Blast you! Are you trying to scare a man to death?' Gilmore stumbled back from the basket he'd just set down. Silas reached out with the hand that held the bandalore, instinct propelling him to attempt to steady the man. Gilmore slapped at the air, warding him back. 'Don't touch me with that damned thing. It's liable to break my bones and turn me into dust.'

Silas drew back his arm. 'It could do such a thing?'

In the distance the troublesome voice returned, bellowing anew about something incomprehensible.

'I don't bloody know, but that's what a scythe's for, ain't it? Death and destruction, and all things no good?'

'Destruction?' Silas's eyes widened. He was faintly aware that the shouting had shifted into song, the sort that a drunken sailor might release after a night in the pub. The screeched notes, though muffled, were hideous upon the ears.

'Well, what do you think death is if not destruction of life?' The indignant man tugged his striped shirt back into place.

'Wait a moment,' Silas said. 'How do you know this? Who told you of the bandalore?'

Gilmore planted his hands on his hips and rolled his eyes. 'Wouldn't you like to know.'

The off-key singing, notes intent on drawing blood from eardrums, grew louder. The singer was somewhere near the main gate but still out of sight. The dreadful pitch only added to Silas's temper.

'Yes,' he declared. 'I damn well would like to know. Is there to be no privacy whatsoever in this damned place?'

'Every time you step out that bloody door, you're in a foul temper.'

'That is hardly accurate, but I have good reason for a sourness of mood. I feel like an animal in a zoological garden here. Now tell me who spoke about the bandalore.'

Gilmore spat on the front step, barely missing the basket of food, which Silas noted smelled especially wonderful this morning. If he wasn't mistaken, there were scones to be had.

'Not that I need to tell you a damn thing, you pompous giant, but if you must know, nobody tells me any bloody thing directly. I have to keep me ears open and take what scraps I can find.' He flung his hand towards the wisteria that draped down the side of Silas's cottage. The flowers shook so hard that a veritable rainstorm of petals descended. 'Tend the garden, Gilmore. Make those plants grow, Gilmore. Feed us well, like a good little gnome, Gilmore, but don't expect to be invited to any meetings or consulted on any matters. Any of you lot ever say thanks to an elemental like me? Not bloody likely. Not even Her Ladyship.'

'Elemental? You're another?'

'Unless you're looking to get those pretty teeth of yours smacked from your head' – Gilmore scowled – 'then you'd do best to stop talking about my kind like they're some kind of plague. There's only four of us in Her Ladyship's service, and you can treat those other bastards as you like, but if you don't show me some respect, your next basket will be your last. The earth won't provide a whit for you. I'll have those hens stop laying faster than you can blink, mark my words.'

Silas raised his eyebrows. 'Now, now. Do calm yourself, sir.' As the petals floated around him, it dawned on Silas that the wretched singing has ceased. The silence was quite divine.

'I'm just making sure you know it. That the earth is a mercurial thing. Good day, Mr Mercer.'

Gilmore spun on booted heels and made his purposeful way along the front of the cottage. He had reached the still-fluttering wisteria when all at once a shadow launched from the cover of the foliage. Gilmore released a high-pitched squeak as the figure enveloped him and sent them both into a rolling tumble. The force of the blow was such that they completed several rotations before hitting the coarse surface of the gravelled path that ran around the extremity of the Village. Gilmore landed atop his attacker, who enveloped him in a bear hug.

'Let me go, you monster,' Gilmore screamed, short legs flailing.

His feet landed more than one blow against his attacker's nether regions, but he was still unable to free himself. Just as Silas decided to intervene, the man beneath the elemental broke into a peel of delicate laughter, as though having his family jewels pounded upon was a laughing matter. A slow crawl of unease played against the back of Silas's neck. The dainty, airy sounds of amusement were strikingly familiar.

'Damn you, Pitch,' Gilmore cried, breathless. 'You are a son of a bitch if ever there was one. Take your dirty hands off me.'

Finally, the small man wriggled free, and his attacker was revealed. Silas fastened his grip around the bandalore, his unease shifting into downright despair. Tobias Astaroth, that most disconcerting of men, lay with legs and arms spread indelicately upon the ground before him.

CHAPTER 11

M r Astaroth did not stay horizontal for long. He rocked to his knees, grabbing a hold of Gilmore's legs before the man had a chance to flee. He sent a wink Silas's way and pushed himself to his bare feet, dangling the unfortunate Gilmore like a duck ready for the plucking. The diminutive man jerked and kicked to release himself.

'Set me down, or I swear I'll set the very earthworms against you,' Gilmore roared, an impressive thing from such a small set of lungs.

Again came the laughter, though this time with raspier, darker notes. Tobias's eyes were dull, there was a cut upon his lips that still bled, and he stumbled as he tussled with the struggling man in his grasp. 'Go on then, you piece of piss.' He slapped Gilmore's arse. 'Show us how fearsome a gnome can be with a piece of dirt.'

Mr Astaroth was clearly drunk. Reason perhaps why he failed to be wearing any shoes. Silas noted the large brown stain upon the white of his linen shirt with great consternation. The mark appeared not dissimilar to blood. His dark trousers bore a tear at his right thigh, and the material at his knees was notably caked with dirt.

Gilmore cried out, more pain in the sound this time. 'You're breaking my leg, you bastard.'

Silas looked to the bandalore, hoping there might be a musical direction sung to him. But the wood was quiet. He should go to the man's assistance, Silas needed no magical trinket to tell him so. Man, or gnome, Gilmore was in clear distress. But Silas hesitated.

'Dear me, do you think I would truly do such a thing?' Tobias's words got away from him, slipping and sliding from his intoxicated tongue. A shadow curved around his right eye, a rising bruise.

'I know you would,' Gilmore hollered. 'You crave harm more than your cock craves fucking.'

With no warning, Tobias landed a punch against Gilmore's belly. Half-hearted as it was, it at last spurred Silas from his reticence. He took a step forward.

'Now, see here-'

'Tobias! Set him down, now.' Jane moved across the green, clad in a nightgown of the most delicate white lace. Combined with her airy way of moving, it was as though a ghost rushed towards them. 'Now, Pitch. I will not ask you again.'

The man's smile was a cruel slash across his damaged face. 'As you wish. Catch him if you can.'

He lowered Gilmore and seemed certain to set him down, albeit on his head, but at the very last moment, he drew back his arm and swung the frantic Gilmore straight up into the air. Without an ounce of effort apparent, Tobias's throw sent the screaming, kicking man skyward. Soaring higher even than Silas's cottage roof.

'Help me!'

Gilmore seemed to hang in the air for a moment. His scream curdled the blood.

'Gilmore!' Silas dashed in beneath the unfortunate gnome, seeking to position himself so he might catch Gilmore when he fell. A dangerous notion, considering the speed of descent, but the man would surely suffer grievous injury otherwise. Silas glanced at the grinning man at his side. The viciousness that simmered within Tobias Astaroth's emerald eyes was breathtaking.

'Stop!' Jane's command came with a rush of violent wind. A great force swept past Silas, lifting the hairs on his head. The gust swept in beneath the tumbling Gilmore, and at once his downward journey halted in a dead stop in midair. The gnome sobbed, hanging limp against his invisible support, drifting slowly down, a leaf upon a gentle breeze.

'Why must you ruin my fun?' Tobias folded his arms, staring hard at Jane as she approached, a pout upon his full lips.

The sun drifted from behind a cloud, its rays setting his eyes alight once more, and marking the pronounced angles of his face. Despite his notable injuries, his odd beauty, accentuated by bowed lips and long dark lashes, was still evident. Rather captivating, if Silas were honest, but he'd just now glimpsed a ferocity beneath the delicate exterior which lent it a certain ugliness.

'You're a mad bastard. A fucking lunatic.' Gilmore's fury erupted with the touch of his feet to the ground. He lined up to level a kick at his tormentor's shin, growling further profanities. Admirable bravery, in Silas's opinion, if not a little foolish. 'If she knew what was best for her, she'd get rid of your damned dae –'

'Gilmore,' Jane said. 'That will be all.'

'Why she sees fit to have him here, I'll never know.' Gilmore glowered, stunted leg at the ready. 'He's a bloody maniac. Too mad even for those high-ups in Arcadia. Look at the bastard. All bloodied up 'cause he ain't happy till he's hurtin'. I know I don't account for much around here, but that don't mean I need to be in fear of my life every day. And that's what I am with that one.' He placed himself at Jane's side before turning to jab a finger at Tobias, who had taken to cleaning his nails. 'Those of us here who ain't so powerful as Her Ladyship are just playthings to him. Like a cat with a broken bird. And it ain't right, he ain't right.'

'Oh by the gods, shut up.' Tobias pressed his hands to his ears, knuckles cut and bruised, and launched into headache-inducing song, swaying as though his tune had any hope of being danced to.

Here stood the dreadful off-key culprit of earlier. Jane ignored the display and leaned down to speak with Gilmore. Silas couldn't catch her words, but they seemed to placate the flustered fellow. He nodded and folded his short, thickset arms.

'That is quite enough now, Tobias.' Jane's nightgown held the pinkness of the sunrise, the satin and lace wrapping each and every curve.

'Fine.' With a languid sigh, he did as he was bid. Letting his hands drop to his sides. 'Now that I'm being a good boy won't you call me Pitch again? I do so enjoy watching your lips when you-'

'Why are you here?' Jane folded her arms across her chest, covering up nipples that sought to pierce through the fine material. 'Or are you too drunk to recall that you do not live in the Village but in the Lodge?'

'Now there's a fine question. Why am I here?' Tobias giggled. His dancing had brought him closer to Silas, the odour of liquor strong. The harsh cruel lines had left his face, and he appeared tired now rather than unkind.

'Must you indulge in your blood sport in your formal wear?' Jane frowned. 'I've asked you, more than once, to consider your dress.'

He fumbled with the buttons on his trousers. 'You are right, I should simply prance about in the ring naked, and alleviate the need for cleaning altogether.' His efforts saw his unsteadiness get the better of him. Tobias tripped over his own feet and collapsed onto the grass, face-first, highly amused by his own clumsy fall. Silas regarded him anew, wondering how this man could have so discomforted him just a few moments earlier. 'I won, in case you'd like to know,' Tobias told the grass. 'Quite think I broke most of the bones in the second chap's body. But they know the whisks...risks...when they step into the bring...sing...ahh, ring. That's it. Ring, with me.' He shoved a hand into his hair, scratching hard at the back of his head. 'I may have indulged to celebrate, bust...just a little...cocaine is medicinal of course.' He rolled onto his back with a dramatic sigh. 'But why am I here? Bloody good question.' He pouted. 'Perhaps we were going to fuck, my sweet sylph?'

Jane wasted no time in answering. 'No.'

'Pity. I did so enjoy it last time.' Tobias launched to his feet with shocking speed and was right up against Silas before he had a chance to draw a breath. The reek of stale beer and sweet things was upon him. Pitch pressed his hands to Silas's chest. 'Were we going to fuck? Now that is something that would pass the time. I'm guessing you have an enormous –'

'Mr Astaroth, remove yourself.' Silas shoved him away. His skin tingled beneath his clothing, where Tobias's hands had lain against him. 'I'd ask that you do not touch me.'

'Well, you're no fun at all.' He cocked his head to one side. 'Satty tells me you had a very successful evening last night. Pray tell, what excitements did you find? Did you bed a whore or watch the baiting of a bear, or perhaps manage both at once? Now there is something I strive for.'

'Satty?' Silas studiously ignored his questions. 'I don't know of whom you speak.'

'Lady Satine.' He made a mockery of his bow. 'She's pleased with you. Well done, boy.' Without warning, he punched at Silas's arm.

'Oh!' Silas cried. 'That is really not necessary.' Bruising was certain to follow, considering the ferocity of the blow.

'None of this is though, is it?' Tobias waved his hand over one shoulder, giving little indication of what *this* was. 'We have that in common, you know. Both of us should by all rights be dead, not prancing about here in these fucking flesh cages.' He pinched at his arm, and his expression darkened. 'But then I suppose this makes for better entertainment, doesn't it? Reducing me to this.' He swept a hand down his front. 'How delightfully comical. They are vicious pricks, they are, vicious.'

Silas blinked, at a loss as to what the man was slurring about.

'No less than you probably deserve,' Gilmore snapped.

For a heart-stopping moment Silas feared that Tobias would launch himself at the reduced man. But that moment passed as quickly as it had risen. Tobias laughed, sharp and bitter. 'No less,' he said quietly.

'If we are all done here I'd like to return to my bed,' Jane said.

'My apologies, dearest one, for inconveniencing you.' Tobias leaned into another gloriously overdone bow. He stumbled, in danger of falling face first onto the ground once again. But this time Silas had to stop himself from stepping forward to assist. It was most peculiar, how this foul-mouthed man could elicit revulsion and pity within the same moment. 'I've no idea why I thought it a good idea to leave the *Spaniard's Inn* to begin with.' Tobias spat, the glob landing dark and thick on the ground. 'I can highly recommend it, Mr Mercer. Wonderful cider cake, and the most delightful array of pussy on offer. Cock, too, should you share my taste for variety.'

Silas stared hard at his feet, studiously intent upon the grass beneath them, and making no reply at all. He was still distracted by Tobias's earlier, cleaner, words. His talk of flesh cages and punishments. As to what a flesh cage might be, Silas did not like to imagine. And if Mr Astaroth were being held here unwillingly, what crime had this capricious man committed?

'Pitch, you need to return to your lodgings,' Jane said, gently now. 'You do look rather dreadful and in need of rest.'

'The night, or day now I suppose, is far too young. Besides, I've just eaten rather more brandy balls than I should have.' His grin smacked of impropriety, and Silas struggled not to wince as Tobias's attention turned to him. 'You are dressed, come and have a drink with me.'

Silas shook his head. 'No, most certainly not. It is barely morning.'

The change in Tobias's temper was as visible as a cloud passing over the sun. But where there had been ferocity before, there was dejection in the slump of his shoulders, the weakness of his grin. 'Sod you all then. I will pleasure myself well enough.'

Damn the sunshine with its manipulating rays, for they chose that moment to illuminate the gathered party once more. Revealing Tobias as fairly hollowed with fatigue, his battered face pale, and an air of quiet desperation about him that caught at Silas in the most peculiar way.

'We could, ah...take a drink in the cottage, if you like, Mr Astaroth?' He marvelled at the foolish invitation coming from his own lips. Was he truly mad with lack of sleep? 'Coffee perhaps?'

Surely Jane would save him from his own empathetic insanity. But she said nothing. In fact she seemed rather to be daydreaming, a vacancy to her gaze, staring towards Silas's cottage in silence.

'Certainly, if that's what you choose to call it.' Tobias clapped his hands, a jovial drunk once again. 'A vigorous rogering is a fine way to begin a day, I can assure you.' His melancholy had vanished entirely. Silas cursed his gullibility.

'Mr Astaroth,' he interjected. 'You mistake my invitation I fear.'

'Oh, my dear Mr Mercer, now that we are to be intimately acquainted I must insist, rather strongly, that you call me Pitch from now on. I do prefer it. And it does sound so much finer when it is being shouted. I quite recall how it burst from Miss Handel's lips as she bucked beneath me.'

Jane's focus returned, and she shook her head. 'That occasion rests in your dreams alone, Mr Astaroth. You were drunk, unsurprisingly, and you were fucking the cushions upon my chaise, all of which were quite silent I can assure you. As impressive as the stories of your vigour between the bedsheets may be, I'm afraid you are simply not my type.'

Good God, nor mine. Silas's silent voice affirmed his denial with a touch more vigour than was necessary.

'I am everybody's type, dear Jane,' Tobias declared.

She laughed, her eyes dancing with evident amusement. 'So it would seem. But still I must decline.' She nodded her chin towards her imposing residence. 'My own bedsheets are being kept warm for me and I must return. Mr Mercer, be sure to make that coffee formidably strong, and take no nonsense from Pitch.'

'Are you certain you won't come in?' Silas wrung his hands. 'I mean, for a coffee of course.'

Pitch staggered towards the front door. Silas regretted ever opening his mouth with the offer.

'Thank you but no, Silas.' She touched a hand to his arm. 'Go ahead. He will not harm you, he will not dare, I assure you. For if he did, it would be the Lady Satine he would answer to and even Tobias Astaroth would dread such an encounter. Spend time with him, learn more about one another now that your eyes are opened, ankou.' Silas did not bother to ask how she knew of his true nature. 'And of course if you wish to indulge in intimacy –'

'Miss Handel.' Silas recoiled in horror. 'I offer coffee. Absolutely nothing more. If Mr Astaroth intends –'

She laughed, the tinkling sound as pretty as birdsong. 'I dare say it would not be the worst experience in your life.' She raised her hands at his sputtered protest. 'Calm yourself, I jest. You need do nothing you do not wish.'

'Gilmore did not wish to sail to such dangerous heights, and yet it happened.' Silas eyed Pitch where he stood swaying over the basket on the doorstep, attempting to use his toes to lift the cloth covering the supplies. What on earth had possessed Silas to offer such an invitation? But he suspected he knew the answer already. It was the hint of dreadful loneliness he'd spied in Tobias's countenance. Silas recognised it all too well, for it lurked within him too.

'Pitch has not long been with us, barely a year, and he's not one to settle easily. He enjoys taunting us all,' Jane said. 'Keeping us set upon an edge where we are most uncomfortable. He rather hungers for it. So do not feed him. Enjoy your coffee, Silas. I will not stand idly by if I hear you scream. Unless of course, your screams are of a more delicate nature.'

'Miss Handel, I told you –'

Jane's smile danced wickedly, and he saw that she played with him. 'All is well, Silas. In fact, I have it on good authority that the Lady Satine approves of your proposal herself.'

Silas frowned, searching out the empty grounds. 'She is about?'

Jane tapped a finger to her temple. 'About here. She likes to be kept informed of Mr Astaroth's adventures.'

'Oh. I see.' He was to have no privacy at all in this place it seemed.

'Good day to you, Silas.'

She swept away, and there was no doubt in Silas's mind this time that her feet did not touch the ground as the sylph moved.

There came a disturbing thud from within the cottage and the tinkle of glasses. The basket and Pitch were gone from the front door. Silas grimaced, his hand moving to the bandalore at rest in his pocket, slumbering after its sudden springing to life earlier with its notes of caution. If it thought his invitation to Pitch a terrible idea, it gave no sign of it now. Perhaps its message had already been relayed as intended. Keep his wits about him when Pitch was near.

Silas made his reluctant way to the front door. The birds were in full song, the sun was weak but the sky had cleared. It was a splendid day, barely begun, and Silas wanted nothing more than to curl back under the covers he had left earlier. He stepped inside, closing the door behind him.

'There's only bloody kippers in your basket.' Pitch stomped into the hall, further down where the entry to the never-used kitchen stood. 'Do you have nothing else? No cake or pastries?' He had, for reasons unknown, removed his shirt. An assortment of tattoos marked both arms, though without staring, Silas could not make out their small forms.

'No, I'm afraid not.'

Pitch was certainly slight, though not without noticeable muscle definition. At his stomach a V-shape of muscle formed a downward arrow of sorts, directing the eye to what lay beneath his waistband. There was not a hair to be seen on his chest, giving him an almost boyish appearance. Almost. There was an air to Tobias Astaroth that could never be confused with youthfulness.

'Fuck.' Pitch slumped against the doorframe, rubbing at his face. 'Where is your bed?'

With a cough Silas readied his answer. 'Mr Astaroth, I have to tell you –'

'Mr Mercer, as much as I'd like to play with what lies beneath those grand trousers of yours, you will have to wait I'm afraid. I'm wrung out, I'm loath to say. I've spent the better part of the last three hours introducing my fists to a variety of faces, and my cock to several assholes.- Unless you have cocaine or cake in this house, we are done for now.' He gestured at the stairs. 'Up there, I'd wager?'

He did not wait for an answer, or protest, turning towards the stairs. With his back bared as he moved away, Silas was astonished to see a most remarkable, if somewhat garish, tattoo there. It was enormous, and no doubt had caused considerable pain to create, but now Silas thought he understood where the man's nickname might come from. The design resembled a pitchfork with the pole running the length of his spine, the two outer prongs across each shoulder blade. The third and central prong was much longer than the rest, its tip lost beneath the length of his hair on the back of his neck. The inkwork was not entirely tidy. Even from where he stood, Silas could see that some of the lines were jagged.

Pitch started up the stairs.

'Excuse me,' Silas asked. 'But don't you have your own bed at Holly Lodge?'

'Why would I bother with this one so close by?' Pitch called over his shoulder. 'I expect it's bloody enormous and wonderfully comfortable.'

'I must insist you stop.'

Of course Pitch did no such thing, reaching the top of the stairs in quick measure.

Silas hurried after him. The corridor, short as it was, was empty, and there were but two rooms to choose from in the upstairs area. Silas made his way to his own bedroom and immediately regretted his decision to look in. Pitch lay facedown on the bed and had discarded his trousers entirely, his buttocks bare to the air.

Silas coughed. 'Do you mind terribly...leaving my bed?'

Pitch patted the pillow. 'Where would the fun be in that? Join me.' He lay with his face pressed into the mattress, his slurred words muffled by the material. 'How long since you've dipped your wick, man? I can smell the rot of you from here.' He chuckled dark and low.

Silas glared down at him, the stench of liquor already fouled the room. He'd not slept in a day and had endured a most incredible evening of revelations. There was little of his patience left to deal with this intrusion.

'I shall not join you and would like you to remove yourself from my bed.' Silas used the sternest voice he owned. 'Now, Mr Astaroth. You have no business here.'

In response Pitch rolled languidly onto his back. Silas quickly averted his eyes, but not soon enough to avoid noticing the man was most adequately endowed. And lazily aroused.

'I have no business anywhere, Mr Mercer. And yet...' He waved his hands towards the ceiling. 'Here I am. Answer me a question, and then let me sleep, because I am sobering at a rapid rate and I'd rather avoid being conscious when I come to.' He scratched at his stomach, his nails leaving red trails on his skin. 'Lieutenant Charters ...you saw him at the ball I believe.'

'Yes, yes.' Silas frowned at the swing of the conversation.

'How did he seem to you?' There was a softness to the question that seemed out of place with the speaker. 'Was he well?'

'Quite well. Aside from far too much drink.'

'Not mad then? I mean in his mind, not in temper. He rarely grows enraged, not when he's himself.'

Silas dared a glance, keeping his eyes lifted from the man's nethers and focusing on his face. Pitch stared up at the ceiling, eyes thoughtful. Wistful even.

'He seemed perfectly reasonable to me. He was very pleasant company.' Silas returned to staring at the floorboards. 'Do you know him well?'

The silence went on far too long. In fact Silas had begun to wonder if the man had fallen asleep when Pitch finally spoke again.

'I know him intimately, and yet not in the slightest. But he is good company indeed. He was a fine choice.'

Studying a whirl in the woodwork, Silas asked, 'A fine choice?'

Pitch released a loud and lengthy yawn. 'Mr Mercer, when I wake, if you still insist you are not in the mood to be ridden, we shall dine at The Atlas and toast your new anointment as death's concubine. Perhaps you will even show me your pretty sickle?'

'I'll have you know it is a scythe.' Silas glowered at the unfortunate swirl in the woodwork. 'Is there anyone in London who does not know of me?'

Death's concubine, indeed.

But there would be no answer from the man in his bed. Pitch began to snore. A sound as loud and preposterous as his singing. Silas darted a furtive glance down to where the man's considerable member rested, half alert, between his thighs. The length of creamy flesh was, as most things about the man were, very pleasing to the eye. Silas hissed between clenched teeth. Sleep, he must have some sleep, for his behaviour grew ever more ludicrous, and abhorrent. With his gaze averted, Silas grabbed at the blanket and swept it up over Pitch's exposed flesh. The man muttered in his sleep, rolling onto his side and curling in upon himself much like a child seeking warmth on a winter's night. Thankfully, he did not wake, and Silas took his leave, treading carefully and quietly down the stairs.

CHAPTER 12

Sleep may have been required, but it was not forthcoming. Silas attempted to settle in his favourite armchair by the unlit fire for some time before abandoning the idea entirely. The cool, dim atmosphere did not make for a satisfying setting in which to slumber, and the knowledge that Pitch lay upstairs kept Silas on edge. He blamed Pitch's awful, sudden temper, of course, for the unrest. Not the man's lurid suggestions and flagrant exposure that had led Silas to act like a vile ogler. Every moment the dreadful snoring ceased, Silas found himself bracing, all at once dreadfully tense. He did not wish to face Tobias Astaroth again so soon.

Rising from his chair, Silas gathered up his coat, and once he had assured himself that the bandalore was on his person, set off into the sunshine. There was a place that could soothe him of these ill feelings. Outside, the October day had begun in a splendid fashion. The air was comfortable if rather brisk, and the sky yawned above without a single cloud to mar its blue canvas. Silas tilted his chin, allowing the sunlight to touch his skin as he made his way towards the east garden. He told himself he wished to sit there, amongst the hedge roses and willows, so they might bring their usual peace of mind. Silas passed by a cottage built in a style reminiscent of the time of the Tudor's, with its white walls and thick, dark wooden beams. No one was in residence, of course. A fact he was growing rather accustomed too, and was not sure he'd enjoy the company should it arrive.

Silas breathed in, the air laced with things of a natural persuasion: lavender here, lilies there, the danker scent of the earth and grass mingling with all. He did so enjoy the balm of nature. His knots unwound, the furrow of his brow uncreased. How easily the names of the plants came to him. Was this connection with the splendours of the garden a hint of his past? Maybe it was that an ankou doubled as a gardener in their spare time. Certainly, he was discovering that anything was possible.

But splendid as it was, Silas could not fool himself that it was the gardens he truly longed for. He removed his coat and draped it over his arm. He dared to unbutton his shirt, just the top three buttons, so that the air might find its way to his undergarments. He reached the first of the willows, where the red brick wall with its sandstone cap gave way to the cruder rock wall. His heart made a notable thump in his chest as he strode closer to where the heavy blanket of ivy concealed the iron gate. The hint of earthiness upon the breeze intensified, and Silas shivered. Beyond the wall the caw of crows reached him, a dry curl of sound so misplaced alongside the gentler chirp of wrens and swallows, but he'd not be distracted now. The ivy began along the wall, growing denser and denser as he approached the gate. His hands began to tremble with the anticipation. By the time he found his place, and swept aside the hang of deep green to peer out into the meadow he was akin to a child upon Christmas morning. Light with excitement.

The golden-headed grasses seemed to bob in greeting, the hint of purple and pinks amongst them denoting the wildflowers who strained against the coming of winter. Beautiful, there was no denying, but this was not what impressed him so. His nostrils flared at the faint scent of rich, dank earth, his eyes would not be drawn from the cluster of stones that poked from the earth. The graveyard drew him as a banquet would lure a starving man. And most especially so today. Of all the times he had lingered here, and there had been many these past weeks, never had he felt such a vigorous urge to tread a path that would lead him amongst the headstones. Perhaps it was the need to distance himself from the man sleeping in his bed, or his own fear of what lay ahead now he knew himself an ankou, but whatever the cause Silas wished to set foot amongst the graves.

He *must* set foot amongst them.

116

Silas did not believe himself a man prone to addiction, but what struck him now must surely resemble the cravings of a drunkard. He glanced at his coat, the bandalore within its folds. There was no song sung to him. No caution or warning. He considered the height of the wall. It was a decent drop, but with his own height it was not impossible. And what harm in such an adventure? The village would be visible from the cemetery. He was hardly vanishing from sight.

Silas sought a foothold within the rough wall. With the aid of the ivy's strong limbs and his own strength and height to assist him further, he managed to haul himself to the top of the wall without much fuss. Negotiating his great frame into position, he pushed off, landing with a thump upon the meadow's thick layers of grass. He cast a furtive glance over his shoulder, half expecting Gilmore or Jane to appear, as though from thin air, and reprimand his wanton escapade. No one appeared. The crows took up their cawing once more, momentarily disturbed by his arrival. Silas grinned. He stretched his arms wide and spun around, releasing a delighted laugh before breaking into a run hastened by the continuing downward slope of the land. Before now the idea of such an adventure had filled him with nerves and dread, but today the pull of the graveyard was so mighty he was giddy with the delight of such an escape.

He made his way across the meadow, meandering this way and that, simply because he could. No one bothered him with instructions or orders, no one demanded great things of him. Silas could travel wherever he pleased. And it pleased him greatly to travel towards the cluster of stones ahead.

As he drew nearer, the generous scent of turned earth strengthened. Silas saw that the cemetery was not so modest as it had appeared from the gardens. The sloping of the land hid a rather grand expanse of headstones and crypts, all enclosed within a simple iron fence. He reached the archway, which held no obvious signage – and would have been no use to him if it had – finding to his relief that it was unlocked.

The moment Silas stepped foot over the threshold, the heady air seemed to sink more deeply into his lungs. He inhaled in greedy breaths. He was quite sure he'd never known such quiet as this. Not even the cackle of the crows reached him here, only the soft whisper of the breeze ruffling a copse of sycamores nearby.

He made his way through row upon row of crooked headstones. Though he could not read the inscriptions upon their faces Silas took time at each one, enjoying the solemnity, and the peacefulness. He was overcome with an odd, and distant sense of satisfaction. A certainty that things were as they should be. There was as much to sooth him here, as there was in the gardens.

'All are found,' he whispered.

For a long while, he walked amongst the dead, the restful dead. The earthy smells were calming, and he relished his oneness with his surrounds. Peculiar, he supposed, considering his violent arrival in just this place. He glanced ahead. Somewhere in this expanse lay his own grave, but he'd make no haste to find it. He could not count himself amongst the restful dead. The goddess had planned another course for him, and he would keep his distance from that bleak hole in the ground, with its plain wooden cross, as well as he could.

Silas halted outside an imposing cylindrical mausoleum, its steps slick with the same green moss that had taken a foothold throughout much of the grounds. He stood with hands clasped behind his back, as though he were visiting a prestigious gallery. It might as well have been such a place, for it was perfection indeed. No tingling took hold of his fingers, no chill upon his neck. No sign at all that a lost soul wandered aimlessly. All here were at peace. Yes, that is what soothed him so. None had escaped Izanami here. Silas gasped, patting at his pockets.

'The bandalore.'

It seemed quite impossible that he could have wandered so long without noting its absence, but now he was aghast. To be so distant from his scythe seemed at once a terrible thing. The cemetery had mesmerised him far too well. Silas abandoned his exploration, stepping over graves and hurrying between tombs to return to the gate. He was quite sure he had come this way, yet he did not recognise the trio of hulking crypts that lay ahead of him.

'Blast.'

He halted, seeking a sign of the outer fence. Somehow he had managed to drive himself deeper into the graveyard, for there was no sign of the perimeter at all. The distant sound of the crows reached him, and he decided to follow their drawl, hoping they had remained near to the outer limits, close to the Village.

Silas hurried along, but he had not gone far before it became very apparent that he had chosen the wrong direction. A crescent-shaped building hugged the pathway ahead, an enormous mausoleum perhaps or a multitude of crypts. Whichever it was, Silas had definitely not happened upon it before. He cursed, grinding his heels into the damp soil of the path, turning this way and that, seeking out some sign of an entranceway. A sea of stone surrounded him. The cemetery was quite enormous. A distant sound caught his attention. A young couple huddled close in shared grief, laying a bouquet upon a freshly-turned pile several rows away. Silas rubbed his hands in anxious contemplation. There was no harm in speaking with strangers, surely. He would ask them the way to the exit. Decision made, he set off towards them.

'Careful where you go. A lot of holes around here.'

He spun around. An empty graveyard stared back at him. 'Hello?' A duo of oaks nodded their branches to his right, their trunks surely thick enough to hide a person. 'Who is there?'

'Me.' A high and childish giggle followed. 'Up here.'

He peered up into the branches of the nearest oak. He saw no sign of the speaker until a flash of colour caught his eye. A young girl clambered down through the branches, jumping between them. She landed with perfect accuracy upon the lowest bough and seated herself, her bare feet dangling beneath her. She was dressed only in a faded yellow cotton slip, with no sleeves to cover her thin arms. As pleasant as the day may be, it was far from suitable attire. She sat at an alarming height off the ground, with her hands resting in her lap.

'That's quite high.' Silas eyed her warily. 'You should come down.'

She tilted her head, and he was reminded of a bird. In fact her hair reminded him of a bird's nest, sticks and leaves trapped in the strands. The girl was on the cusp of womanhood, he saw now, but was in dire need of a meal. 'Why is that?'

The danger seemed fairly obvious to him. Maybe the woman was of unsteady mind. 'Well, if you slip, it's a long way to fall.'

She burst into singsong laughter, holding her hands to her mouth as though she'd been told a delicious secret. 'Do you think I would fall?' She lifted off the branch in a most peculiar way. She did not use her hands to bolster herself but quite simply rose, settling her feet upon the branch. 'Well, I did not fall.'

Again her head tilted in that pronounced way, and a greater stirring of consternation filled Silas. It occurred to him that he might have assumed wrongly that no lost souls wandered here. But if this girl were such a creature, she was nothing like the ghost at the baron's residence. Gaunt as she was, she was entirely solid, not vapourish as the other had been. Whatever the truth, one thing was certain, Silas's peaceful haven had been disturbed.

'No, indeed,' he said. 'You did not fall. That was most fortunate.'

He squinted, trying to learn if there was a shadow at her feet, for the way she moved belonged to no one of true human birth. But with the dappling of light and the swaying of branches around her, he could not tell. Never was he more desirous to leave, and chanced that the creature might answer his question. 'Would you be so kind as to direct me to the exit?'

'Oh, don't go so soon, you do amuse us.' A man stepped from behind the other oak tree. Equally as gaunt and as slightly clothed as the girl. His dirty brown hair, too, was dotted with twigs and leaves, but he appeared older than the girl by some years.

'I'm afraid I must. I'll be going now, if you don't mind.' Bandalore or no, chimes of alarm were ringing loud and clear now.

'We mind.' Another voice, somewhere right, and this one sterner than the others.

Silas backed away, hoping that a headstone did not block his path. His jaunt into the outside world was fast becoming a terrible mistake. He was being surrounded, he was certain, like wolves descending upon prey. The girl danced upon her branch as easily as the bird she so reminded him of. Silas's heart raced beneath his ribs. He should run. But in what direction?

'He's so big,' someone exclaimed from overhead. A fourth assailant lurking in shadow.

'Perhaps the Nephilim remain amongst us after all.' This reply brought a chorus of squealing laughter, sounds that peppered down on him from every direction.

'What do you suppose he is?'

'It was human once, it smells bad.'

'Should we make the giant run and scream?'

'I'd like to see what giant tastes like.'

Silas turned and fled. He dashed with mad abandon through the tombs and headstones that stood to block his way. His headlong journey saw him turn an ankle in an unseen divot. He grunted, biting down on a curse, and pushed on. His ankle throbbed with pain, but there was as much chance of him stopping as there was of the sun falling on him in that moment. His pursuers made no secret of their chase, laughing and calling to one another as they followed after him, leaping over the grave markers with ease. Silas's dread deepened. They were indeed like wolves, predators who bided their time to strike.

Squeezing through a narrow gap between two granite tombs, he burst out into an open space, a space in the graveyard that had not been already taken up by the dead. He glanced back over his shoulder, seeking out his hunters. The man bounded up onto the tombs Silas had just passed, as though wings lifted him. His malicious grin was the last thing Silas noted before the ground disappeared from beneath him.

Silas tumbled down into a pit of darkness.

Well, actually not so dark as it seemed, nor so deep. He hit wet earth with a muffled thud and splash, the air knocked from his lungs. The water at once clung to his trousers, its chill soaking through to his skin. He attempted to push himself to hands and knees, only to find that he was in a space barely bigger than himself. His shoulders grazed the rough soil around him, and it rained in tiny pieces into the water he knelt in.

'Dear god,' he cried hoarsely, a great wave of terror clawing its way forth.

Silas had fallen into an open grave. The horror of it drenched him, stealing the bountiful air from his lungs. The waft of the earth now suffocated him. In jerking motions he managed to turn himself and dig his fingertips into the dirt walls, pulling himself into a kneeling position. His ankle berated every move. Those who hunted him gathered around to peer down at their imprisoned prey.

'Well, aren't you in just the spot?'

'Rather thoughtful of him, I think.'

One of them leaned too hard upon the loose edge and showered Silas with dirt.

'Leave me be!' he shouted. 'I've no quarrel with you, whoever you are.'

'Who said there needed to be a quarrel?' The group laughed, though this time the sound resembled all too well the rasp of the crow.

Silas fought to hold his nerve, no easy task with the weight of his memories ten times that of any gravestone. He judged the height of the hole to be no greater than his own. He could stand, on an ankle that could barely hold him, but then what? He'd only succeed in bringing himself closer to those taunting him, and who could tell what assault they had in mind? For it was an attack they rallied for, he had no doubt. But dear God he could not stay where he was. He remonstrated his decisions of the morning, beginning with the ludicrous invitation to Tobias Astaroth to enter his home. If not for that, then Silas would be safe and slumbering in his own bed.

A sharp pain sliced across his shoulder. He cried out, throwing himself onto his back, attempting to move beyond reach of what had struck him. Light spilled across the features of those watching him, perched on the edge of the grave as crows might perch upon a branch. How horribly they had altered. Gone were the sly grins on human faces, gone was any trace of their humanity at all. Creatures most foul formed a living halo around Silas's grave. Instead of human feet, now thick scaled legs tipped with enormous claws stood at the edge, each easily the length of Silas's own forearms. Multitudes of teeth filled their lipless mouths to bursting, their eyes sagging as though melting from their faces. And instead of hair, now dirty, lank feathers formed a thin layer over their heads and bodies. The flimsy yellow shift dress was nothing now but shredded rags upon the girl's body. A dark shape filled the air behind her, and Silas breathed in shuddering gasps as he recognised the plume of black-feathered wings.

A moment later one of those very same wings thrust down into his dirty prison. Silas covered his head, curling in upon himself. He was struck across the back of the neck, the feathers as sharp as knives. The heat of his own blood warmed his shoulders.

'Stop!' Silas cried. 'Someone, help me!'

In answer a new assault was launched. Silas pressed himself into a corner of the grave, covering his head as best he could. Hot agony spread across the tops of his hands as the knifepoints made their mark. Another caught his cheek, and the warmth of blood once again made itself known. They toyed with him. Any one of the strikes might have been the killing blow, so razor-like were the wing tips. They laughed at the amusement his torture was providing, drowning out his pleas for them to let him be.

Mother Nature chose that moment to add her hand to the fray, releasing a torrent of rain down upon them. Heavy drops ran red with his blood. Rivulets streamed down his temples, a coppery tang rising above the freshness of the water. Had he imagined his second death, it would never have been this, set upon by winged daemons, and him putting up the most pathetic of fights. Silas licked his lips, tasting blood and rain. He shook hard with the visions that came to him. The memories of the drowning that had taken his first life. Now here he cowered, his history set to repeat itself with greater brutality. Mr Ahari had made it clear, Silas was not immortal. If he did not move himself, he was set to have his life ended once again, this time already in his grave.

Voices rose amongst his attackers, shouted words he could not discern, and there came a blessed pause from the slashing of their blades. He seized the moment, and his courage. Silas launched himself to his feet with an unsteady cry, his injured ankle singing with pain. The rain stopped at once, and one of his taunters released a screech that could have resurrected all the dead within the cemetery. Silas threw up his fists, readying to strike. Instead, he found himself dodging a fast-moving object, one that barely missed him before glancing off the edge of the grave and landing with a deadened thump at his feet.

'Oh my god.' Silas shrank back, bile harsh against his throat.

There before him, lying in the blackened water, was the head of the young woman he'd first encountered. Eyes wide open, her mouth caught in her final scream. Sounds of pure chaos rained down into Silas's grave. Hell-risen screams cut off at their quick. The scuffle of feet, and the grunts and groans of a fight rang out. Shapes moved above him, darting back and forth across the hole where he huddled, ripe with fear. Feathers rained down on him, and other things. Meatier things. Wet and unyielding upon the mud.

The silence hit as suddenly as the chaos had begun. Stillness returned, the drip of water marking each moment. Silas trembled in his confines, taking short sharp breaths lest he make too much sound and draw the attention of those above. Pressure landed upon his shoulder, and he was hauled from his pit, soaring some distance before he made contact with the ground once more. With a grunt and cry conjoined, he landed on his stomach. Instinct rolled him onto his back, fists bunched. Someone set upon him, their figure bathed in a sunset's glow. Warm hands found Silas's neck, clutching with a strength that left him immediately breathless. All too clearly he saw his attacker. Pitch's stunning emerald eyes were blazing, their centre burning with flames of gold. That same glow of flame, as though he stood in front of a great fire, was evident around his body, naked but for the open coat he wore. The creatures' blood was spattered all over his face and caked in the waves of his hair. A nasty smile played at his lips, revealing teeth also stained with blood. Silas tried to speak the man's name, but there was no air to exhale. His vision was dotted with specks of white.

'Fucking harpies,' Pitch growled.

Silas's crushed throat allowed no reply.

Was Pitch blind? Or mad? Silas was fast becoming certain it must be the latter, for Pitch's eyes were truly frightening. Widened and glazed. And his grin was awful in its width, stretching his lips until they seemed set to split. With the sounds of his own struggle growing faint, Silas gasped, an ugly gurgle coming from him. He was on the cusp of losing consciousness. With his world darkening, and his body weakening, he levelled lacklustre thumps against Pitch's chest. He managed barely two before all strength was gone.

Silas's hands fell. His right brushed against the draping side of Pitch's coat, and the soft and glorious sounds of the bandalore's song filtered down into Silas's shrinking world. Blinking through a haze of white, Silas caught the flash of royal blue. With a last desperate twitch of muscle, he thrust his hand into the folds of familiar material, finding the pocket where the bandalore nestled. His fingers clenched around it. Impossibly, thankfully, the bandalore lay in his grasp. Ears buzzing, chest set to explode, Silas thrust the device at Pitch's head.

He let loose a startled cry and flew sideways, soaring some distance before he landed with a heavy, comforting thump upon the ground. Silas sucked in a huge, gulping breath, and the air poured into his lungs. He clutched at his throat, wincing at the bruised flesh there.

'What is wrong with you?' he rasped.

Pitch, his strange glow now disappeared, muttered an angry reply, but it was lost to Silas as he caught sight of the scene around them. Scattered around the open grave were the dismembered limbs of the creatures. Flesh and broken bone carpeted the sodden earth, with the feathers lying like crushed coal atop them.

'Dear god,' he whispered. A wild and rabid animal could not have done more damage.

'What the fuck did you hit me with?' Pitch sat up, swiping at his chin and smearing blood further along his jawbone. He wore Silas's Inverness coat and nothing more, save for great smears of blood and disconcerting flecks of white and pink. The coat itself was ruined, great rents in the back that allowed hint of the large tattoo upon Pitch's back.

'What have you done, Tobias?' Silas attempted to rise, leaning hard upon a nearby headstone to relieve his ankle of the pressure. He was surprised to note that his hands appeared merely nicked with shallow cuts, and not slashed deep as he had feared. There was no sign of the couple who had been tending a grave earlier, and he hoped they had been spared the grisly battle. But surely someone had heard the screams. He and Pitch would hardly be alone for long.

'Nothing more than was intended.' Pitch flicked at a gelatinous glob upon the cuff of Silas's coat. 'Is that how you thank all your rescuers?'

Silas stared at him. 'You do realise that you just tried to strangle me, after your so-called rescue?'

Pitch shrugged, pulling the folds of the coat tight about himself, for which Silas was both grateful and horrified in equal measure. 'So I got caught up in the moment. Can't blame a man for being passionate about what he does.' He touched at his head, where the bandalore had made contact. 'But it appears you can stop a berserker in his tracks. What is that?' He gestured at the bandalore still in Silas's hand.

'It's mine.' He enfolded it in both hands, clutching it to his chest. He would face those dreadful creatures again rather than allow Pitch or anyone else to have it.

'Oh gods, settle down, big man.' Pitch rose to his feet, making a rather futile attempt to tidy his bedraggled hair. Nothing short of a thorough bath would remove the signs of massacre from him. The coat was several sizes too large for him, running along the ground like a lady's gown. 'No one is taking your toy from you. Perhaps you should have used it earlier.'

'I didn't have it earlier.' Silas attempted a step forward and hissed at the effort. His ankle bothered him far more than the grazes and cuts upon his skin. 'Do you have any idea what just happened?'

'Yes. You were cowering in a hole like a weeping babe while a cluster of harpies made sport of you. Are you coming? I doubt very much it's a wise idea to remain here.'

An understatement if ever there was one, but Silas was not enjoying the rude cramp of muscle that radiated from his ankle.

'I did not cower,' he muttered. Then louder, he asked, 'How did you find me?'

Pitch gestured to the sky. 'Rainstorm drummed me out of the most pleasant dream, which I will not thank you for. Who knew there were such uses for the common milk bottle? Once I awoke, Matilda led me here with her dribbling sun showers. What is wrong with you, man? You will need to let go of that headstone, we aren't taking it with us.'

'My ankle,' Silas growled. 'I've injured it, and don't believe I can walk upon it.'

'By Gabriel's sphincter, you are an enormous bother.' Without warning Pitch weaselled in beneath Silas's arm, draping it across his own slender shoulders. In another life Silas might have laughed at such a slight man's attempt to assist him, but he knew better now. Pitch righted, and fairly lifted Silas onto his tiptoes. 'Is your blood pumping, Mr Mercer? For mine is flowing to all the right places,' he said. 'Shall I take you to your bed where we can expend our energies?'

'What on Earth is wrong with you?' Silas would have given his own soul to be yards away from the man at that moment. 'What of the carnage?'

'Rest assured, that does not qualify as carnage.' Pitch tugged at the length of the coat with his free hand. 'A skirmish, no more.'

'Surely it will be discovered.' Though how it had not been already, he was at a loss to say.

'Oh, Satty has her troops well versed at cleaning up. Don't worry your large but attractive head about it.'

They made slow progress past the grand curving mausoleum, and to Silas's great surprise, he saw that beyond its furthest edge rain still fell in a heavy sheet upon the graveyard.

'It does not rain where we stand?' he said with wonder.

'Of course not. Matilda would piss upon me at her peril. I despise having my hair ruined in such a way. It takes time to cultivate this perfection.'

That perfection he spoke of was far from evident after his encounter, darkened black in places by blood. Not to mention the state of Silas's coat. What had possessed the man to clothe himself in it anyway? A fortunate though strange decision. But Silas was more puzzled by the conversation.

'Matilda?'

'Part of Satty's elemental foursome. Water, in case you could not surmise. Matilda is an undine with the most astonishingly agile tongue.' Pitch shifted his grip on Silas's arm, somehow managing to heft him so that only Silas's tiptoes scraped the ground. 'Oh, remove that frown from your face, it does you no favours. The rain sent everyone scurrying, and now Matilda shields what remains of those fucking harpies from view behind a downpour. The corpses will be dealt with by the appropriate people. Wouldn't want any of the precious humans to see what we are really capable of, now would we?' His bare legs shifted in and out of the folds of the coat, thankfully now buttoned low enough to cover his most intimate parts.

'Harpies?' Silas marvelled.

'Did the encounter render you a moron? I just told you that is what they were.'

'What did they want with me?'

Pitch uttered a sharp and vulgar curse. 'Gods, you are insipid. I am not your personal font of knowledge. Do me the greatest favour, and shut your pretty mouth until we reach the Village. Then you can bore the eyeballs out of whoever you wish. Understand?'

Of course he did not, but Silas was not about to test the man's fragile patience. He nodded, fingering the bandalore, calmed by its return to his person. Silas could not say for certain, but it seemed to him that the cuts on the backs of his hands were fewer than he had imagined earlier. And certainly not deep enough for concern.

'Good boy.' Pitch patted Silas's chest.

'You're not going to the Village.' The surly voice startled them both, and even Pitch jumped at the sound.

Isaac, buried beneath his usual layers of dark fabric, stepped out from behind a formidable sycamore.

'Bullshit we aren't,' Pitch declared.

'I'm to take you to The Atlas. Mr Ahari would have a word with Mr Mercer about his sojourn to the cemetery, and you're to join him, Astaroth.'

'Fine.' Pitch sighed, putting up surprisingly little protest.

Silas stared down at his muddied, bloodied attire. 'But my clothes –'

'Don't matter,' Isaac grunted 'Now hurry it up. You've left us with enough bloody work to do here as it is.'

Silas bristled. He was hardly to blame for the destruction. 'I cannot attend like this. I am a dreadful mess.' He gestured at Pitch. 'And he is quite naked under that coat.'

As much as Silas adored the garment, he was not so sure he wished to wear it ever again.

'Do I look like I care anything at all about him?' Isaac growled. 'Just get to the carriage. Both of ya.'

Silas worked against Pitch's attempts to move him on. 'We are covered in...rather dreadful things. This is ridiculous.'

'You'd be surprised how wonderful those dreadful things are for your skin,' Pitch replied. He grasped the waist of Silas's trousers, lifting him clear off his feet, causing his undergarments to wedge rather painfully in the crease of his buttocks. 'Now, come along, Silas my dear. Let's not keep Mr Ahari, or his pints, waiting. I have rather the appetite.'

CHAPTER 13

The Atlas was closed. The morning had not yet given way to midday, and not a single patron graced the seats or slumped at the bar. Only the bartender, Kaneko, was in attendance, and when he looked up from his glass polishing, his face grew dark.

'Mr Astaroth, back so soon?'

'I simply cannot stay away from your pleasant self.'

Kaneko's scowl deepened. 'I'd be more pleasant if you did not insist on breaking my glasses every time you grace us with your presence.'

'Well, Mr Talbot should not insist on accusing me of cheating every time we play cards. Your misfortune can be blamed on him.'

Kaneko gave a slight shake of his head and turned his attention to Silas, who used the aid of a walking cane Isaac had handed him as he stepped down from the carriage. In truth, he was not sure he required it at all. Silas's injured ankle did not bother him nearly so much by the time they had made the journey from the cemetery to The Atlas, but he dared not refuse the surly coach driver.

'Mr Mercer,' Kaneko said, 'I must warn you, your choice of company may lead you into some trouble.' He selected a pint glass and pulled an ale, the deep brown liquid frothing as it poured. Kaneko made no mention of the state of either Silas or Pitch. 'He's not one to waste your time with.'

'Oh, do be a good tsukumogami and piss off.'

Pitch settled into one of the armchairs by the fire. Save for a missing pair of shoes he was, thankfully, now fully clothed. In the strangeness of things that Silas was fast becoming used to, the carriage Isaac fetched them in had held some items of clothing in a storage compartment, a pair of brown trousers and a light yellow shirt, all of which fit Pitch perfectly. Isaac had mumbled something about this being a common occurrence, the need to dress Mr Astaroth, and it was evident he thought little of the service. There had been a lack of shoes available though, so Pitch remained barefoot, but it was a welcome relief to see him shrug off the coat. Even if it did mean Silas was forced to endure a lurid show of flesh for far longer than necessary, whilst Pitch dressed in the confines of the cabin on their journey. Silas's coat now lay waiting in the carriage for the return to Holly Village and Gilmore's attentions. Sadly, there had been no emergency provision of clothing for Silas, and he stood now most uncomfortable. The mud had hardened distastefully upon his trousers, and down the length of his shirt.

Kaneko set down the pint of ale, doing so with enough gusto to send froth spilling down its sides. It was too early for such an indulgence, but with the bloody encounter still so fresh, Silas was not about to refuse.

'Oh, thank you very much.' Silas was quietly impressed that the bartender remembered his ale preference.

'Can I get you anything else, Mr Mercer?'

'Well' – he tugged at the foul material of his shirt – 'I was wondering if perhaps there were some –'

'We're hungry,' Pitch called out. 'Is Mr Harrison in the kitchen?'

Muscles at Kaneko's square jaw tightened. 'You know full well he's on the evening shift. You ask every time. We're not even open for another hour, you're lucky I'm serving you at all.'

'Lucky?' Pitch sniffed. 'You gib-faced twat, talking as though you have a damned say in the matter. Ahari says jump, the umbrella jumps.' He slid deeper into his seat, his backside barely upon the cushion. 'Mercer, let me tell you. Mr Harrison knows his way around a kitchen. The man's cakes are more angelic than a single one of those celestial assholes.' He snapped his fingers. 'Umbrella, you got anything that passes for food in that kitchen then?'

Kaneko glowered, his lips pressed white-tight, and looked set to tell Pitch exactly what he could do with his demand when Silas's stomach launched into a fervent growl. The bartender's sour mood lightened, and he gave a wry smile.

'Mr Mercer, could I interest you in a kedgeree perhaps? It was on the menu just last night. I could warm it for you?'

'I'm not sure I've ever eaten such a thing. What might it consist of?' Though in truth he'd have eaten a piece of dry bread readily enough.

'Pure delight, an exotic mix that's been brought all the way from India, can you imagine?' Silas could not. 'Smoked haddock, some rice, and wonderful spices of curry and coriander and turmeric.'

The bartender seemed so delighted by the dish that Silas had no heart to decline, even if it sounded far too rich for his tastes. 'How wonderful. I would love some.'

Kaneko fairly danced behind the bar. 'Please take a seat. I'll see to the food. Mr Ahari will be down momentarily.'

At least there would be no stairs to deal with, a small mercy.

'Of course,' Silas said. 'But I wondered if I might bother you for...' He brushed at his shirt. 'A change of clothing?' He touched at his cheek, where there had been a definitive cut earlier, though now his fingers did not find any broken skin, just a crust of dried blood. 'Some water perhaps?'

'Of course, of course. You have had quite the day of it, haven't you.' The bartender's smile had returned in full.

'Wine.' Pitch called from where he lounged. 'Red. With a serve of strawberry tarts.'

Kaneko's smile slipped like an egg upon an oily pan.

'Allow me,' Silas said. 'I'll take him the wine if you'd like?'

Kaneko threw him a grateful look and leaned across the bar. 'You're too good for the likes of him, Mr Mercer. Stay well clear would be my advice. He was not made for niceties.' He withdrew, gathering a bottle of wine and a glass. 'For His Highness.' Kaneko smirked at his words.

Pitch sat upright, a thunderous look upon his face. It seemed he might launch himself across the room at the bartender. 'Shall I wipe that grin from your face entirely?' The sound was as of distant thunder, rumbling and low.

Silas hurried to stunt the mercurial rise of Pitch's temper, too exhausted, hungry, and tender to deal with its display.

'Thank you, Kaneko. We are most grateful.'

He negotiated the wine, glass, and pint, as the bartender repeated his discomforting disappearing act. One moment there, the other simply not.

Silas hurried to where Pitch had returned to his slumped position. His shirt had ridden up and his trousers had slipped low, revealing a fine fuzz of light hair just below his waistline. His eyes held a gleam of gold that did not come from the meagre fire.

Setting down the wine and glass on the small rounded table at Pitch's elbow, Silas said the first thing that came to mind. 'I'm rather glad we don't have to climb those infernal stairs.'

'When one has no talent for small talk, one should not talk at all.' Pitch gestured at the bottle, and the cork escaped its top, flying into the hearth, a tiny plume of scattering embers marking its landing place. He poured himself a full glass of crimson wine, tilting it to his lips and downing the contents entirely, save for the few droplets that ran down his chin and marked his fresh shirt.

Silas took a much more modest sip of his ale. As Pitch poured himself another, he touched his free hand to his own neck. 'You have bruised up quite nicely.'

'Yes.' Silas desired to set the blame on Pitch, but with the man's temper so recently cooled, the idea was foolish, if not dangerous.

'Delicate flower, aren't you?'

The sigh left him before Silas could contain it. He was tired beyond all measure, his clothing was damp, and the memory of the horrors of the graveyard were ripe and fresh. Maintaining civility in the face of Pitch's constant bad manners required a strength that was fast waning. 'A bruise is a normal enough thing, considering the force used.'

'Normal for you perhaps. Despite my best efforts to cause myself great injury, the blood barely spills before the repair begins. They have reinforced my prison well.'

'Your prison?' Silas took a glorious sip of warm ale, the froth touching at his nose.

Pitch rolled his head so that he looked on Silas without shifting in his chair. 'I am beautiful as I am, I'm sure you'll agree, but I am breathtaking in my true form, I can assure you. Oh, Mr Mercer, you would be entirely speechless if you set eyes upon me, were I able to discard this flesh. But alas I cannot, as they are not done toying with me just yet. My penance continues.' A muscle in his jaw flexed, and he sucked back the remainder of his glass as though he wished to punish the droplets. 'If I had known I was to be confined to this form for so long, I would have given myself two cocks and several assholes to while away the time.'

Silas stared at him, the pint glass near his lips forgotten. What creature did he find himself in the company of? Aside from impossibly vain and arrogant? 'This is not your true form?'

'Why do you insist on speaking in a tone that suggests you do not believe a word I say? It's really quite irritating.'

There it was again, the faint rumble of menace that rose from the man like frost on a winter's morn.

'My apologies. I can assure you I do not intend to patronise you. This has been a decidedly fraught few weeks, and I am faced with fantastical situations that I'm struggling to comprehend.' Silas contemplated his half-drunk ale, the warmth of it already spreading through his belly, bringing enough ease with it for him to continue. 'I don't believe I thanked you for aiding me today.'

Pitch snorted. 'Aiding you? Christ man, I saved your bloody life.'

'Of course, yes. You did. And I am so very grateful that you heeded my calls for assistance.'

Pitch ran his tongue over the rim of his glass. 'It is not as though I had a choice.'

'I beg your pardon?'

'I have no duty to you, Mr Mercer, and no interest in extricating you from the situations you lower yourself into. I followed orders simply because I have no other choice, for now.'

'Orders?'

'Our dear and illustrious lady of the house had Matilda stir me, at a rather inopportune moment I must say. Might I say, you should probably have Gilmore launder your sheets before you next sleep upon them.'

Silas coughed into his ale, the last of the froth lifting from the glass. 'The Lady Satine is in London?' he said, recovering.

'I didn't say that. I said she had Matilda rouse me. And she could have done so in far more pleasant ways.'

'But if Lady Satine is not in London, how did she know I was in peril?'

Pitch rubbed at his face. 'Gods, man, you were in spitting distance of four of her elementals. Likely one of them watched you. Can you please stop talking?'

'Gentlemen!' Mr Ahari's voice, so close behind, nearly lifted Silas from his chair. 'Oh apologies, Mr Mercer.' He chortled. 'I do tend to be light-footed as a fox.' He lowered himself onto the hearthstone, a familiar bottle of brandy in one hand, a glass in the other. 'I did not expect to have you back here quite so soon. You've had quite the adventurous time of it, my boy. How are you?'

'Well, I would say I have been better. That encounter with the –'

'Fucking harpies.' Pitch spoke into his glass, which was all but empty.

'The harpies.' Silas nodded. 'It was frightening indeed, to say the least of it.'

'Quite, quite. I imagine it was very upsetting.'

Kaneko appeared without warning, right alongside Mr Ahari. Silas barely held on to his pint. The bartender carried two open trays. One held an enormous slab of Victoria cake, three layers of sponge filled to bursting with cream and strawberries. The other was a heaped dish of yellow rice smothered in a rich brown sauce and filled with chunks of fish and other things Silas could not make out. The waft of smoked haddock caused his mouth to water.

'Oh, by the gods.' Pitch wrinkled his fine nose. 'Did you insist on choosing the foulest-smelling dish on the menu?'

'Mr Astaroth , now now. That will be quite enough.' Mr Ahari's smile was pleasant, but warning laced his words. 'And don't be giving Kaneko any strife for failing to deliver strawberry tarts. The cake will have to do you. Another snide word from you and I will have him remove it entirely.'

The possibility pleased Kaneko visibly, his eyes brightening.

'Suffer the consequence if you try,' Pitch snarled, snatching the cake from the bartender and moving to sit at the opposite end of the hearthstone. As far from Silas's curry as possible apparently.

'Here you are, Mr Mercer.' Kaneko's face filled with a smile as he set the remaining dish on the side table. 'I do hope you enjoy.'

'Where is the cream?' Pitch demanded. Kaneko made such a furious face, Silas was forced to stifle laughter.

'He insists on three times the amount of sugar be added to any recipe,' the bartender whispered. 'It's disgusting. Just as well his body is kept by means other than natural, or his teeth would have fair rotted from his head.'

'My unnatural ears can hear your snivelling, you rotund asshole. Now where's that cream?'

'I fear you did not understand my words, Mr Astaroth.' Mr Ahari spoke lightly, but Pitch stayed silent, the message received.

Kaneko patted Silas's shoulder. 'When you have eaten, I'll show you where you can change your clothes. I presumed you and your stomach were needing food first and foremost.'

'Thank you very much.' He wasn't wrong. Silas could barely get his forkful to his mouth fast enough. Upon delivery a steaming, flavourful heaven assaulted his senses. The dish was magnificence on a plate.

Kaneko left them, walking this time rather than simply vanishing. Mr Ahari regarded the fire, sipping every so often at his brandy. He took the poker and stoked what remained of the embers.

'Now you have finished insulting my employee, Mr Astaroth, I would like to speak with you both of the events of this afternoon. My apologies for the hasty request that you travel here, but I'm not one for travelling about this early in the day, and I thought it best we spoke where there is no chance of being overheard.'

'Not much to tell. The harpies knew a giant imbecile when they saw one and decided he was easy sport. They did not live to regret it.' Cream filled the corners of Pitch's mouth. 'Oh, by Lucifer's balls, Mr Harrison knows his way around a cake tin.' He dropped his head back, groaning as he chewed the mouthful.

'Don't mind him.' Mr Ahari chuckled. 'Our friend here has quite a serious addiction to the sweeter things. But I'm afraid he does underplay the attack on your person somewhat. Mr Astaroth, tell me, did you frequent this world much in the days before your…ah…current situation? Because I can assure you what the harpies did today was most uncommon.'

A hardness set itself into Pitch's features, his sugar-dusted lips tight. 'Though it is none of your business, yes, I frequented this world. But such visits were undertaken for pleasure, and pleasure alone. I could only have given a damn what harpies were doing, if they were doing me.' He laughed, but the sound had no substance and quickly died. 'And if by my current situation you refer to the fact that Lady Satine holds my leash, thank you so dearly for the reminder.' Daggers of emerald were sent the old man's way. 'Make your point, for you are boring me.'

Mr Ahari selected a log from the pile stacked by the fire and cast it onto the rising embers. Sparks danced in a brief flurry. 'My point is that though the harpies are prone to being bothersome, such bold violence is quite unheard of.'

'How dull.' Pitch sighed.

Mr Ahari showed the first sign of frustration, a muscle in his cheek twitching before his smile settled back into place. 'Mr Mercer has had an awful lot of information to absorb of late, so for his sake I shall reiterate. The Order of the Golden Dawn has existed in this world for a very long time. It was not set up purely to indulge and exploit the latest obsession in this society for all things of the paranormal nature, though granted that has been a financially fortuitous coincidence. Members of the Order are monitors, if you will. Guardians who police the supernaturals who reside here in this world and ensure that their coexistence alongside the humans runs smoothly. And it is rather a case of vice versa, too. Humans are fearful creatures and will tend to do some rather unsavoury things to those they do not understand. The Order keeps the balance, punishes those who stray into nefarious ways, and protects those not capable of doing so themselves.'

His soft brown eyes settled on Silas, who shovelled another large spoonful of rice into his mouth. The kedgeree was quite astounding. Kaneko was right to have been so enthusiastic about the dish.

'I am very thankful that Mr Astaroth came to my defence.' Silas's words were hindered by his mouthful, and not entirely truthful.

Certainly he was grateful for the rescue, but the ache at his throat as he swallowed reminded him of the pain of Pitch's assistance.

'Since when am I part of the bloody Order?' Pitch scoffed.

'Come now, Mr Astaroth,' Mr Ahari said. 'Did you believe yourself to be on a sojourn where you could do as you wished indefinitely? Everyone has their place.'

Pitch stayed silent, and the quiet was almost as troubling as when the air was filled with his snarled replies.

Silas took one last mouthful and sniffed, his nose running from the heat of the curry. 'So, I was not singled out?'

'We don't believe so, no,' Mr Ahari said. 'The village tends to draw the less civilised of the supernaturals to its doorstep, on account of the energies that go into its protection and fortification. Much the same as The Atlas, really. Moths to the flame, as it were. Moths seeking a high, I'm afraid. But such deliberate violence, such a coordinated attack, was unheard of until recently.'

Pitch set his empty plate upon the hearth, the crack of porcelain on stone sending a shiver across Silas's shoulders. 'Care to inform us as to what is going on? Don't dally with dramatics, Mr Ahari. Why did those harpies lose their minds, before they lost their heads? '

Mr Ahari set down his glass and templed his fingers, studying them. 'Mr Mercer, you must heed my instructions in the future, for I did say that you should not leave Holly Village unless told. But I believe you've learnt your lesson well enough. I advised such caution to begin with as there have been several unsavoury incidents reported of late, and we are yet to find a definitive answer as to their cause.'

'I'm quite happy to kill as many fucking harpies as you like. Their stench is ridiculous.' Pitch refilled his glass.

'That won't be necessary, Mr Astaroth. At least, we sincerely hope not.'

Pitch ran his fingertip through the last remnant of icing sugar upon his plate. 'You're as great a showman as those bloody Americans, the Fox sisters. Enough with the mysterious allusions, spit it out. What is the problem?'

Mr Ahari's withering gaze would have caused Silas to cower, but Pitch simply belched and rose to his feet. Making his way to the bar where

Kaneko took his order for a bottle of port wine with a scowl. After a great pause Mr Ahari cleared his throat and poured himself more brandy. 'Now that you have been awakened to your role, Mr Mercer, and a place has been found for you, Mr Astaroth, upon our little team, allow me to educate you further. The heart of this world holds a turmoil. A darkness that has resided there for time immemorial, as much a part of the landscape as a storm or an erupting volcano, and just as powerful.'

'A darkness?' Silas repeated, rather dumbly. Like a person new to language reciting a word he does not understand.

'It is named the Blight. The Lady Satine contains it for the most part, but there are certain weaknesses within the Earth where such a task is near on impossible and faint traces of it escape. These places are well known to us, and it is simply a matter of monitoring it and dealing with any...abnormalities it may cause. You see, there are some who react rather unfavourably to its touch.' He took a long, slow sip. Silas wanted to knock the glass from his hand and demand he speak on. 'The Blight is bothersome certainly but has failed to cause any great concern in nearly two thousand years, just a few outbreaks here and there. Certainly nothing so great the Order and the Lady Satine could not deal with readily enough.'

'Ah, but now Satty is losing her touch, so she has claimed me so I might clean up her mess for her.' Pitch sauntered back to the armchair, bottle in hand.

'I have no idea why Her Ladyship saw fit to bring you into service. I truly do not.' Mr Ahari shook his head, the look upon his face leaving no doubt he rather thought the idea ludicrous. 'But there we are. You are here, and we must make the most of it.'

Silas took in Mr Ahari's words, but the strangeness of what he was hearing belied belief. A darkness at the core of the world?

'Mr Ahari, I'm afraid I don't quite understand –'

'Now there's an oddity.' Pitch smirked.

Silas did what he was growing ever more adept at doing. He ignored the man. 'What effect does this...Blight...have upon the land?'

'It varies.' Mr Ahari pursed his lips. 'And its effect is felt by human and supernatural alike, and can be as mild as a headache or as severe as unnatural fits of violence, paranoias, or madness. But where you will note its effect most readily is upon the souls of the dead. The human dead, of course. Lost souls left to wander too long are terribly susceptible. The Blight will transform meek and harmless souls into...well, into rather unsavoury things. Teratisms, they are called. Mindless creatures with violent intent. All that remains of their humanity has rotted away, leaving a monster in their stead. Ensuring teratisms do not develop is at the crux of why ankou exist to begin with. You must move on the lost souls before the Blight can take hold. Once the souls are fouled though, the ankou lack the ability to destroy a teratism. The Lady Satine deals with those creatures. Every world holds its share of monsters you see, Mr Mercer, and they are watched and dealt with accordingly.'

'That's a wonderful story, old man,' Pitch said. 'But I do so wish you would make your point. I'll hazard a guess here and say that you are suggesting a link between the Blight and the behaviour of the harpies.'

'I am indeed,' Mr Ahari said with a solemn nod.

'Let it be said I have beauty and brains in equal spades.' Tobias sank low into his armchair, his eyes bright with self-congratulations.

The curry stirred in Silas's gut. 'But what sort of link exists?'

Mr Ahari tilted his glass to and fro, allowing the vanishing ice cubes there to tinkle back and forth. 'I can assure you that such a pointless yet vicious attack upon yourself is most definitely not the usual behaviour of the harpies. Even those who indulge themselves in the protective energies around the Village. From what Matilda shared with us of what she saw, they were quite callous, and acting with a wild violence we would expect of Mr Astaroth perhaps but not the harpies themselves. We are concerned, Mr Mercer, I'll not lie to you. But it would appear that the Blight rises more frequently than before. '

'Oh bloody hell, you melodramatic old bastard.' Pitch released a vehement belch, and the sweet scent reached Silas where he sat. 'Just direct me to where you wish your monsters taken care of.' He raised his glass. 'I shall cut down whoever needs cutting. You know, you could have just sent word to the Lodge. No need for all this clandestine rubbish.' He waved at the surrounds. 'But seeing as we are here, I'd like to order another serving of cake, some eclairs if you have them, too.'

Silas's thoughts swam like tadpoles, darting this way and that. He wished to run from here. Disappear into the crowds beyond the pub door where there was no talk of real monsters and awful dark energy seeping into the world.

'Mr Astaroth, I have some news for you that I fear you shall not enjoy, but there is no room for debate.' Mr Ahari paused, and Silas had to agree with Pitch, the man tended towards dramatics. 'You shall kill only those who seek harm to Mr Mercer. You are to be his guardian.'

'What?' Pitch and Silas spoke in perfect unison, their voices raised.

'You heard me well enough, Tobias. It has been decided that you shall remain at Mr Mercer's side for the time being, while he is still rather vulnerable with youth, and the Blight shows itself to be so unsettled.'

'I am to be a nanny to the giant oaf?' Pitch perched on the edge of his chair, the sharp lines of his face tense with anger.

'If you so wish to view it that way, then yes.' Mr Ahari was an oasis of calm.

'I'm sorry, Mr Ahari,' Silas stuttered. 'But I'm not sure what concerns me most, another such attack...or...' He glanced at Pitch and went no further.

'Certainly Mr Astaroth can be...challenging at times.'

'I will happily grow to be unbearable.'

'Mr Astaroth, please.' Mr Ahari grew stern. 'Your prowess for the fight is without equal, but if you have issue with the request, then you can take it up with the Lady Satine, for it was she who decided upon this. She would see Mr Mercer protected in these uncertain times. His ability to handle you, Mr Astaroth, has proved impressive so far, but she worries he can handle himself far less well, as today's events suggest. As wondrous as one of Izanami's scythes may be against the dead, it is a paltry defence against the living. Aside from giving one a nasty knock on the head. How is your head, by the way, Mr Astaroth?'

Pitch sneered and touched his temple where Silas had struck him, but remained silent. The bandalore pressed against Silas's hip in the folds of his trouser pocket, and for a moment he enjoyed the memory of Pitch being hurled through the air with the force of Silas's strike. Despite what Mr Ahari said, the scythe had served him well.

Mr Ahari continued. 'The lady and I agree that Mr Mercer must hone his skills quickly so that he can do his death-given job and no greater number of teratisms can be birthed. If the Blight does indeed grow more intense, we should endeavour to ensure we do not have a host of lost souls for it to feed upon.'

The heat of the fire failed to reach Silas, as though the room had grown too vast for it to penetrate. 'What is it exactly, this Blight?'

'A part of this world, my friend,' Mr Ahari said brightly. 'Just as the skies cast catastrophic storms, and mountains on occasion spew forth, so too does the core of this world have its own natural violence, and we have always dealt with it. I'm sure these measures are temporary. So there it is. Mr Astaroth shall deal with natural monsters, you Silas, will deal with the lost souls, and the teratisms shall fall to Lady Satine. I've no doubt we shall reminisce on this before too long and laugh at our concerns. Are you quite well, Mr Mercer? You've gone an odd shade.'

'I'm not sure I am equipped to deal with all of this.' Silas Mercer was far from well. He was quite sick to his stomach.

'No, you are right. Which is why we shall begin your training in earnest the day after tomorrow. There is an appointment that I think will suit you. I had thought to attend to it, but instead you shall both head north, to Leicester.' With a lot of grunting, Mr Ahari wobbled to his feet. 'Fear not, Mr Mercer. It is a simple enough task. An undesirable haunting such as you attended to at the baron's.'

Pitch groaned, pressing his glass against his forehead. 'North? The weather is so dreary –'

'I shall arrange first-class seating on the train.' Mr Ahari stretched his arms. 'I must leave you for now. Mr Mercer, enjoy the rest of your meal. Mr Astaroth, I shall see to it that those eclairs are delivered to you, along with another bottle of red. Try not to look so concerned, Mr Mercer.' He laughed as though Silas were a child refusing to take their first pony ride. 'I understand this must all sound quite overwhelming, but I've no doubt you'll find a way to deal with it. May this be the start of a fruitful partnership, for the Order of the Golden Dawn, and for you both.'

'Oh for the love of Raphael's asshole, stop prattling,' Pitch growled.

'A pleasure as always, Mr Astaroth.' Mr Ahari's rich brown eyes sparkled with bemusement, his irritation subdued. 'Mr Mercer, I will assume you would like another ale? Perhaps some eclairs as well?'

Silas shook his head, wondering if he would ever again harbour a desire to eat. 'The ale alone will suffice.'

'Wonderful. Good day, gentlemen, and best of luck.' Mr Ahari left them, breezing out of the room at quite the speed, as though he were tired of being there.

Unsure if he should wait for his new ale or retrieve it himself, Silas got to his feet and made his way to the bar. He was watching Kaneko pour the next pint when it suddenly occurred to him that he'd walked across the room without any discomfort. Silas touched at his neck, where Pitch had so violently assaulted him. There too the flesh was bruised no more.

He was, quite miraculously, entirely repaired.

CHAPTER 14

The morning of their departure for Leicester, bound for the residence of one Mr Alfred Donisthrope, Silas awoke bleary after yet another restless night. His head was far too full of monsters and oozing darkness to grant him decent rest and for the past two nights he'd tossed and turned more times than he could count. He found a dreary day awaiting him. And it did not improve. By midmorning it appeared as though the day were close to dusk, the cloud cover so thick, the rain so constant and heavy. The coldness of the day was more reminiscent of the heart of winter than mid-Autumn.

Silas shrugged deeper into his coat, freshly laundered and with much mending work done upon the awful rips it had borne after Pitch's graveyard confrontation. The back had taken the brunt of the ruin, with two near identical tears running from shoulder to waist. There had been a moment, the image of Pitch standing naked and bloodied in the folds of the royal-blue Inverness coat fresh in his mind, when Silas considered telling Gilmore he could discard the item. Burn it preferably. But that moment had quickly passed despite Gilmore's clear annoyance at being asked to repair it.

'You've got a cupboard full of bloody coats,' he huffed.

True enough, but Silas found a strange comfort in the Inverness coat. A sense of familiarity that he enjoyed though could not place in the slightest way. There was every chance his mind threw up false sensations, as a way of dealing with a vanished past, but at least this one kept him very warm. Most particularly now, for the coat's thick weave aided Silas in not freezing entirely as he sat in the carriage, waiting on Tobias Astaroth. He was equally grateful for his choice of headwear, a homburg of black wool that was rather stiff but barred the chill from his crown.

Isaac had halted the carriage—the same impressive Clarence with its gold trim and set of chestnuts geldings that had borne Silas and Pitch to The Atlas—beneath a covered area of driveway directly in front of Holly Lodge's front doors. It was the first time that Silas had been this close to Lady Satine's residence. For all the talk of her power and importance, the house was rather modest and inviting. More akin to a summer home than the imposing fortress he might assume she would reside in.

The carriage shifted with the movement of the horses, grown restless after near on half an hour of waiting. Isaac murmured to the animals, soothing them into steadiness with ungloved hands. Silas supposed the man did not notice the cold. Surely being a fire elemental meant heating simply came with being.

Silas pressed down the window, a pane of glass that was next to useless in blocking out the chill.

'Do you think I should go and hurry him along?' he asked of the driver. In truth he expected no answer. Silas was simply looking for an excuse to move before he lost sensation in his toes.

Isaac released a gruff laugh. 'You've a lot to learn if you think that a good idea. He ain't been home since you left The Atlas two days ago. Jane only pulled him out of someone's bed about an hour ago.'

Grasping at the rare conversation, Silas asked, 'Will we still be able to make the train?'

'That's why we're here three hours before it goes anywhere.'

'Oh.' Now Silas was not so keen for Pitch to arrive. The train journey would be arduous enough, an hour or so in that unsettling man's company, without draining conversation dry in the wait beforehand.

As though he sensed Silas's hope that he might take longer to ready himself, the front doors swung open, stained glass sending a swathe of coloured patterns rushing across the ground. Jane strode out first. She carried two large brown leather suitcases. Pitch was just a few paces behind, clad in a coat of the most stunning teal, with a black satin shirt beneath, and a scarf of checkered red draped around his neck. He wore black gloves, and his hair was slicked against his skull, highlighting the drastic angles of his face. His cheeks were flushed pink, as though he had run to meet them. A scenario Silas doubted very much was the case.

'Right,' Jane declared. 'That was much more arduous than it needed to be.'

Silas moved to alight from the carriage. 'Can I help with—'

His sentence could not be completed before Jane was at the luggage hold. She unstrapped Silas's small solitary case, setting it on the ground, and hoisted Pitch's much larger cases onto the storage rack at the back of the carriage.

'I'm fine, thank you, Mr Mercer.' She dusted off her hands against her day dress, a pretty white cotton with a dusting of pink flowers. He had barely seen her these past few days, save for a single visit where she had advised him about a particular cafe in Leicester she thought he should try to visit while there. 'Tobias, you are going for several nights, not months. You do realise that, don't you?'

'Aren't you preciously amusing.' Pitch's gloved finger touched against her nose before Jane had an opportunity to swipe him away. She did so a second later and only fended off thin air. 'This is my first official appearance for the Order, and both they and I have reputations to uphold. How am I to know what dreadful things the weather has in store for us?'

'What would your reputation be?' declared a gruff and familiar voice. 'Most adept at dropping to your knees and sucking a—'

'Gilmore.' Jane sighed. 'The sooner you hand over the lunch basket, the sooner you and Mr Astaroth can part ways. Wouldn't you like that?'

'More than all the gold in the world.' Gilmore stepped from behind Pitch, ignoring the sly and frightening gaze being directed at him as he focused on the large wicker basket he carried. He lifted it as high as his stature would allow towards the carriage. 'Here you go, Mr Mercer. There's some wine in there I think you're going to need.'

Being as he was mostly still inside the carriage, Silas had to lean at a substantial angle to accept the gift. The basket was heavier than he'd anticipated, and he almost succeeded in dropping it upon the diminutive man. Gilmore scowled up at him.

'Some bloody thanks that is. Crush a man, why don't you?'

'Thank you, Gilmore. This is very thoughtful of you.'

'Wasn't my bloody idea.' He turned on stubby legs to be on his way.

'Get in,' Isaac grunted. 'We are leaving.'

Silas shifted into his seat, taking the forward-facing bench seat as was his preference. Jane stood just behind Pitch, who had taken it upon himself to remove his black gloves, finger by finger, before he got in the carriage. She waved her hand, looking for Silas's attention. When she had it, she pointed at the seat on the opposite side of the carriage. Silas pointed to himself. Was he to move? A firm nod. He considered remaining where he was. But the rebellion was fleeting.

He shifted into the other seat. He'd deal with the nausea of travelling backwards if and when it arose. Pitch pressed his gloves into Jane's hands, despite her frown.

'Use these as you wish while you think of me,' he declared.

Pitch entered the carriage, smelling faintly of lavender. Far more pleasant than stale whisky, Silas supposed.

'Goodbye, Gilmore.' Pitch blew the departing man a kiss, but Gilmore shoved open the front door and disappeared inside without glancing back.

'Good luck, gentlemen. If nothing else, it will be interesting.' Jane gave Silas a meaningful glance. 'Don't let him bully you, Silas. Let your instinct take hold and guide you. It is there, you just need to listen for it.'

Though he nodded, Silas was not certain. And with the added weight of what Mr Ahari had told him about the Blight, he felt even less so.

'So terribly dramatic, sylph. I'll only bully him if he asks me sweetly and pays me well.' Pitch sat heavily in his seat, lifting his legs up beneath him, settling his head into the crux between the seat back and the side of the carriage. 'Mr Mercer, wake me when we're at the station.'

Isaac set the chestnuts into motion with a sharp whistle, and the carriage jerked forward.

'Goodbye, Jane.' Silas was surprised at the sudden pang that came at parting. In the midst of his strange transition, Jane had been a constant presence. And, he realised, a very welcome one. But as Isaac set the horses into an eager trot, the carriage curved around the circular drive and Jane was lost from sight. By the time they reached the main road and set off in earnest, Pitch was snoring in soft, rhythmic waves of breath. His lips were an unnatural shade of red, as though a winter wind had left them chapped. With his head tilted to one side, his neck was bared, revealing several thin marks upon his alabaster skin. Scratches. Fresh enough that Silas did not believe they were remnants of the fight with the harpies. Silas's own cheeks reddened as the reason for such markings, and red lips, dawned upon him.

He transferred his scrutiny to the outside world. It rushed by as the horses pulled them towards central London. Isaac had to slow as they travelled down Highgate West Hill and approached the intersection with a wide avenue where a funeral procession held up the traffic. A hearse of spotless glass and a beautifully-carved black and gold exterior was drawn by six magnificent midnight steeds with lashings of mane and tail. Plumes of black feathers were attached to their bridles, as though great birds sat between their ears. A walnut oak casket sat in place on the carriage, an enormous bunch of white roses resting upon it. Silas twisted in his seat so that he might view the procession as far as possible as it made its way down the avenue. Highgate Cemetery was situated further down that same road. The place where Silas's grave rested amongst so many others, and the guts of the harpies had been so brutally spread. Jane had informed him of its name during her brief visit after the bloody incident, describing the grounds as quite beautiful. Clearly, she had not been involved in any clean-up.

Silas tugged at the window, pulling the glass down so that he could thrust his head out into the elements, straining to catch sight of the main entrance. Despite the trauma of his last visit, the hunger to step foot amongst the graves swelled within him. He bit his tongue so he would not call on Isaac to take a detour and follow that corpse in its polished wooden box. The Clarence gathered pace once more, and the hearse and any chance of glimpsing the cemetery were stolen away. Silas withdrew into the cabin, his hair damp and eyes watering with the cold air. He exhaled and the strange longing ebbed into nothingness. Pitch stirred in his sleep, his lips forming around words uttered too softly to reach Silas's ear.

They moved closer to the heart of the city. It was near to midday and, despite the drizzle, the streets were busy. Ladies in their finery walked quickly alongside stiff-suited chaperons who held dainty parasols over their companions. Dirty-mouthed children in their soaked rags darted bare-foot into alley ways, or across the paths of strident horses, earning the bellowed curses of drivers who did not slow despite the human obstacles. The stench of horse manure and woodsmoke was heavy upon the air. On they travelled. Silas rode through the world, both a part of it and yet utterly distanced. Searching the shadows of those they passed. But in the strained light of a rainy day, it was difficult to note either the lack or presence of those shadows.

Pitch sighed, muttering something in his sleep, a coy smile playing at his lips.

'Come back?' This time Silas heard the words clearly.

All at once Pitch's smile collapsed and his eyes fluttered madly behind closed lids. 'Why not? Raph…not my fault…Raph, no!' Pitch's eyes flew open, his chest rising and falling as though he'd chased after the carriage all the way from Holly Lodge. His gaze darted about, and though it fell upon Silas, he had the sense Pitch did not see him at all.

After a few moments of breathy silence, Silas asked, 'Are you quite all right?'

Pitch coughed, pressing a curled fist to his chest. 'Of course.' He shuffled along the seat, settling himself against the opposite side of the carriage, folding his arms tight in front of him, eyes closing once again. 'Why do you ask?'

'You seemed most upset.' Silas couldn't help but press him further. Curious about anything that would disturb Tobias Astaroth in such a way. 'You were calling to someone, rather urgently.'

Pitch stiffened and his eyelids slid open to reveal just a hint of emerald. Silas could not help but feel he was being regarded by a viper. 'Is that so? And who pray tell did I seek so desperately?'

Silas's curiosity was fast being overtaken by trepidation. He waved off the question. 'Oh I couldn't be certain.'

'You're a fucking dreadful liar,' Pitch snarled. All at once the confines of the carriage were entirely inadequate in size. Pitch's seething temper crowded in upon them. 'Speak. What do you think you heard?'

'You said…something wasn't your…fault.' Silas eyed the floor, eager for a hole to appear. 'And a name…Raph, I think.'

Pitch stared at him for a long, long moment. He passed his tongue over his red, chapped lips. 'Do me a great favour and don't think.'

He tugged up his chequered scarf so that a good portion of his face was covered, and huddled tight into his corner.

Clearly, the conversation was over. Which was fine by Silas. A singular question had often nagged at him since his first encounter with Tobias Astaroth. What was the man? Supernatural, of course, but what particular kind? There had been opportunity to enquire, certainly, but as well as being caught up in his own peculiarities, Silas would admit to himself that he was rather afraid to know.

The rest of the journey to St Pancras Station passed by without conversation and only one significant incident. There was considerable traffic. An overturned milk cart caused issue near the canal and forced Isaac, with much cursing, to alter their route. This saw them arrive in a fluster at St Pancras a mere fifteen minutes before the train's departure. Pitch proved interminably hard to rouse from slumber, and the throng of people moving about the station set multiple obstacles in their hurried way. They settled into their first-class compartment only a few minutes before whistles blew. Station attendants called for all passengers to board and all nontravellers to leave the train. With a great, heavy hiss the train pulled from the station, and they were on their way.

CHAPTER 15

They were not ten minutes out of St Pancras Station, the clack of the train's wheels quickening, when Silas had a rather depressing realisation.

'Blast,' he cried. 'The luncheon basket. It is left beneath the seat in the carriage.'

And contained the wine, the precious wine. A juice that might ease Silas's nerves.

'By the gods, man, that is hardly something to lament,' Pitch said. 'You have dined on the gnome's gastronomic disasters, surely? I would bet all the diamonds upon me that he spat into every morsel packed, and included not an ounce of sugar amongst the ingredients, just to vex me. The only loss is the wine, I can assure you.'

Pitch rose to his feet, and Silas shrank back into the cushioning of his seat, heart thudding. Would the man strike him so easily? But Silas's fears were without warrant. Pitch pushed open the door to their compartment. 'You there,' he called to someone in the corridor. 'We would have some red wine and a selection of all the cakes and slices on offer.'

There was a muffled reply, and Pitch slid the door closed and returned to his seat. Once again he had taken the forward-facing seat. Granted, there was another on offer alongside him, their cabin able to accommodate four travellers, but Pitch had taken the preferable window seat, and Silas would not entertain the idea of requesting a swap. Wishing to admire the passing scenery, he resigned himself to travelling in reverse once again. It was warm in the cabin, too much so for the heaviness of his coat. He hung it upon the hook provided, slipping the bandalore into his trouser pocket before returning to his seat.

'Should I fear to sleep, lest you strike me again with your little sickle?' Pitch's grin fought with a snarl.

Silas glowered. 'Of course not. And I've told you once already, it is not a sickle, it is a scythe.' Had he spoken with a note of pride just then?

Pitch made a dismissive sound. 'You can hardly lay claim to the greatness of death when you barely survived four measly harpies.' He clapped his hands with a sudden and startling slap. 'But how brilliant am I? For there is your new name. Sickle!' He giggled at his own jest. 'It's perfect. A lesser name for a lesser servant of death.'

A sudden and fervent brush of anger came upon Silas. 'That is quite ridiculous.' He pressed his hand to the bandalore.

'It's barely different to your name now, you won't even notice.'

'I believe I very much shall. Why must you mock me?'

'Why ever not?' Pitch swung his legs to rest his shoes upon the seat beside him. 'And besides, I think it has rather a nice ring. Pitch and Sickle, esteemed members of the Order of the Golden Dawn.' He pursed his lips. 'Rather long though, might have to work out something else for our calling cards.'

Silas did not laugh as Pitch did. 'I don't expect there will be any need for calling cards. I suspect they will be rather disappointed with my performance, or lack of.'

'That's the spirit, old chap. Resign before you begin. Well done.' Pitch blew a noisy breath at the luggage rack above him. There had not been enough room for all his cases, the rest being stored elsewhere on the train by displeased porters. 'Gods, you are a bore.'

Silas ignored the slight. 'Why do they call you such a thing? Pitch, I mean. Is it for the tattoo upon your back? For I would say, it rather resembles a pitchfork.'

It was a jibe borne from Silas's smouldering temper, an attempt to irritate Pitch just as Pitch irritated Silas. So he was rather surprised – and mildly relieved – that the look that swept the man's delicate features held no sign his temper was stoked. There was another, gentler expression there instead. Melancholy, perhaps? Whatever it was, Pitch quickly wiped it clear.

'Aren't you adorably perceptive, Mr Mercer. In a way, yes, it is indeed what inspired the name.'

His gaze shifted to the passing scenery, and Silas was quite certain he saw it again. A wistfulness utterly uncommon to the man. The crass words that followed though were far more expected.

'Once, I knew a man who fucked me rather well and did not bore me at all. I admit I indulged him for it and did not protest when he bestowed the name upon me, foolish as it is.'

It was the gentlest smile Silas had yet seen upon Pitch's face, softening the wildness that usually clung to his features. And although Silas squirmed at the thought of two men so intimate, he could not help but wonder who such a lover might have been.

'But tell me, Sickle.' Pitch's smile drowned beneath a slier rise of lips. 'How have you seen the tattoo? Have you been watching me sleep? For I do so naked. I cannot think where else you might have gazed upon me. When I bathe perhaps? Gracious, are you quite taken with me, sir? You only need ask and I'll bend for you.' He dropped his hand to rest it between his thighs.

'Of course not.' Silas bristled, cursing the heat that came upon him. 'What nonsense you speak. Clearly you were too intoxicated to recall that you cast yourself into my bed, entirely naked –'

Pitch gasped. 'Are you saying you took advantage of me when I was intoxicated? I did wonder why I was so tender –'

'Stop! You are truly an incorrigible man.'

'Incorrigible I shall allow, but kind sir, my manliness is only skin deep.'

A light tap at the door interrupted any reply Silas may have had. An attendant entered the cabin, pushing a silver cart bearing a plethora of cakes and slices, at least half a dozen set upon plates of the most delightful patterned china. On a lower shelf sat a bottle of red wine and two glasses. The attendant, a youthful man with a complexion almost as dark as Isaac's, wheeled the cart into the narrow space between the facing seats, and Silas could not help but notice how his eyes found their way to Pitch and seemed unable to shift.

'Would you like me to pour the wine for you?'

He lifted the bottle with shaking hands. Silas could hardly blame him for his nervousness. Pitch regarded him with that viperish stare he held, one that seemed to devour a person whole.

Silas sought to put the young man out of what he assumed was his misery. 'No, that will be quite fine, thank you.'

But the attendant did not scupper away as Silas thought he might.

'Is there anything else I can do for you, sir?' The question was quite clearly aimed at Pitch, who now regarded the man with a lazy grin.

'Yes. There is actually.' He waved the man closer. 'Lean down, I have something for your ears alone.'

The young man set down the wine, rather too heavily. 'Sir?'

But he did as Pitch bid and, being rather stocky and short, did not have to lean far to find himself face-to-face with the man addressing him. With whip-like speed, Pitch's hand wrapped around the man's neck and pulled him forward to press his lips against the attendant's own. The younger man struggled lightly and then seemed to grow limp, bracing one hand to the back of the seat to prevent himself from collapsing onto Pitch's lap entirely. There was the dreadful, intimate sound of lips seeking one another, air making its way between hungry teeth and tongue. Silas knew he should either look away or attempt to extricate the man from Pitch's hold. But he did neither. In truth, the attendant did not appear to desire saving. After excruciating minutes, or perhaps just a few seconds, everyone inhaled. Silas included. The attendant stumbled back, knocking into the cart.

Pitch waggled his fingers at the unfortunate boy. 'Goodbye then.'

The man's legs did not seem to want to hold him, and he staggered, sweat visible upon his wide forehead. His hand trembled as he pulled the door closed. Leaving Silas and Pitch alone once again. The thundering clack of the wheels upon the tracks was the only sound for a short while.

'Pour the wine, will you, Sickle?'

Pitch helped himself to a huge slice of vanilla creme cake, adding an extra dollop of cream upon the heap. Silas did as he was bid, but not through any sense of servitude. He too required a drink, and required one now. He poured himself a generous glass and set the bottle down, leaving Pitch's glass unfilled. Pitch eyed him with a bemused smile.

'Something wrong?' he asked.

Fingers tight around his bolstering drink, Silas nodded. 'That was unseemly, what you just did.'

Through a mouthful of sponge, Pitch replied, 'What? Taking such a big mouthful?'

'Attacking that young man.'

Pitch laughed and flecks of cake escaped his mouth. 'Did he look under attack to you?'

He had Silas there. The attendant had not struggled long or hard. But Silas was quite sure that did not equate to full consent. 'You...bewitched him...'

'How quaint, you think me a witch?'

Silas indulged in another generous sip of wine, for this was a conversation that filled him with both dread and overwhelming curiosity.

'Is that not possible?' he said at last. 'If ankou and elementals and harpies exist, why not a witch or a sorcerer? For clearly that man was beguiled beyond his control.'

Pitch dug his finger into the centre of a bright pink tartlet. 'He was quite willing. His desire was there beneath the surface. I simply removed his inhibition. Don't tell me you could not see the want in him? Are you that chaste and delicate?'

For some reason Pitch's accusation irked him, and Silas shook his head firmly. 'Of course not. But it is hardly the done thing to impose yourself like that.'

'We are hardly the done thing, sweet Silas. Let go of that world, and you'll enjoy yourself far more. Humans and their rules, their etiquettes, are tiresome not to mention tedious. I have my needs, and I will fulfil them, it is really quite as simple as that. Who would stop me? A fool perhaps, but none that would prove a real bother.' He sank his finger again into the rich pink filling, gouging a portion free before running his tongue slowly along the length of his laden finger. 'I used to frequent this world on occasion, you know. And it amused me. I would even go so far as to say I rather enjoyed it once, but that was in different times, and with far different company.' His words were gossamer soft. Pitch sucked at his teeth, and continued. 'The human world is rather less attractive when one is forced to stay in it, so I do what I can to amuse myself.' He kissed the tips of his fingers. 'Cakes and carnal knowledge. What point existing without them? They bring fire to my blood, and I do so enjoy the warmth.'

'That is quite apparent,' Silas muttered.

Pitch's laughter held a note of surprise. 'What an odd creature you are. Afraid of your own reflection mostly, yet every now and then a braver spirit appears. I know I frighten you, Sickle, but don't worry, you are not the only one.' The pink tartlet suffered a most vigorous bite from white, perfectly aligned teeth.

The conversation paused, and the monotonous clack of the train's wheels on the rails proved quite hypnotic. The rain pounded down heavily, slanted against the glass by the speed of the train, obscuring the view of the outskirts of the city beyond. Silas took a long sip from his glass. The wine was pleasant, fruity at the back of his throat. He waited until it warmed his stomach before he dared speak again.

'If you are not a witch or sorcerer, then might I ask what your true nature is, and why you are made to stay here?' He felt rather ill as the questions left him, as though he stood upon a dark precipice and might soon fall.

Popping a candied strawberry into his mouth, Pitch regarded him through lowered lashes. 'They would prefer I did not say, so as not to frighten their precious new ankou.'

Silas glanced at his coat where it hung with the bandalore hidden in its folds. 'Is that so? Are you that frightening, Mr Astaroth?'

'What would you say?'

Pitch was frightening in the way the dark of night was, but if Silas did not take hold of his trepidation, this partnership would dissolve into a nightmare he could not wake from. He could not be afraid of the dark. 'I would say that you aim to be quite a horror, and achieve it very well.'

Pitch tipped his chin and nodded. 'Quite astute, Sickle. Though to be fair, that is exactly what was intended for me from the very day I was birthed.' He moved on to a stacked jelly of the brightest orange, the gelatine wobbling with the movement of the train. 'How ironic that when one is made for violence, they are then punished for a job too well done.'

Silas's hesitation gave way to rapid curiosity. 'And that is why you were banished from Arcadia? Gilmore spoke of this place.' He was acutely aware that his first question was yet to be answered.

'Gilmore should keep his tiny mouth shut.'

'Where is this Arcadia?' Silas set down his glass. 'I'm quite sure I've never heard of such a place.'

'I'm quite sure of that too.' Pitch sucked back a glob of jelly. 'Fear not, it is not somewhere you will be forced to endure.'

'Was that person you spoke of in Arcadia as well?' It was a terrible long shot, but as much as he dreaded answers, Silas craved them. 'The one you called for, in your dream...Raph, was it?'

Perhaps the reason for Pitch's expulsion lay here. Had he not cried out about something not being his fault when the bad dream shook him?

A spoonful of jelly came to a sudden halt at Pitch's parted lips. 'You truly heard that name from me?'

Silas swallowed. 'I believe so...yes, though I'm not certain I heard correctly. Perhaps my –'

'Overly large ears deceived you? Highly likely, you are quite inept in all else, why not hearing?'

The man's composure had slipped, and Silas could not read the signs so well now. If he was angered, the usual caustic air was absent, but nor was Pitch entirely at ease, the muscles in his jaw flexing with tension. He appeared rather confused, if Silas were to name it. He breathed carefully, quiet as the proverbial mouse, and waited. After an interminably long time, Pitch shoved the jelly into his mouth and threw the spoon down onto the plate.

'I rather need to piss.' He stood. 'Touch a single morsel upon the tray and I will know about it.' He stepped forward, and lowered his face close to Silas's ear. 'My nightmares are my own, Mr Mercer, and you'd do well to stay out of them, for I am no witch, nor sorcerer.' He drew closer, their cheeks brushing. 'You are right to suppose that all manner of things exist, and you can count daemons amongst them.'

He brushed his lips to Silas's cheek and stepped away, winking as he stepped through the door.

The air rushed into the compartment once again. Silas's knuckles were whitened by their fast hold upon the arms of the seat. Did Pitch toy with him? Silas reached for his wine, trembling every bit as hard as the attendant had. This was exactly the type of taunt that Pitch adored, one that had a man near to loosening his bowels with fear. Slugging back the remainder of his wine, Silas eyed the bottle. A daemon. Was it impossible? A small and uncomfortable voice echoed back at him. He himself had been raised by a death god, what was not possible? But damn Mr Ahari if it were so. To be sent off with such company without warning was abhorrent. If they had kept the truth from Silas for fear of terrifying him, then they had been astute in that at least. Silas was not sure how much more of this peculiar world he could bear.

The minutes stretched into an hour, and Pitch did not return. The wine bottle sat empty now, its contents relaxing Silas enough that he now eyed the cart and its remaining delights with some fervour. Two of the six plates still held desserts: a chocolate cake with glistening frosting and a small bowl of trifle.

Did he dare?

He grabbed the tiny silver fork alongside the cake and dug into the thick, rich depths, cursing Pitch. Cursing the daemon, if that was his real nature. But in truth it was not hard to imagine that a man so prone to cruelty and rage might be the very devil himself. A low anger built within Silas at his predicament. He had been partnered with a sinister creature, his choice in the matter nonexistent. Well, both Mr Ahari and Pitch be damned. He raised the forkful to his mouth. If Tobias Astaroth would kill him over such a thing as the eating of a dessert, then best this whole predicament be done with now. He shoved the cake into his mouth, one eye still upon the door. The chocolate clung to his tongue and buried itself between his teeth. Utterly divine and decadent. Before he knew it, he had consumed the entire slice, his gut now turning for a very different reason. He had purposely set out to goad a daemon. What bloated, sugar-mad fool was he?

But he need not have worried about Pitch's return, for there was no sign then, nor fifteen minutes later, of the man. Another attendant returned to remove the cart a short time later, a woman this time. Just as well Pitch was absent, for Silas could not imagine what he might have led the young woman to do.

'We'll be arriving at Leicester London Station very shortly, sir,' she advised. 'I'll have your cases seen too.'

'Very well. Thank you.'

The attendant backed out with the trolley and rattled off down the corridor. Some ten minutes later the train slowed, and the call went down the carriage that Leicester London Station was imminent. Silas stood, gathering his coat and hat, once again reassuring himself that the bandalore was still upon his person, ever more comforted by the disc of wood since Pitch's revelation. The bandalore had very ably protected him whilst the daemon was in the throes of a berserk rage. A porter arrived at the cabin to collect their luggage, just as a scream of whistles announced their arrival. The carriage shuddered to a stop. The platform was not quite as crowded as St Pancras, but there were people enough. Perhaps, Silas mused, he could lose himself in their midst. Step off the train and vanish into the everydayness of life around him. Run far, far away from lost souls and teratisms and darkness rising from the heart of the Earth. Run far away from his partner.

'I'd locate you, you know.' Silas whirled to find Pitch in the doorway, the heady waft of cigar smoke coming from him. 'You rather stand out. And I'd be as unhappy about you attempting to run away as I am that you ate the chocolate cake.' His voice sank lower. 'I'll punish you for that later, you know.'

'You'll, you'll...what?'

'Whip you quite soundly or throw you into a pit of scorpions. I haven't decided yet.' His lopsided grin returned. The dark mood of earlier was gone without trace, Pitch's eyes alight with amusement, a carefree air about him. Whatever he had been doing the past hour or so had served Silas well. 'Oh come now, Sickle. Don't pale so. Perhaps you shall not be such dull company as you first seemed. Any man who would defy me after learning who it is they defy must have an astonishingly large set of balls. And who does not enjoy playing with balls? Come now. We wouldn't want to keep Mr Donisthrope waiting, would we? Let's not give the Order any reason to return you to your grave.'

'Stop talking rubbish.' Silas blamed the wine and excess of sugar for his curt reply. 'I know you seek to unsettle me, but I'll not have it. The Order would do no such thing.'

'We are all dispensable, Mr Mercer,' the daemon said. 'Believe me, I should know.'

CHAPTER 16

Their employer, one Alfred Donisthrope, had sent a chaperon. A thin, freckle-faced young man with a shock of orange hair.

'Gentlemen, I'm Clarence, Mr Donisthrope's valet. Welcome to Leicester.' He touched the tip of his fingers to his black felt hat and nodded, a jerky movement of his head reminiscent of a collared dove. 'We are all well pleased you made the journey. This is quite the honour, to have the Order here. I don't mind telling you, I'm thrilled by the notion.' He tugged at one of the brass buttons on his coat, a cloth of heavy speckled brown that bunched at his shoulders.

'We are at Mr Donisthrope's service.'

Pitch was the epitome of grace, exuding charm. It caught Silas quite by surprise and left him to wonder once again if talk of daemons was simply a cruel attempt to frighten.

'The Order prides itself on attending to matters with the utmost urgency wherever possible. I am Mr Tobias Astaroth, and this is my companion, the spiritualist, Mr Silas Mercer. It is he who will be attending to the bothersome spirit. I am merely here to ensure that as a novice at the task, he does nothing untoward.'

Silas released an inward sigh. The man was not congenial at all, rather insufferable.

'A novice you say?' Clarence pinched his nose, red-tipped from the cold. Silas was mildly insulted by the note of concern in the man's voice.

'Don't let that bother you, Clarence my boy.' Pitch added to his charm offensive. 'It is a very new policy of the Order that we should travel in pairs to our appointments. So new in fact, we are the first to work under these instructions.' What Pitch thought of those instructions was evident only in the slightest tilt of his nose. 'Mr Mercer is a rising star amongst the Order's members, I can assure you. You need not look so concerned.'

He touched lightly at the man's arm, and Clarence flinched ever so. Which Silas enjoyed very much. At last, someone who was not so easily swayed by Pitch's charms.

'It has been a troubling few weeks, don't mind me.' Clarence laughed with unsteady sound. 'I apologise for my rudeness, Mr Mercer. I'm sure you are ever so good at what you do. Right this way, sirs.'

Silas hardly knew if he was ever so good or terribly bad. There had not been time to determine such a thing, but he accepted the apology with a genuine smile.

Clarence led them through the station, a grand affair of quite new construction. As Silas studied the high ceiling and elaborate chandelier that threw gaslight across the open space, he sensed the stares of passersby, levelled at Pitch and himself in equal measure. True to form, Pitch tipped his hat and threw out the occasional wink at those who presumably took his fancy. Which meant there was much winking being done. The coy smiles that were returned to him were not so readily on display when gazes shifted to Silas's imposing figure. A wide berth was taken by many, and a businessman intent on his paper quite noticeably jumped upon seeing who he had almost run into.

'Did that child just hide behind its mother's skirts at the sight of you, Sickle?' Pitch said in an ill-concealed conspiratorial whisper.

'No.' Silas frowned, though that's exactly what the small boy had done. 'I should think it more likely he sensed your true form.' Blast it, could Silas not stifle his irritation with the man?

'Oh, he'd do more than hide behind a swathe of useless material if he saw my true likeness.'

Pitch offered the child's mother a smile that was more angelic than daemonic, and the poor woman almost tripped upon her own feet in her resultant fluster. With dismay Silas noted her childish giggle and beaming smile. Pitch certainly seduced with sinful ease.

Their carriage, a rather stunning enclosed landau with contrasting light wood spokes, was led by a pair of impressive dappled grey horses. The driver tipped his hat with a gloved hand as they stepped aboard, and though he did not quite smile, Silas suspected him of having a far more charming demeanour than Isaac. The rain that had followed them most of the way from London had abated here, though the number of muddy puddles on the road suggested that respite may be momentary.

They settled into their seats, Silas forced to sit beside Pitch when Clarence seated himself with his back to the driver. 'Have either of you visited Leicester before?'

Silas shook his head, arms pressed into his sides. With his bulk the seating was barely adequate for the two of them if they sought not to lean against one another. Despite his efforts to avoid such a thing, he could not seem to achieve his freedom, and was quite certain that Pitch leaned on purpose towards him.

'I've never had the pleasure of a visit to this...illustrious city.' Pitch plastered his words with a sarcastic note that Silas was coming to recognise, even if Clarence did not.

Outside, the midafternoon sun made a valiant and short-lived effort to break the cloud cover. Along the roadside calls went up from the various sellers of warm chestnuts, shouting at passersby that they'd be foolish to miss out on such a treat.

'It is full of industry here, with some massive factories. Mr Donisthrope owns three of them.' The tentative man's olive-green eyes lit up when speaking of his employer. 'He specialises in boots and shoes.'

Pitch leaned his elbows on his knees, head resting in raised hands. 'Shoes you say? Well, I never. If I'd known, I would have insisted the Order claim payment for services rendered through footwear entirely.'

He laughed gaily at his own humour, and after an initial hesitation, Clarence smiled too. Despite his earlier observation of Clarence's reticence around Pitch, Silas had returned to believing himself and Gilmore the only ones who found the daemon's presence so disconcerting.

'Clarence,' Silas said, 'might I be so bold as to ask about the hauntings we are here to deal with? I believe the household are of the mind that more than one spirit plagues the residence?' Mr Ahari had said that much at least, but little more.

Clarence cleared his throat. 'Yes. Yes. That's right. There are at least two of them, I've been told.' He frowned down at his hands, not meeting Silas's gaze as he spoke. 'There is definitely need of you here.'

'How long have you worked at...' The name of the residence escaped Silas.

'Knighton House? That would be four years now. And the strangeness of Leicester has grown with each year passing. Never more so than now.' Clarence breathed the last few words, wringing his hands.

'You do not speak only of the spirits at Mr Donisthrope's residence?' Silas said.

Clarence did not answer straightaway. He peered out the window where the sun had lost its battle with the clouds, though the air remained dry. As the silence continued, a curl of concern rose through Silas. The man's face had grown very pale, quite an accomplishment considering his already-pasty pallor.

'Not entirely.' He made an odd face, as though his stomach pained him. 'You seem like a reasonable man, Mr Mercer. I must confess I have not been altogether truthful in bringing you here.' He raised one shoulder as though expecting a blow, and Silas could not help but notice it was the shoulder nearest to Pitch. 'I'm so sorry that I...' Clarence's tongue failed him, and his eyes glistened with what Silas was startled to realise were tears.

'Is everything all –' he began.

'I note that you do not include me in your summation of reasonable nature, Clarence,' Pitch said. 'Very astute, but might I add that I detest tears and whimpering also.'

'Mr Astaroth,' Silas said, as firmly as his unsettled nerves would allow, 'I'm not sure that is a productive line of conversation.'

'If you'd allow me to continue, Mr Mercer, you would know that I intended to ask him to get to the point. So, Clarence, make your point before I am forced to slap some sense into you.'

'Mr Astaroth!' Silas cried. 'That is enough. Please, Clarence, pay him no mind. Do go on.'

Swallowing hard enough to bob his Adam's apple, Clarence bothered at his brass buttons and took a deep breath.

'I confess I put the idea in Mrs Donisthrope's head to contact the Order. I kept telling her of the marvellous seances and such that were being had in London and that maybe we needed to do the same, on account of our household ghost.'

Raising his brow, Silas asked, 'You said you were not truthful, are you suggesting there are no ghosts in the household?'

'Oh no, sir. No, no. They are there all right. But truth be told, they are no bother at all, and we wish no harm to them. But I was most grateful when Mr Donisthrope at last agreed your employment. He thinks all talk of the supernatural rather foolish, but he does not deny his lady anything.'

'Rightly so.' Pitch nodded sagely. 'No doubt he desires not to be cast from between his wife's legs –'

'Tobias,' Silas hissed.

Clarence gaped. 'I beg your –'

'Please, Clarence,' Silas said, 'ignore my companion, and I apologise for his rudeness. He is here as my escort certainly, but Mr Astaroth is on probation, and I shall report all of this to my superiors.' Pitch exhaled a brittle laugh, but said nothing. 'Now, do go on. If not the ghosts, then what is it that propels you to bring us here?'

Clarence may well have wasted his master's funds. Silas could barely deal with lost souls, let alone any greater mystery. His longing to return to the sanctity of Holly Village was growing with a vengeance as the horses pulled them deeper into the city.

'You see, Mr Mercer, Mr Astaroth' – Clarence leaned forward, lowering his voice – 'there are some awful things afoot in Leicester, more terrible than a harmless ghost in the cellar.'

'Wonderful. Shall there be bloodshed?'

Pitch's grin was quite unwholesome. How Silas wished he could edge further away, but he was pressed hard against the side of the carriage as it was.

'I beg your pardon, sir?' Clarence frowned.

'Again, never mind him.' Silas grew more alarmed with each moment. 'What awful things do you speak of?'

The man's gaze darted to the window, his thin fingers raised to flick at something upon his shoulder. If Silas was not mistaken, he believed Clarence had just warded off evil. 'Black Annis is back amongst us. I'm certain of it.'

'Black Annis,' Silas said. 'Who is that?'

Clarence winced, as though the very words he spoke tasted bitter. 'She's a terrible thing, sir. A nasty spirit that has haunted the Dane Hills for many years. Till now though, she's not set her foul eyes upon more than the livestock. There hadn't been true sign of her in a very long time, decades. She'd become little more than a story. Until this last year. There are those of us who are certain she skulks beyond the Dane Hills and commits unspeakable horrors.'

Pitch crossed his legs. 'Perhaps this visit shall not be so dull as I imagined.'

Silas fixed his attention on the frightened valet. 'Unspeakable horrors? Clarence, I would insist that you give me more detail.' Before his own imagination had him curled more deeply into his corner.

'Around the Hills they've always guarded against her. You'll see it in the windows there, with how high and narrow they are, built so as she can't reach right in. She has nails of iron, and arms so long they scrape the ground when she walks.' Clarence was clearly fearful, but was delivering the tale with relish. 'Horrid long arms so she can reach in through any window, steal the livestock straight from their pens.'

'Oh do tell me she uses their bones for toothpicks.' Pitch clapped his hands. 'How delightful that would be.'

Silas could not discern if he enjoyed mocking the man or was delighted at the idea such a terrible thing might occur.

'Tobias, please. Clarence, do continue.'

Clarence's lips made a downturn, and his eyes glistened once more. 'A walking nightmare, she is. Blue as a bruise and she sets her teeth cracking so you know your time is coming.' The man appeared quite unwell, and Silas wondered if they were in danger of being vomited upon.

'She sounds ravishing.' Pitch laughed. In that moment Silas could have thumped him, daemon or no.

'Anything but ravishing, sir.' Clarence shuddered. 'You see, until most recently, she only ever came for the beasts. Leaving her marks upon the walls, but content with whatever animal she got her claws into. Back in the day when she was terribly hungry, it was said some houses set out a goat or a pig when they heard talk that the crack of her teeth had been heard in the area. Thought to keep her satisfied that way, you see. There are old tales that she took a man or two, but they were hunters trying to rid the Hills of her. And it's a pity they never did so.' His voice dipped low and fragile. 'Because her appetite is fiercer now. Gentlemen, Black Annis has come for our children.'

'Children?' Silas enjoyed this conversation less and less. Had Mr Ahari not said the Blight could turn a lost soul into a monster? Perhaps one with blue skin and iron claws?

'In this past year, an uncommon number of little ones have gone missing,' Clarence said, perched on the edge of his seat. 'And there are those who believe it is Black Annis who's taken them.'

Silas tugged at the collar of his shirt, giving himself a moment to think. This appointment had taken quite the turn. 'Do you have some proof of this?'

'Very sensible question.' Pitch nodded with a put-upon frown.

The carriage made a sudden neck-cricking halt, the driver letting his displeasure be known before they continued on.

A distressed Clarence continued his breathless story. 'Since the thawing of last winter there have been half a dozen disappearances, and no end to sightings of Black Annis.'

'I'm certain there hasn't been,' Pitch said, scrutinising a nail. 'Humans do so love an excuse to scare the wits out of themselves. Are we almost there, dear fellow?'

'Yes, sir. Only a few more minutes –'

'Will there be cake?'

Clarence's mouth bobbed opened as a goldfish's might, thrown by the sudden shift in conversation. The carriage hit a particularly deep pothole, throwing them all around in their seats. Silas took hold of the leather strap over the window, just in case Leicester's roads worsened.

'Clarence,' he said, 'what of those disappearances has you convinced Black Annis is responsible? Are any of the sightings of merit?'

And if they were, what in heaven's name was Silas to do about it? If this creature were a teratism, Mr Ahari had said, quite clearly, that ankou were not able to remove them from the world. Silas's maddened thoughts settled on something of more comfort. If Black Annis did exist, was it not possible she was a monster entirely? Not a lost soul gone foul? And if the monster did exist, would this not become a case for the smooth-faced monster killer seated at his side? Silas quietly marvelled at the ridiculous nature of his own thoughts. Here he was, hoping for the existence of a true-born monster.

'And will your master serve cake for tea?' Pitch flared his fingers before him, surveying the state of his nails. 'Vanilla slices will do, I suppose. I'm dreadfully hungry.'

Silas glared at him, having less and less trouble believing that the man was indeed a spawn of Satan.

'Clarence, please tell us what has you believing Black Annis is responsible for these disappearances,' Silas said.

'Not three months back, two young-uns had been out to collect firewood and didn't return. The only trace they found of them was a scrap of bloodied clothing on the edge of the woods where Black Annis's bower lies.' He touched at his throat, tears welling once more. 'Only a few dared search too deep, and even then they didn't linger long. Nothing was found, but the parents of those little ones heard strange things the night before the children disappeared. They live mighty close to the woods, and say they heard her wailing and gnashing her teeth till dawn. Her nails marked their walls too, cuts in the stone that hadn't been there a day before.'

'Did they see her?' Silas asked.

'Not directly, sir, no.'

Silas relaxed his grip on the handhold. Perhaps Pitch was right about the human propensity for fright. The children had wandered into the woods and were lost. The parents were stricken with grief, searching for cause. Silas stared at the passing scenery, seeing none of it. All at once Clarence reached for him, pressing his hand down upon Silas's own.

'Mr Mercer, my brother's girl is another who has gone missing.' His voice cracked and wobbled. 'She's barely five years in this world. But the authorities just as soon believe my brother responsible, killing his child to ease his cost of living, and won't hear word of Black Annis. The Order will believe us though, won't they, sir?' His fingers tightened against Silas's before he released his hold and sat back. Teardrops dangled from his chin, and he made no move to wipe them clear.

'Oh by the gods, must you cry?' Pitch pulled his checkered scarf to cover his mouth and nose. 'It's not terribly fetching.'

Silas moved before he could think his actions through, throwing his elbow hard against Pitch's arm. He was rewarded with an almost comical look of astonishment.

'Clarence, I am terribly sorry for the loss your family has endured,' Silas continued. 'But I'm not sure that we can assist in this matter. We were brought here to attend to the spirits of Knighton House.'

The carriage began to slow, the clip of the horses' hooves changing pitch as they met a new surface, one less resonating than the cobbles.

'And I'd not ask you to ignore your task, of course.' Clarence's hands returned to toy with the brass buttons upon his coat. 'This evening will go as planned. I would never dream of interfering with that –'

'Because you lack the power to do so,' Pitch said, with blunt efficiency. 'You are a servant.'

'Yes, yes...that's right, sir.' The poor man finally held colour upon his cheeks. 'Of course. But on the morrow, might you come with me before you depart back to London and see Dane Hills for yourself? Her Ladyship has heard of the stories. She would be amenable to you pursuing such a tale. Perhaps, if men of such...standing...can place themselves nearer to Black Annis's bower, they might learn the fate of these children.'

Pitch wrinkled his nose. 'I can tell you now if it's not one monster that has taken them, it's another. And likely human at that. There are many with a taste for fresh young meat.'

'Tobias, please.' Silas spoke through grit teeth.

The driver brought them to a standstill with far more grace than Isaac seemed capable, a gentle nudge that did not threaten to heave them from their seats.

'Please...sirs...my brother and his wife are fair out of their minds...Bethany is their only babe –'

'Do stop begging, it's turning my stomach,' Pitch said brightly, buttoning up his teal coat in preparation to alight. 'If I am not provided with a slice of pie or a decent hole to bugger I may snap that skinny neck of yours –'

The man flinched, pressing into his seat. 'What –'

'Tobias!' Silas pondered when the next train to London might be, for he wished more than anything to be upon it.

'I jest,' Pitch said. 'Of course. We will go to these precious hills of yours, Clarence.'

Aghast, Silas stared at him. 'What?'

'We will go to Dane Hills is what I said. Mr Mercer, are your ears failing you yet again? We will go, and if there is something that needs killing, then I shall kill it.'

'Thank you, Mr Astaroth.' Clarence appeared ready to cry all over again.

'But what if it turns out to be a...' Silas muttered. 'What if there is a chance that it –'

'Is a teratism?' Pitch threw all discretion to the wind. 'Then we inform our illustrious masters.' He frowned. 'Really, are you quite that stupid? I suspect we will find nothing but the shadows of wild imaginations, perhaps some tiny corpses floating in a pond in the woods, but if not, it may well be something I can drive a blade into, and I don't see why I should not be able to find amusement on this trip. Now, Clarence, pray tell, what desserts are on the menu this evening?'

'Ahh, there's...I'm not sure –' Considering the look Pitch levelled at him, it was a wonder Clarence did not soil his trousers then and there. 'But, but rest assured, Mr Astaroth, I will personally see to it that you have more sweetness than you can abide.'

'Then you set out on a mission bound to fail, I'm afraid, but at least my belly will fill,' Pitch said. 'Shall we go in?' He rose, hunching over in the confines of the carriage.

A full-cheeked footman opened the door and greeted them with a nod. All Silas noted of Knighton House was that it was grand and imposing and he did not wish to set foot inside. The whole visit felt as though it were spinning out of his paltry control faster than he could blink.

Clarence gestured for Silas to step out before him. 'Sir, could I ask you just one more thing?'

Silas nodded, though he'd rather have delivered a firm shake of the head.

'When you cast them out, the ghosts here I mean...it won't...won't hurt them too much, will it? Because they truly have been no bother.'

Silas struggled to find an answer. It had not even occurred to him to consider how a lost soul might feel when the scythe found them. He recalled the young girl at the baron's home, and decided upon his answer.

'No. I do not believe it harms them. They are lost, and I make them found. It is as it should be.' He blinked, quite pleased with his eloquent answer.

'Everything must die and rot and vanish into nothingness, Clarence,' the daemon declared from his position outside the carriage. 'Now, Silas, get your great arse off the seat, man. There is blood to let and cake to be eaten.'

CHAPTER 17

T he lady of the house, Mrs Evelyn Donisthrope, was quite beside herself upon their arrival. They stepped from the carriage and made their way through the grand sandstone arch that framed the solid oak entrance to find her rushing at speed down the staircase to greet them. Her gown of butter yellow and black lace flared around her as she moved across a superb rug of vibrant reds and blues. Mr Donisthrope's factories were doing very well indeed, if Knighton House were any indication.

'Mr Mercer, Mr Astaroth, it is so wonderful to have you here.' Her chestnut eyes flitted from one to the other, barely resting a moment on Silas before moving on to Pitch. 'Oh my, you are both so...' She giggled, most unbecomingly, and did not bother to finish her declaration.

'So appealing?' Pitch took her hand and pressed it to his lips, gazing up at her from beneath lowered dark lashes. A world away from the rather cruel beast who had just taunted Clarence so.

Mrs Donisthrope tittered again. 'It is said that I am to be wary of you, Mr Astaroth.' She batted her eyes in return.

Silas shuffled his feet, discomforted at being in the midst of such clear flirtation. If only the woman knew quite how sound the advice was.

'Wary?' Pitch gasped, still holding fast to her hand. 'Whatever for?' They laughed softly together, the sense of a shared secret between them.

'Oh, Mr Astaroth.' She touched at his arm, her neck pink with a blush. 'You are delightful.'

It was far more than Silas could bear. He coughed, interrupting the excruciating moment. 'Mrs Donisthrope, the Order thanks you for setting your trust in us to assist you with these, ah, hauntings.'

'Of course.' Her attention moved to him for a fleeting moment. 'I've just recently heard about your work at Baron Feversham's. It's said you were quite remarkable. Many a London acquaintance of mine is quite jealous of your presence here, at our humble Knighton House.' With that, Silas's moment was over, her gaze returning to Pitch. 'I do have so many questions, Mr Astaroth.'

'And I can assure you, my answers are astoundingly varied.' Pitch tossed his head, and a perfectly curled tendril of hair fell down the side of his face.

To Silas's astonishment, Mrs Donisthrope's fingers darted to it, shifting it to rest behind his ear. The move seemed to startle her as well, for she sucked in her breath and took a step back.

'Forgive me, I am rather too hysterical with excitement.'

'Nothing to forgive.' Pitch's words slipped like oil from his Cupid's bow lips.

Silas decided he was feeling quite unwell. 'Madam, might I enquire as to where our rooms are? It's been rather a long journey, and I had hoped to freshen up.'

Pitch lifted a slender brow. No doubt Silas had breached a rule of etiquette with such a request. Their host would show them to their rooms eventually, but if Silas did not extricate himself from Pitch's company, he might cause a scene. Added to that, he rather wished for the chance to muse over what Clarence had told them and consider a course of action.

Mrs Donisthrope, if she were insulted by the slight, showed no sign. 'Of course, Mr Mercer. Clarence, would you be so kind as to make sure that the cases are delivered to the rooms immediately?'

Silas had quite forgotten the man was still standing with them.

'Yes, ma'am.' Clarence's colour had not much returned, and he appeared even more road-weary than Silas felt. He hurried back out into the chilly, sunless day, hat in hand, darting an unreadable glance at Silas as he went.

'Sophie,' Mrs Donisthrope called.

A solemn woman with sharp features and brown hair pulled back tight from her face, appeared from another room. 'Yes, my lady?' She seemed to start at the sight of Silas, but quickly gathered herself and bobbed to her mistress, the hem of her simple grey dress cupping the floor.

'Would you please see Mr Mercer to his room and attend to his needs? We could have a bath drawn for you if you wish, Mr Mercer?'

'No,' Silas said, the single word sharp as a knife. 'Please forgive me, I don't travel well, I'm afraid.' A blatant lie of course. Considering the company, he'd managed well enough, but the idea of stepping into a pool of water brought with it the very same cold rush of terror it always did.

'Terrible traveller, I can vouch,' Pitch said. 'Spent most of the journey locked in the lavatory.'

Silas held his tongue, not keen to joust with the daemon in the foyer. He was still not certain Pitch didn't intend to punish him as promised for the consumption of the chocolate cake.

Mrs Donisthrope smoothed her skirts. 'Mr Astaroth, would you like to take to your room as well? Or could I interest you in some tea?'

'I have rather more stamina than my companion. I'd be delighted to join you, on one condition,' Pitch said, brandishing the lopsided smile that seemed to be his signature weapon of seduction. 'Clarence made a promise of cake, and I am rather partial to the sweetness of such things. There was some to be had on the train of course, but Mr Mercer is ever the glutton and I was left sadly denied.'

Mrs Donisthrope returned to her childish giggles. 'You shall not be denied here, Mr Astaroth. You've come to the right place if sweetness is what you seek.' There was a lowering of lashes yet again. Silas could barely contain his sigh. 'Cook is quite the hand at desserts. I'll have them serve tea in the front parlour. Are you sure you won't join us, Mr Mercer?'

'Quite sure, as delightful as it sounds.'

'Very well, thank you. Sophie, you can be on your way now.'

With a nod and a swish of her grey cotton skirts, Silas was at last led away. He spared Pitch no time, though the man wished him well with his rest.

Silas followed the maid up the grand staircase that dominated the foyer. It, like the building it was situated in, was white. Silas swept his hand along the railing and found marble beneath his fingertips. Evidence yet again that Mr Donisthrope was doing very well indeed with his boots and shoes. Sophie led him down the corridor in silence. They walked along a runner cluttered with exotic flower motifs, and he recognised only dahlias amongst the elaborate pattern. The hall held a multitude of heavily framed landscape paintings upon its walls. Amongst them was a wonderful castle perched upon the flat peak of a rocky hilltop. He halted in front of it, enraptured by the scene.

'Quite beautiful,' Silas muttered beneath his breath. An odd sensation came over him with looking at it. Not recognition, not exactly. If he were to say what he felt as he stood there he'd think it closer to comforted, rather than familiar. Not much different to how it was when he wore the royal blue coat. Silas stared at the painting. He could fairly taste the crispness of the air and hear the distant call of birdlife. 'Excuse me. Where is this castle located?'

Sophie had moved some distance ahead and had to retrace several steps to make out the artwork. 'That's Edinburgh Castle, sir. I've heard tell it's most lovely to see.'

'I imagine it would be.' Silas said absently. 'Where is it located though?'

The maid did not answer straight away and he turned to ensure she had heard the question. Sophie was eyeing him with a most befuddled look.

'Why, it's in Edinburgh, sir. Scotland.'

'Scotland.' It were as though saying the word out loud opened some small door in his mind and the knowledge of such a place set itself like a tiny sun in his thoughts. Scotland, the land to the far north. Of course. How had he ever forgotten such a thing to begin with? 'Of course, of course.' He cleared his throat and gestured for the maid to continue. 'Shall we?'

She nodded, the confusion not quite wiped from her face, and moved on.

As he followed behind his escort, her shoulders rigid, her posture most upright, Silas cast a glance over his shoulder, considering the castle once more. What about it had captured him so? Had he enjoyed visiting that place in his past life, or had he owned such a painting, perhaps? He returned his attentions to the corridor. It always gave him an unpleasant shiver to consider too deeply the life he'd lost. A distasteful emptiness at his core that he'd rather avoid. Silas retrained his thoughts onto the matter at hand. It might be wise to have a message sent to Mr Ahari. Best, surely, to inform him of what Clarence had said.

'Here you are, sir.' Halfway down the length of the hall, Sophie pushed open a door. 'There's a basin inside. I'll bring some warm water for you right away.' She stood back to allow him to pass, and as with most people, she had to tilt her head to make eye contact. 'Can I bring you anything to eat or drink, sir? I suspect you have a fine appetite.' The stern-faced woman smiled. Quite unexpectedly and rather sweetly. 'I once worked with a woman in Inverness who had a young son large as life, just like you. He was barely in his fourth year and he was nearly as tall as someone double his age. She could never keep up with feeding him.' Something in his own expression must have concerned her because her smile dipped. 'I'm sorry, sir, did I speak out of turn?'

Silas gathered himself. Her words had served to remind him that he had been someone's child once, and he'd dared imagine for a moment that she spoke of his own mother. There it came again, the scratch of the emptiness within him, the great hole where his life must have been. But what would his own mother even think of him now? The strange anomaly he'd become. Here Silas stood, a step away from a living, breathing human being, but the divide between them yawned like a chasm.

'Forgive me, I have had a harrowing time of it of late and have not slept well.' Silas stepped into the room. 'I won't be needing any food, but thank you.'

She dipped her head, a faint wrinkle of concern still upon her face. 'Very well, sir. I hope this evening goes well for you and is not too taxing upon you.'

'Thank you, you're most kind.'

Silas closed the door and released a long, slow breath. Melancholy would only serve to make his life intolerable. He decided then and there that he would not contact Mr Ahari. If he dared, Pitch would likely accuse Silas of cowardice, and he was not certain he would disagree. Silas could not be afraid of the dark, whatever form it took, if he was to endure this life. He shrugged off his coat and dropped it upon the bed, which was a lavish affair with a cream-coloured canopy and matching curtains. The bedspread held an intricate floral design (flowers were evidently of import to the household) and more pillows laid upon it than a handful of people could deal with. The fire danced in the hearth, filling the room with a comfortable warmth. He moved to the window, pushing back the heavy forest-green drapes to allow what meagre light there was to fill the room. His view reached out onto the main street, where hansom cabs hurried their passengers to and fro. A growler led by four white horses made noisy progress along the cobbles, its seats full to capacity. Across the way, the park was equally bustling. Several women in starched black and white uniforms pushed wide-wheeled perambulators with their charges nestled inside. Ladies strolled and chatted in elaborate shawls and dresses that swept the ground, and an artist had set up his canvas by the fountain at the heart of the gardens, working furiously with his colours.

It was while Silas stood there, observing the normalcy of the world outside with hands clasped behind his back, that the tips of his fingers awoke with a tingling. Quite suddenly, the warmth in the room vanished, replaced with a draught that caressed his skin with icy fingers. Silas curled his fingers into his palms, ill at ease. He knew this sensation. This very same affliction had come upon him, both in the library at the ball and at Baron Feversham's. He waited, his lungs devoid of air.

'Who is there?' For there was someone, he knew it. Someone not of this life. 'Show yourself.'

The air at the foot of the bed grew dense, as though a lone cloud had found itself trapped in the room. The mass contorted, bulging and contracting, until a discernible form grew. Silas took a step back, finding himself against the window ledge, and praying he might go further.

The stocky, wide-shouldered man was translucent but vivid in detail. A balding head, a chin that blended into his neck, eyes like black coals. But it was the gaping wound upon his neck that caused Silas the greatest consternation. The gash was wide as a finger and spilling a torrent of blood that soaked the man all down the side of his light brown waistcoat and onto his trousers. Death by slit throat, clearly. And it was a very unpleasant affair to gaze upon. Teeth near to chattering, Silas considered his next move. And decided upon the simplest route.

'Good afternoon.' He swallowed. 'I am Silas Mercer.'

The blood streamed , pooling around the man's feet. 'The ankou.' It was more hiss of escaping air than speech.

'Yes.' Silas nodded, uncertain if he should expect violence. He eyed his coat, and the bandalore within its pocket.

'You have finally come.' The hiss shifted to something akin to a person speaking underwater. 'I sensed your blade.'

Silas nodded, rigid as a statue. What rhetoric was suitable here? He tightened his fist. Mr Ahari must have taken leave of his senses to give Silas no training to speak of. 'So you understand then...that I come to...send you...on your way.'

At the very least, Mr Ahari might have said that such a conversation was even possible.

'At long last.' The reply held more than a smudge of frustration. 'But you'd do well to turn your attentions elsewhere first. There is great need of you, ankou. But not for us that lie within these walls. There is a creature far fouler to be dealt with.'

Silas might tear his skin if he clenched his fists any tighter.

'I don't understand, what creature?' His teeth chattered, the chill of the room rising. And there was a coppery tang upon the air.

'He spoke of her, I am sure.' The man swayed, as though hit by the gentlest of breezes. 'Clarence.'

Not only could the lost souls converse, they understood things of the world around them. Pulling at his collar, seeking greater ease of breath, Silas said, 'Are you speaking of Black Annis?'

'A monster's been made of that soul. A darkness took her.' The flow of blood from the man's neck pulsed, sputtered, then resumed its cascade. His arm was a crimson length of limb. But his words were more disturbing.

A knock came at the door, and a voice called out, 'Mr Mercer, I have your hot water.' But it was not the voice Silas had expected. He stared straight though the unfortunate apparition to the door where Clarence stood beyond the oak.

'I am no threat,' the soul gurgled. 'Nor does he fear me. Clarence is touched. Not all must be a creature of the supernatural to know them, and he is one who sees between the layers of the veil.'

'Mr Mercer?' came the call again. Another knock. 'Is all well?'

'Yes, yes, everything is...fine.'

The apparition contracted, shifting and contorting once more. 'Bid him enter. You must listen to the man.'

After the slightest hesitation, Silas summoned the new arrival. 'Come in.'

Clarence fairly burst into the room, bucket in hand. He shuddered. 'Oh, has your fire not been set? I did...' His sentence died as he regarded the hearth, the swell of flames abundant behind the brass firescreen. He turned to Silas.

'He's here, isn't he?' His breath was a soft white upon the air, his eyes searching. 'Simon?'

'That is not my name.' The lost soul folded his bloodied arms , and thankfully the movement did not set off another spurt of crimson. 'He might be touched but he does not hear. Tell him I have no liking for the name I've been given.'

Silas, somewhat flustered, ignored the apparition's request. 'You are right, Clarence. We are not alone.' Though it appeared the valet would have to take his word for it. Clarence peered around the room, overlooking the soul right before him. 'The spirit says I should listen to you.'

'My name was Addison.' The hiss was high and irritated.

'Addison,' Silas muttered. He was not sure he preferred to know such a thing. Such intimate detail would make drawing the bandalore very much harder. 'He said to tell you that his name is Addison, and not Simon.'

Silas – the great servant of death, and messenger boy of lost souls.

'That so? Tell him I'm terribly sorry.'

'There is no need. He is capable of hearing you.'

'Oh, of course, of course.' Clarence hurried to the rosewood washstand on the far side of the bed and poured the steaming water into the large ceramic bowl there. 'I'm sorry I doubted you, Mr Mercer. Seems you are the genuine article, just as I was hoping. Blast, it's cold in here, worst I've felt in the whole house. Is he...Addison, I mean, is he stronger around you then?'

A sound enough theory, though it was not one Silas was sure he enjoyed. Messenger, servant, and now energy source?

'Perhaps, I'm not sure.' The tingling in Silas's fingers was truly bothersome. 'You can sense the soul, but you cannot see him?'

Though really the answer was obvious. If Clarence could see the sanguinary mess , Silas would know it.

'No.' Clarence shook his head. 'Though I wish I could. I've only seen the writings.'

'Writings?'

'In the mirror, one morning about a month ago.' Even though the water had long emptied from the bucket, Clarence still held it tilted over the wash bowl, his attentions elsewhere. 'I should have mentioned it when –'

'What did the writing say?' Silas frowned. Indeed, Clarence should have made mention of this during their carriage ride.

'She is lost. Bring the Order.' Clarence and the lost soul spoke in unison.

Clarence's features twisted. 'Took me a day or two to get over the shock of it. I'm not proud to say I trembled like jelly when it happened. Screamed too, I think. But when it happened again the next day, same words, I realised what it was trying to do.'

'Which was?' Now Silas faced a lost soul that could communicate, had a name, and a skill that he himself did not. The ability to write.

'Help.' Clarence shrugged. 'I felt it, in my bones, as they say. That this wasn't a nefarious spirit –'

'Astute man,' Addison wheezed.

'I was in no danger,' Clarence continued. 'None of us feel in danger here, never have. Just spooked sometimes. Anyway, it wasn't until my brother's Bethany went missing that I decided I had to try and do what they said, and bring the Order here. But it took me some time to convince Mr Donisthrope that a seance here was something worth considering. I was desperate in the end, and I let slip to Sophie that the master was being quite the ratbag of late, coming in at all hours from the club, knowing full well she couldn't keep a secret if we stitched her lips together. Not long after, Mr Donisthrope was making arrangements for the Order to visit. As I said, Mrs Donisthrope is quite obsessed with the whole spiritualism movement and the parties they hold. She forgave the man all manner of sins when she learnt he'd put in a request for your services.

But that was a ways back, and it took some weeks before we got word that the Order would be coming.'

'The delay has cost dearly,' Addison bubbled. 'A terrible mistake. Delay no longer.'

'I'm sorry but I –' Silas said.

'Not your fault, Mr Mercer,' Clarence cut him short, wrongfully assuming the apology was for him. 'You're here now, and that's the main thing. So, the ghost truly says you should listen to me? Simon knows who I am?'

'Addison,' the lost soul growled.

'He does.' Silas cast the gruesome apparition an anxious glance. 'And as I mentioned, his name is Addison.'

Clarence winced. 'Addison, of course. Forgive me. Hold on. Addison...the name is familiar. Was he the stable hand who met his end in a fight with the blacksmith a few years back?'

The sudden unsteadiness of the apparition, his head blurring until all features were lost, left Silas suspecting an answer in the positive.

'It would seem so. Knife wound. Terrible sight.' Quite stomach churning really. What fresh horrors awaited Silas with other lost souls?

'You can see the injury?'

'I'm afraid so.'

Clarence shook himself. 'That can't be pleasant.'

'You waste time, ankou,' Addison hissed. 'Go now to the bower and draw your scythe.'

Silas rubbed at his chin with pained fingers. 'Why do you rush me there, spirit? I would not walk so easily into a trap.' It seemed easier to accuse the soul of trickery than admit that Silas was useless if it was indeed a teratism at large. And with each word spoken, it seemed more and more likely.

'Rush you? There has been need of haste for far too long.' Addison's face lengthened as though melting. 'I do not wish Black Annis's fate upon me, do you hear? She was the oldest of the lost souls around here, and though she was a changed thing, she still held her humanity. But in this past year she's became a horror, there's nothing left you might call human inside of her. Black Annis is foul with rot and darkness, and all of us that linger here keep as far from her as our positions will allow.

But it ain't easy. You failed her, ankou. Your scythe should have found her long before this. I'll not have it happening to me. Deliver your death blow now, death's servant, I offer no protest. Then be on your way.'

'Have you seen this creature yourself?' Silas asked quietly.

The blood-soaked man regarded him. 'I have not set eyes upon her, and nor do I need to. Things work different here behind the veil. All I need to know is that she exists. You can feel her rotting. Her presence is the heaviness in the air before a storm, it is a mould that clings to the ether. Surely you feel her, too? She is one of your children, after all, bloated and distorted as she may be. Why do you hesitate, ankou? This is your purpose, why do you shy from it?'

Silas stayed silent. In truth it was not his purpose. The lost soul's desperate hopefulness was ill-placed upon him. If Black Annis was indeed a teratism, then the Lady Satine was his hero, not Silas.

Clarence fairly danced from foot to foot. 'Mr Mercer? What does the spirit tell you? You will help us, won't you?'

Silas's nerve shook as hard as his body, and he yearned for the life he must have lived, whatever shape it took. Even if he had been a wicked man in life, a miser who feasted as others starved, or a brute who showed no mercy to a debtor, Silas yearned for it still. But such wistfulness was pointless, selfish. He knew it.

He moved to the bed where his coat lay and dug until he found the bandalore. The moment the smooth wood slipped into his palm, a sliver of his apprehension evaporated. Silas grew more rigid, and his mind more settled. He may not be able to face a teratism, but he could determine its existence in relative safety, surely?

'There is time before dinner, is there not, to go to Dane Hills?' He stood with his back to Clarence and the lost soul, his eyes upon the bandalore, which lay quiet and tepid in his hand. Was it the scythe that urged him? Created that nagging itch that drove him now? For surely it was not his own courage leading him.

'Yes, yes, indeed,' Clarence said, breathless. 'I'm most grateful to you, Mr Mercer. I truly am.'

'Inform Mrs Donisthrope that I wish to take some air and tour the city as part of my ritual for this evening. I will do so in your company alone.' Perhaps he was going quite mad, pretending bravado, but Addison's quiet desperation unsettled him. And his words still lingered. *You failed her, ankou.* Biting, and not a little unfair. But were they truth? If not his truth alone, then that of the Order? The notion did not sit easily with Silas.

'Very well, Mr Mercer. I'll inform her straightaways. Thank you.' The door handle squeaked as Clarence turned the brass knob. 'But what about Mr Astaroth? Shouldn't he travel with you? For safety?'

The man was entirely correct. That was the whole point of Pitch's presence on this trip, after all. And if ever Silas might require protection, it would be now, chasing after the very creatures he was tasked with preventing. He closed his eyes. For all the sense it made, Silas had little desire to return to Pitch's company. The man may well be more dangerous than any tcratism.

'I'm sure I'm more than capable.' He sighed. 'But if Mr Astaroth can be drawn from his tea, then yes. Have him ready himself to depart with us.'

'Absolutely, Mr Mercer. I'll be back to collect you presently.'

Clarence made no attempt to leave quietly, thundering down the hall as he ran.

'Now, Addison,' Silas said with a determination he did not entirely feel. 'Shall I bring you to your final rest?'

The lost soul regarded him with eyes black as pits. 'Best you be saving me for your performance this evening, wouldn't you say?' The apparition flickered, like a cloud in a lightning storm. 'We can give them a show they'll never forget, you and I. I didn't leave much of a mark on the place when I was in it, wouldn't mind making a grander exit. What do you say?'

For all his talk of being freed, of Silas's failure to provide release, now that death's servant was beside him, the lost soul was not quite so willing. And Silas could not begrudge him that. Besides, it was the very first time Silas could make a significant decision that was entirely his own.

'I say that sounds a very fine idea, Addison.' He bowed to the apparition whose long-ago shed blood did not seem quite so terrible to behold now. 'A very fine idea indeed.'

CHAPTER 18

Silas soon regretted his decision to include Pitch on the journey. Pitch tapped out an irritating rhythm with his shoe upon the floor and sang a tune beneath his breath, a lewd tale that centred on a farmer's daughter's breasts and other bodily regions of desire. Clarence grew pale with the graphics of it, but Pitch himself seemed to barely notice he sang at all. The fix of his emerald eyes was upon the view outside the carriage, though they did not appear to take note of the scenery there. Rather he seemed focused on something within his own mind, or it was simply the effects of far too many of Mrs Donisthrope's offered treats. After near on a quarter of an hour in the carriage, with the combined rumbling of the wheels upon the road, the clatter of the horses' harnesses, and Pitch's magnificently dire singing, Silas could bear it no longer.

'Mr Astaroth, enough!' he shouted.

There was a terrible moment when Silas feared those words may be his last. They provoked a festering stillness and a glare from Pitch that was capable of stripping the very varnish from the wood around them. Clarence braced as well, as though expecting a strike.

'Is there a problem, Sickle?'

There was. It sat before him, eyes fairly glowing in the dimness of the cabin.

'I should not have yelled. For that I apologise,' Silas acquiesced. 'But I am rather on edge, and would ask that you stay still for at least part of this journey.'

'Whatever are you nervous about? It is either a child-devouring teratism or a monstrous fiend we seek. The latter is mine to deal with, the former is yours to scurry home and cry about to Mr Ahari. How is that frightening, dearest whore of death?'

Silas swallowed hard. Daemon or no, he was set to wallop the fellow before long. 'I am simply asking that you sit still, and perhaps lower your voice when you sing. So that I can think of what lies ahead.'

'What lies ahead is you showing off those lovely balls of yours for once. Look at you, brave Sickle, setting off to see what lurks in the woods. And with it being entirely your idea to go now, as well. I'll admit, I'm impressed. But don't allow that to go to your head. It's far too large as it is.'

Silas worried his tongue at his bottom lip. 'Perhaps I *should* have sent word to Mr Ahari first. This is not the appointment he set for us.' His earlier gumption had suffered with the journey.

Pitch sighed. 'By the gods, you'd fit in well with the bloody Archangels. Gabriel cannot shit without consulting with Metatron about the time, place, and duration.'

Silas stared at him. Archangels? He squeezed his eyes shut and rubbed his face, deciding in that brief moment of darkness that he'd not question Pitch further. Not today. He had quite his fill of extraordinary to deal with. A potential child-devouring teratism for one. All at once he recalled that Clarence sat alongside him, and the man had not breathed a word in some time. Opening his eyes, Silas regarded him. Clarence stared beyond the window, lost in his own musings.

'Should we speak of such things in his presence?' he whispered, low as he could manage.

Pitch was staring at Silas in a most discomforting way. At least, more discomforting than normal.

'He does not hear me,' Pitch said. 'My words *should* fall on deaf ears. Tell me, Sickle, what is it you heard me say last?'

Silas did not answer the odd question immediately, quite intrigued by the suggestion that Clarence could sit so close and yet not hear a word. But it did indeed appear the case. The young man was quite oblivious to his companions, working upon a dirty nail as though no one spoke at all.

'Sickle, pay attention,' Pitch snapped. 'What is the last thing you heard me say?'

'Should I too be deaf to your words?' He shook his head, utterly confused.

'What did I say?' Pitch hissed, the viper rising. The prickle of unease that came so readily in Pitch's presence now charged its way along the back of Silas's neck.

'You spoke of archangels, one named Gabriel, and Melatron another, I think?' Silas tumbled over his words in his haste to release them.

'Metatron,' Pitch said slowly.

'That's right, Metatron, my mistake.' Though Pitch's expression was most peculiar, Silas could not help but continue on. 'There are truly archangels...in this Arcadia?'

That he should ask such a question and wait on a genuine reply showed that all sensibility had fled from his world.

Pitch ran the tip of his tongue slowly across his teeth before he replied. 'Most unfortunately. Archangels, and all the rest.'

'And yet...you are...' He coughed against the roughness of his throat. 'You are a...daemon...'

Pitch nodded, far too slowly, and the hairs on Silas's arms stood tall. 'I am. I am the...' His mouth hung open, and he appeared to strain, as though on the cusp of either speaking or throwing up, Silas could not tell for sure.

Pitch touched his fingers to his lips, and his eyes glittered. 'What is your point, Sickle?'

Whatever had just occurred did not please him, the low burn of his temper unfurling from him like a flag struck by a breeze. The hairs on Silas's arms joined those on the back of his neck that stood to attention.

'Is everything all right?' he ventured.

'Quite wonderful.'

'Might I ask...what is it you were about to say?'

'You can ask, but I cannot say. They are no longer my words to speak.'

Silas nodded. 'I see,' he said, but he could not have been more lost.

'Ask me something more,' Pitch demanded. 'Let us see where my boundaries lie.'

'Boundaries?'

Pitch stared at Clarence, who had not shifted his attentions from the passing world. 'He is deaf to all talk of the supernatural world, as are all humans. And the same power that enables such a thing has rendered me mute with regards to...certain aspects of my sorry life. Pity, don't you think, with a mouth so beautiful as this? But there it is. And that is how it has been. Until you.'

'Me?'

'So many redundant questions.'

'I'm sorry if I seem confused, but that is precisely how I am. Why can you not speak of certain things?'

Pitch groaned. 'And there you go again. You idiot.'

Silas took the criticism and did not protest at it, seeing full well that he was right. How could Pitch explain the things he could not speak of, if he could not speak of them?

'All right then.' He clasped his hands. 'I shall ask you something more. How is it that angels and daemons reside in the same world together?'

Pitch curled a tendril of his hair about his finger. 'Because the human lore of heaven and hell is all utter bullshit.' He kissed the air. 'Wonderful, I can tell you of how ridiculous the notion is that there is a heaven where beautiful beings of white and light flutter about and play their harps all day, complete and utter tommyrot.' He laughed, hard and short. 'The only smidgen of truth is those bastards do tend to sit on their arses far more than is necessary. Sending daemons to the Hellfield to have *their* arses blown apart, rather than face the fight themselves.' His face hardened, a shadow dimming the glow of his eyes.

'Hellfield?' Silas leaned into the conversation, quite entranced.

'A quite wondrous place of perpetual bloodshed and endless loss. The last existing front between Arcadia and the Nephilim.' Pitch pushed at his cheeks, as though urging the words clear. 'It is where I should be, and would be, if...'

He gagged against the unseen binds that held his words in check. They had found another of his boundaries. Outside sounds came from what seemed a distance, as though the carriage were wrapped in layers of cloth. Silas took short, quiet breaths.

'Nephilim?' he whispered. 'They are an enemy?'

186

Pitch closed his eyes, slumping back against the seat. He nodded. A tiny trickle of blood started from his nose.

'Pitch, you're bleeding.'

'Very observant of you. We are done with this conversation for now.' His alabaster skin held an unpleasant green tinge, and his breathing had grown laboured. From where he sat, Silas could hear the wheeze of air through his chest.

'Getting close now, gentlemen,' Clarence suddenly declared. He did not appear to note the state of Pitch, who wiped at his bloody nose with a lacy kerchief. 'I'd say no more than a few minutes. We're approaching the meadows that sit between the woods and the town's edge now. We'll need to travel to the bower by foot.'

Pitch sat up, some colour returning to his cheeks. 'Walking? Not far I hope?' Whatever affliction had come over him appeared short-lived but decidedly brutal if it were to quash the life out of someone like Tobias Astaroth.

'I shouldn't think so, sir.'

'You're not required to think, you're required to know.'

Clarence gave the outside world a longing glance before he replied. 'You see, no one is sure where the bower is, exactly. It's not like anyone who's seen it has lived to tell. All's we know for sure is she lives in that wood up ahead.'

Pitch pinched the bridge of his nose. 'I can assure you, Clarence, I am not one for trudging through the woods. If I wished to get hot and bothered, this would be the very last method on my list.'

'If no one has seen it,' Silas said, 'how do you know it exists?' With each press of a horse's hoof to the road, Silas grew more doubtful of the sensibility of their trek here. The carriage bounced along the uneven surface of the road, throwing its passengers about. Outside, the huddle of houses and factories had given way to open pasture.

'Well, we learned from tales passed down.' Clarence huddled, miserable, in his seat. 'I suppose someone must have found it. But you see, Mr Mercer, I was hoping that, well, with your talents...perhaps, you would just know? I presumed the Order to have ways and means of doing such things.'

'I'm not certain that I...'

Silas grew rigid, all the hairs upon his arms standing hard against the material of his shirt. The tips of his fingers were painful with their tingling, a sharper edge to the sensation than when the bloodied apparition had appeared. He might as well have been digging them into a seamstress's pin box.

'Are we to guess what you are not certain of?' Pitch spoke casually enough, though his gaze was narrowed as he watched Silas. 'A long list that would be indeed.'

'You sense nothing?' For Silas the heat in the air had been replaced by a razor-sharp iciness, cutting through the layers of his clothing as though he wore nothing at all.

'I sense that you are quite beside yourself with some peculiar frenzy, that is all,' Pitch replied.

'Stop the carriage,' Silas croaked, the air white with his breath. 'Stop the carriage.'

Clarence pounded at the wall. 'Stop the carriage!' he yelled. The driver did so with impressive speed and a suddenness that could harm one's neck. 'Mr Mercer? Is everything all right?'

Outside, the horses whinnied and stomped their hooves. Silas expected some droll, derisive retort to come from Pitch, but the man was silent. Watchful as a bird upon a worm.

'Clarence,' Silas said, 'you and the coachman should go no further.'

The red-headed man's eyes widened. 'Really, sir? Are you certain?'

'Quite certain.' And quite terrified, though Silas could barely wait to step foot from the carriage. 'This is where we will begin.'

Clarence nodded with a grim set of his mouth. 'Very well, Mr Mercer. We shall wait here for you.'

'Shall we hunt, Sickle?' Pitch adjusted his scarf, settling it more tidily against his throat.

'We shall begin, that is all I know.' *Out, out,* his tumbling thoughts urged. Silas must get out of this carriage.

Buttoning his coat, he disembarked. The clouds were being pushed by a breeze that tugged at his hair and coat folds, the strength of the wind enough to allow the sun to peek momentarily from its hiding place. But the rays held no warmth, most certainly not enough to bring relief to Silas, whose shivering body bristled with gooseflesh. The driver stood alongside one of the dapple greys, one wide hand stroking the beast's sweat-soaked neck. The other steed tossed its head and flicked its tail as though it were a whip.

'Easy now, steady up,' the driver murmured in a deep and rumbling voice. The man was well-built, at least in comparison to all but Silas himself, and his hands were calloused with use.

'Something unsettles them?' Silas said, though the answer was quite clear.

'Indeed, sir. Young Tuppence here doesn't take well to new roads. I usually keep him to the city. If you listen to the gossip and the whispers though, people would be telling you it's those woods that have set them off. Excuse my boldness, sir, but are you here to search for the old witch? Have the whispers spread as far as London town then?'

'I'm not sure about that.' Silas surveyed their surrounds. The cultivated fields gave way to meadow, where a scattering of wildflowers still tilted their colourful heads to the sky. Some distance ahead, the road disappeared into a wooded area, where the trees formed an arched canopy over the path. 'We were informed of the disappearances of the children when we arrived here. Clarence asked that we might use our, ah, expertise in the matter and investigate for ourselves.' Each exhalation of breath moved as a white cloud from his mouth. Something which, he noted, did not occur when the driver spoke.

'Well, I don't mind telling you, you're a braver man than I to go into her woods.' The driver shifted his peaked cap, a red line across his forehead where it pressed too tight. 'Not many are travelling this road these days. They take a longer route through the church grounds a bit west of here.'

Heavy cloud cover snuffed out the sun, lending tenor to his words.

'Because hallowed ground might save them?' Pitch stood a short distance away, relieving himself in the tall grass and taking no care to stand at such an angle that his privates would not be exposed. He subjected both Silas and the driver to a full view of his generous member. 'Best of luck with that.'

The coachman patted his horse with a firm palm. 'Well, whether it's a murderer using legend to frighten everyone senseless or an honest-to-god witch in those woods, no one is going in there who wants to come out. That place will give you the shivers, make no mistake.'

Silas would agree with him on that. He shook as though he stood in an ice bath. There was a darkness here. A stirring that was chilling his body to its very heart. But lurking in the depths of his fear was the growing urge to lose himself in the strangeness of the place. He wanted to enter those woods. His muscles twitched to move forward. Silas slipped his hand into the pocket where the bandalore lay. The wood was warm but only from being in the folds of material, nothing untoward. What gripped Silas was something internal, instinctual.

'Well, come on.' Pitch strode up the road. 'Who doesn't enjoy a good shiver?'

Silas hesitated, studying the woods. With the paltry sun now gone, the depth of the shadows within the trees intensified, as though one of the storm clouds had descended and moved in amongst the trunks and branches.

'Here, boy, come on, boy.' Pitch mimicked a master calling to his dog. 'And hurry it up, Sickle. I don't intend to miss supper. For anyone, or anything.'

Silas felt Clarence's gaze upon him. The young man's desperation evident in the lick of his lips, the wringing of his hands. The naked vulnerability was disconcerting, and Silas turned away to face the woods. A shadow darted along the tree line. It was not Pitch. He sauntered up the dirt road, his whistling as horrendous as his singing. Silas fixed in on where the sudden movement had occurred. Was it merely a branch swaying? One of the horses let loose a shrill neigh. Silas glanced back to see the animal rear in a half-hearted attempt to escape its harness. While the driver tended to the beast, Silas turned once again to the woods. There was nothing there now to give him pause, only the sullen, still darkness of nature. He hurried after the daemon, a great urgency pushing him on, and a growing hunger he did not recognise, rising up to take hold.

CHAPTER 19

After breaking into an undignified run to catch up to Pitch, Silas reached two great hornbeams whose arching boughs formed a vast green umbrella over the road. Stepping beneath them, it was as though he passed through an invisible barrier, one that banished the weak light of the cloudy day. He was quite stiff with cold, its grip upon his skin and bones more than a little painful. He grunted, rubbing with vigour at his arms, quite startled at his own rush to enter the place.

'Why are you just standing there? Do you think the wench will come to you?' Pitch moved further and deeper down the road, his teal coat the only note of bright colour in the dullness of the woods. The shadows curved around him, not quite touching his body, as though they dared not. Pitch, of course, threw no shadow himself, which created a peculiar sense of him not being entirely present at all.

'Have some caution, Pitch. If it is a teratism, neither you nor I can confront it.' Silas did not move from where he stood, one hand pressed into his pocket, rubbing a thumb over the rim of the bandalore. 'Do you detect anything untoward?' The device did not release any notes of caution, nor did it warm at his touch. Was there another sign he had overlooked? Silas had paltry knowledge of how the scythe worked. He may well be ignorant to subtler signals. Or perhaps the scythe assumed he needed no one to tell him what was as blatant as the prickled flesh on his body.

This was not a pleasant place to be.

'Mr Astaroth, I asked if you sensed anything of note?' Silas repeated his question with vastly more irritation.

'It is dank and cold and smells of foetid rot in here. There you are, my notes in their entirety.' Pitch stood at the centre of a road which could barely be classified as such. Two narrow tracks dug deep into the muddy earth, a trap for carriage wheels if ever there was one. 'You are the one with a nose for death, Sickle. It is I who should ask the question of you. Did you think to ask your ghostly friend of the bower's location?'

'No, I did not.'

'And your little trinket there tells you nothing of note?'

'No, it does not,' Silas said, with a pathetic note of despair. 'I see the place as you do, and it's cold to the point where I cannot feel the tip of my nose any longer.'

Pitch sighed. 'Wonderful.' He cupped his hands around his mouth. 'Child-murdering bitch, show yourself!'

'What are you doing?' Silas hissed. 'Stop.'

'Oh, I'm sorry.' Pitch blinked prettily, quite returned to his bothersome self. The hint of vulnerability that had appeared when he tried to speak of his life now buried. 'You have a better idea? Come on, move. I wish to know now whether we shall enjoy sport here or not. For if we do not, then I have much greater things to indulge in. And they involve far less clothing and dirt.'

He flicked his scarf, as though to mark his point, and continued down the road, leaving Silas no option but to follow or find himself quite alone. His initial drive to enter the woods had dimmed, and although he was likely as frightened of Pitch as he was of Black Annis, Silas hurried after him. The man's lean figure spliced its way into the gloom, following the curve of the road as it wound to the right, heading ever deeper into the woods.

Silas could not help but feel that this place was perpetually damp, the sun never able to force its way through the tree canopy. The drip of water against leaves played on the air, though there had been no rain falling when they left the carriage. There was a distant twitter of birdlife, but he could not say if it was within the woods or without. As they moved steadily on, less and less light made its way through the gnarled boughs and heavy foliage. Silas clucked his tongue, frustrated at futile attempts to keep his boots clear of the mud. He had just extricated himself from a deceptively deep puddle when a vicious ache struck his wrists. The joints of his fingers joined in a moment later. The cold that troubled him flickered deeper, finding its way into his bones with an ice-blue flame. He ground his teeth.

'Pitch, would you –'

His words were buried by an awful renting scream. The sound tore the air to shreds, reaching a magnitude that threatened to shake the leaves from the trees.

'Good god,' he gasped.

The agonised notes came at them from all directions: above, to the right, to the left. There was no telling where the culprit lay. On and on it went, with no drawing of breath to give reprieve. Silas pressed his aching hands to his ears, seeking escape. Pitch did not appear as effected. He stood with hands on hips a few paces ahead, surveying the forest the way a general might survey a battlefield.

Silence collapsed upon them. Silas's ears rang with the echoes of the gut-wrenching scream. No human mouth could produce such a cacophony, of that he was certain.

'Well, then, not a wasted journey after all,' Pitch declared. 'There is to be a hunt, Sickle. This is indeed a good day. This way.' He moved off the road, pressing on into the depths of the woods.

'Where are you going?' Silas cried.

'Did you not see the scattering of birds?' Pitch slid between two saplings, using the very tips of his fingers to hold a slender branch at bay so he might pass without contact. 'They fled from something in this direction. And I suspect that it is the something we seek. Use your brain, man. It's not difficult.'

'I'm not sure we should track it down. That sounds like no lost soul I've met.' Silas could barely set one foot in front of the other for the tremble that gripped him. The tingling upon his fingers was more akin to the prick of pins.

'Let us be honest, Sickle, you are hardly an expert on lost souls at this point.'

Scowling, Silas hurried after him, the mud and debris sucking at his feet, fallen branches cracking with his weight. Pitch released a branch he'd pushed aside, and it swung back at Silas, swatting him square in the chest.

'I am right behind you,' he grumbled.

'Truly? I had no idea. The lumbering through the undergrowth didn't give it away at all.' Pitch made light of an enormous fallen tree, a grand old elm, dancing up onto its rotund girth as though he'd grown wings. 'If you truly have no inkling of this creature, then I shall indulge myself with some bloodletting this afternoon.' He was like a child at the foot of a Christmas tree, green eyes brilliant with anticipation. 'Are you certain your hackles are not raised?'

Silas's body shook as though gripped by a fever. It pained him to bend his fingers. He might as well have been an old man run rife with arthritis. It was the chill of a lost soul for sure, but of a magnitude Silas had not yet encountered. 'My hackles are well and truly raised, and it is with far more violence than I've known before.'

Pitch snorted his displeasure, his hopes of bloodletting apparently dashed, and again in a light and controlled way, stepped from the log and drifted to the ground on the other side. Silas surveyed the fallen tree with concern. He did not trust his trousers to withstand the strain of such a leg lift. They were burdened enough as it was around his muscled thighs. He made his way around the root system, which had been torn completely from the dampness of rotted leaves and soaked soil. The tangle of roots had spread wide when the elm lived, and now rose higher than Silas's head, frozen in death. When he emerged from behind the dirt-clogged shield, Silas found himself alone.

'Pitch?' There could not have been time for him to go far. Likely, he had chosen this terrible moment to toy with Silas and was hiding in the undergrowth nearby. 'Come, this is no time for stupidity. I know you watch me.'

For someone did. Silas felt it as certainly as the ache in his knuckles.

'Mr Astaroth, enough.' He was pleased with how firm he sounded, considering his stomach had tied itself into a knot. 'It was you, was it not, that wished this to be done with sooner rather than later?' His voice echoed back at him, bouncing off the canopy. Silas kept close to the bulk of the fallen tree, taking comfort in the solidness of it.

The splintering of wood came from somewhere up ahead. Perhaps Pitch did not hide at all, and was so eager to be done with this adventure that he'd run off ahead. The man had certainly kept a clipping pace so far and appeared to find no part of the scenery an obstacle. Silas pressed away from the fallen tree with no small amount of anxiety. He was under someone, or something's, watchful gaze. How had he ever thought it a bright idea to enter these woods? But he had his answer already. Tangled there amongst the knots in his belly. The pull of the place was like a rope tied around his innards, dragging him deeper.

Silas had grown so cold that it seemed no fire could ever be hot enough to warm him, and his fingers curled with the pain at his joints. He stomped through the undergrowth, attempting to appear in utter control of his faculties, while his pulse thundered and his ribs were held so tight he could barely draw a breath. With his head lowered, Silas stole furtive glances at his surrounds. Eyes were upon him, and their weight pushed the goosebumps on his skin higher. But whose eyes? And where from? He cursed Pitch with every step. The foliage took on a life, and their sole purpose seemed to be to snag him, pulling at his hair, snatching at his coat, wrapping around his legs.

He was certain he was treading a far too calamitous path through the forest. Even if he were not so sure he had already been spied, whatever had emitted that god-awful sound had no need to hunt him. It could simply listen for his approach.

A wretched scent engulfed him, one of meat beyond rotting. Silas pressed a balled- up fist to his mouth, gagging at the ferocity of the odour.

'Oh my god,' he whispered. But opening his mouth allowed the putrid air to cling to his tongue.

He gagged, his throat constricting and his stomach contents warning of their impending ejection. He crouched low behind an elm tree, his aching knee joints protesting the movement. The elm was young and barely wide enough to conceal his frame, but Silas desired protection of any kind. All his natural alarm bells rang as though played by someone quite deranged. *Danger*, they declared. *There is danger here.* The very air in this place, foul as it was, tore at him. Seeped into his pores and made its way through his blood with intent to harm. Silas shook, not with cold alone, though that was piercing enough, but with the biting clutch of panic. What lurked in these woods was monstrous. A teratism. And neither he nor Pitch could defeat it. Mr Ahari had told them so. Now that Silas's body told him the truth of what lay here, they must leave this place. Cursing Pitch anew for his abandonment, Silas searched for sign of the road, but the woods were thick about him.

The soul-searing scream rang out yet again. He leapt to his feet and plunged headlong into a crazed run. He ran with a heart set on breaking his ribs, and lungs that could not gulp enough air to keep him from dizziness. Around him it appeared all the plants had fangs, tiny tearing teeth that took hold of his clothing, ripping at the fabric. The sleeve of his coat tore open on his left arm, the thorns of some green fiend digging into his flesh. If he did not find the outer reaches of these blasted woods soon, he might well find himself fleeing naked. Yet another horror of this place to contemplate. His eyes watered with the wretched odour that permeated the air. It was the sewers on a heated day, mixed with the discarded entrails of a day-old kill. The scent alone threatened to bring him to his knees.

'Pitch!' he roared.

But he did so at the same moment the scream tore the air anew, that horrendous sound swallowing his own voice whole. This time the despairing wail was joined by something new. A grating, rasping cacophony that reminded him of a metal shovel finding rock, magnified tenfold. Where was the creature whose call sent shock waves through the woods? Surely it was enormous and should be shattering its way through the foliage?

'Damn you, Pitch! Where are you?'

A sudden, terrifying thought gripped him. Perhaps Tobias Astaroth had fallen, and the coarse grinding was a herald of his demise. Dear god, if this creature could fell a daemon, what hope did Silas have of escape?

'Take hold of yourself.' He pressed his wayward thoughts back where all logic lay cowering in fear at the back of his mind. 'Move. Move. Move.'

The mantra aided Silas in setting one foot in front of the other, forcing back the panic that threatened to paralyse all movement. The coarse grind of metal upon stone erupted yet again, though it was with a modicum of relief that Silas recognised its change of position. Further away.

He ran, a great crashing oaf indeed, and he did not care one iota. Arms flailing to make a pathway for himself, coat flying out behind him to be torn to ribbons by nature, on Silas ran. Headlong into a thick scrub of dogwood. His shins met with something solid, and with a curse flying from his lips, he tumbled forward. His landing was devoid of grace, crashing on all fours in a sludgy concoction of mud and debris. His fingers sank through grit and sharp things, and with wide-eyed alarm, Silas realised his downward motion had not stopped entirely, his weight pressing him into the great puddle of mud.

Wrenching his hands free of the dark soil, he sought out an anchor. The mud sucked at him, drawing his lower legs into its embrace entirely. Nothing solid met his feet. Silas was set to drown in a vile muddy grave if he did not find a way to free himself. The length of his coat vanished beneath the surface, the material hard against his shoulders as the quickmud fed upon it. Struggling, Silas barely took note of the sudden heat against his side. He was vaguely aware of the soft note of the bandalore in his ears, but the mud presented a more immediate issue. One of survival. He heaved himself this way and that, grabbing great fistfuls of gritty mud in the paltry hope that perhaps a tree root lay beneath, anything that might secure him to the land. He continued his slow descent into the quagmire, the notes of the bandalore steadily rising. Their song of warning growing richer, until he could deny them no more. Silas gave up his struggle, and at last saw where it was he had landed. A rocky clearing in the thickness of scrub.

'Good lord,' he whispered. Without a fight, his slow descent grew slower.

Opposite him, an enormous oak perched atop a low, narrow outcrop of rock. Hanging from several of its boughs were small, dirty brown shirts, swinging with a wind that did not touch Silas. The thread of the oak's exposed roots wound through the crevices in the jagged rocks and curved their way around the entrance to a crude cave below. The opening was not considerable. He doubted he could right himself fully if he were to enter. Rubble lay at the cave's entrance, as though the hollow itself had only been created in the recent past. Silas's gaze fell upon one of the greater pieces of broken rock at the entrance. Nightmares would plague him from that day on.

The body of a child lay there, as broken as the crude altar it rested upon.

Crimson blood stained the rock and the ground around it. All but the crown of the child's head had been flayed. A rise of bile burned its way up Silas's throat. He understood now what it was he saw hanging from the boughs. Not dirty shirts at all. Silas retched, coughing yellow stains upon the dark mud as it continued to entomb him. The dead and mutilated child upon the rock had long, knotted brown hair, and the wind played at it, giving the awful impression that the child yet lived.

The tales Clarence told, were dreadfully true.

Silas had found Black Annis's bower.

CHAPTER 20

S ilas had nothing left in his stomach, but that did not matter to his body, which heaved his innards in clenching waves, trying to dislodge the horror of the sight. The godforsaken stench sucked at his nostrils and drained him of all strength to fight the mud as it sank him ever downwards.

Let it do so. Let him leave this life. Christ almighty, Silas groaned, let him leave this life. For he had no wish to live in a world such as this. An image of Clarence came to him, the poor, unwitting man pacing beside the carriage. Desperate for word of the child that had been lost. Was that Bethany's skin swaying in the branches? Was it her blood that formed a dark curtain around the stone where the ruined body lay?

Silas's very bones rattled, come loose beneath his flesh with the shock of what he had stumbled upon. It was no monster or teratism here, but the very devil himself who held sway in this clearing. Children's flesh upon his tongue.

The mud crept to the top of his thighs and rose up his arms, almost to his elbows, yet still Silas found no urge to shift. The intolerable cold and the pain in his joints was a distant thing to him now, vague sensations barely a part of him. All the while the bandalore hummed, its notes ripe with urging. He should move, if he was ever to do so again. Yet Silas could not stir. It was as though his limbs had forgotten how to move themselves, the darting message from his brain unable to command his hands to lift, nor his feet to press and find purchase in the quagmire. He was frozen in a state of disbelief.

But not so the wind. A breeze caught the skins hung like discarded linen in the branches. The fluttering ribbons of moist, heavy flesh swished back and forth, back and forth, a grotesque metronome. Silas stared, transfixed by the macabre display.

And still the bandalore sang to him.

Move. Move. Move.

The very same mantra he had used upon himself earlier, his advice played back at him from somewhere far, far away. But his own sensibilities might as well have been touched by the Blight itself, for Silas could find no resolve to do what a sensible man might. Fight. Struggle.

Hush. Hush. The very fabric of the child swung back and forth, skin stained dull brown by the loss of its own blood.

Hush. Hush.

Silas bowed his head, and a sound rose from him, from the very pit of his gut, clawing its way through his chest and splitting his throat wide open. He wailed. Keened as the very best of the banshee might do. He *was* sorrow, he was despair. It splintered him into pieces as it furrowed deep, rancid water carving its way through rock. And still the interminable wind would not let the child rest. His cry reached its peak, and a thunderous crash came from a place behind him. Loud enough that he coughed down on his cry, biting into the grief that had taken hold of him.

'Get up, you fucking fool.'

Pitch came hurtling out of the forest, barrelling down on Silas. To say he was wild-eyed would be to vastly understate the situation. Pitch's emerald eyes were wide as half-pennies, and his body glowed with an internal light that pushed free of his skin, of his clothing, and shone like a halo around him. Just as it had done in the cemetery.

'I said get off your fucking knees, ankou.'

Pitch threw himself at Silas. He landed with the force of a steam train moving downhill, propelling Silas from the grip of his muddy cocoon. Silas screamed at the pop that came from his shoulder under the tremendous force.

'My arm!' he cried as they landed in a tangled heap.

Pitch grabbed hold of the limb that Silas nursed and threw his weight against it. Bone crunched as the shoulder slipped back into place, and white spots filled Silas's vision.

'Bloody hell –'

'On your feet!' Pitch shouted. 'She's coming.' He was framed by light, a sheen that clung to his form, as radiant as the very angels he had dismissed.

'Then dispatch her, Tobias!' Silas shouted right back.

Another great crash and crack of trees came from the woods. And the return of something far worse. That unholy screech, despair and hatred and ferocity rolled into one great, terrible sound. Silas pressed hands gloved with mud to his ears.

'Not I, Silas. My part is done.' Pitch grabbed Silas's lapel and dragged him to his muddied feet, having no issue despite their contrasting size. Silas's trousers were weighed down with the thickness of what still clung to him, and one of his shoes had not made the escape. He stood dripping with mud, one foot bare.

'Your part?' he spat. 'What are you talking about?'

Wood snapped, not a mere stick or twig, but a great towering tree that must have brought down a dozen others with it, such was the calamity of the crash.

'You were to face Black Annis by whichever means I saw fit. Your spectral friend has my thanks for seeing you here sooner than I hoped.' Pitch swept a hand through his hair, as though now were the time to attend to such things. 'You are the servant of death, and that' – he jabbed a finger in the direction of the shattered woods – 'that is a dead thing. Now see that you rid this place of her, Silas.'

Mouth agape, Silas swayed on his feet, overcome by the stench, the pain, the sheer madness of it all. 'Are you mad? I cannot face a teratism. Mr Ahari –'

'Mr Ahari desired this meeting, Sickle!' Pitch shouted against his ear, his spit warm against Silas's chilled skin, his light bright enough to cause Silas to squint. 'This encounter is no accident. Now play their bloody game, and win. Use the scythe.'

No accident? The Order knew of this horror and did nothing, save for sending a man who was little more than a newborn himself to dispatch such a monstrosity? Fresh, heated blood rose through Silas's veins, his anger chasing back the interminable cold. He slapped his hands to his pockets, searching the folds with mud-caked fingers.

'Where is it?' he hissed.

Beyond the clearing it sounded as though the entire world was collapsing upon itself. And the cries, the terrible cries, continued. Silas dug now in his trouser pockets. Dismay blanketed him, adding to the weight of the mud.

'It's not here,' he cried. 'It's not here...the mud...the mud...'

'Are you out of your mind? You lost it?' Pitch stamped his foot, his eyes blazing at their centre with a bright orange flame. 'You have one task, idiot, one.'

He spoke with such derision, such utter contempt, that Silas's temper caught and flared. 'Then why don't you do it, daemon? Why are you hiding behind my skirts? What kind of hell creature has such miniscule balls?'

A growl, an actual growl, came from Pitch. The flecks of orange in his eyes devoured the emerald until no trace remained, each pupil now entirely on fire. Silas had never been more aware of Tobias Astaroth's lack of humanity.

The ground shuddered.

Pitch cursed ferociously under his breath. Silas flung out his arms, at the ready to brace should the reckless movement of the ground strengthen. Black Annis was desperately near, and Silas, fool he was, had lost the bandalore and it's song.

'Find the scythe, Silas.' Pitch spoke too low, and far too calmly, a pot ready to boil over.

Pitch dropped to his knees, a torrent of curses suitable for the worst of the alehouses flowing from him, as he drove his hands into the mud. Silas followed suit, not bothering to try to save his own shirt sleeves, which were a certified ruin.

'Can you not sense it?' Pitch demanded, the glow from his body dissipating.

'No,' Silas snapped.

The cold, the stench, his pained body all taxed him. If the bandalore called to him through that noise, Silas did not hear it. Certainly not over the destruction coming from the woods, and Black Annis's screams which flew at them from differing angles, as though a horde lay in wait, not a solitary monster. What did she wait for? He ignored the small voice that said perhaps she had no need to hurry at all. Her insects were already caught in her web.

'How can you be such an inept moron?' Pitch hissed.

'Shut your bloody mouth.' Pitch's ceaseless badgering fuelled Silas's anger. He sat back on his heels, jaw tight, and thrust his hands at the mud. Channelling the hot rage of desperation towards that which eluded him. 'Come. Come to me...now!'

The bandalore shot up from the mud, bulleting into his waiting hold.

'I've got it!' he cried. The loop of string slid down the length of his finger, fastening tight.

'Move,' Pitch cried, scrambling to clear the mud.

The limb of an enormous oak flew at them, arrowing through the air with astonishing speed. Silas had no time to run, so he settled for a violent lurch sideways, mercifully finding firmer ground. The branches whacked the mud mere inches from his face.

An erupting scream, more raucous than any before it, tore through the clearing. A fearful apparition emerged from the woods. A woman once, perhaps. Taller than Silas by a decent head, although her own was anything but decent. Black Annis was as Clarence had said. The work of a nightmare. Her skin blue as a late summer sky and as wrinkled as a crone's, her beakish nose running to a hooked point that dripped with foul blackness, and her huge eyes a dull silver. Her hair, what of it could be called such a thing, ran with the same fluid that came from her nostrils. The strands reached to her feet, their ends clogged with the debris gathered off the forest floor. But it was her nails, no, her claws that captured Silas's attention. As long as half her arm, and with sharpened tips that a swordsmith would be jealous of. She set her silver eyes upon him. Her wretched body, not much more than skin and bone, held dreadfully still. A predator ready to strike. Despite the assurance of the bandalore in his grasp, Silas was paralysed with fear.

'Pitch, help me,' Silas cried.

'You must –'

Whatever Silas *must* do was lost to the moment. The creature standing so statuesque in the shadows now burst to life. Arms spread, slender claws reaching, her dank hair flowing around her like a tattered coat, Black Annis lunged at Silas. Her cry was a far-reaching note that sailed ahead of her, splitting the air. Silas's own scream rose with it, his voice hoarse from wailing, from fear and horror, cracking as the tormented soul flew at him. He sought to find his feet and at least make a show of defending himself from what surely must be his end, but his muscles spasmed, his arms locking rigid. His fingers bunched into rigid claws around the bandalore, and a single, solitary note rang out.

Silas leapt to his feet, just as Black Annis was upon him. He threw up his arm and swung wildly. His fist struck her middle, where the flesh had no give, as hard as the bandalore that struck it. She did not fly through the air as Pitch had done in the cemetary, but she did stagger. Black Annis shattered the air with an enraged howl, her bladed claws sweeping desperately close to Silas's shoulder. He ducked, for once finding himself not to be the tallest in the company he shared, and managed to slip beneath her outstretched arm, twisting around to position himself in behind her. The blood roared in Silas's ears. This was insanity. What had Mr Ahari thought would happen here? Silas was fighting a battle that he could not win. And Pitch, damn him, did nothing to aid him.

He let out a frustrated bellow, and it was met by one of Black Annis's own. She turned on him, and the stench of her drove ahead of her, pressing at him. Silas ran, choosing a direction blindly – seeing too late where it had led him. To the bloodied and broken body of the child. He blinked down at the senseless carnage. The hair lifted with the ever-growing strength of the wind, and he found himself staring down at eternally sightless eyes. Barely had the child lived and she was gone.

Addison had laid blame upon Silas for this. Blamed those who should have seen to this creature long before she killed in such an appalling way. His anger was not misplaced. And Silas's own now joined it. If the Order saw fit to make the children's lives a part of their game, as Pitch claimed, then Silas would play for them. The bandalore's string tightened around his finger. The opening notes of a new melody rose sweetly against his ears, and Black Annis's scream reached higher, as though the notes tortured her.

Silas uttered a silent prayer that they might. He stood still over the child, the wind slapping his coat against the rock. From somewhere, far away, Pitch shouted at him. Urged him into the fight.

But Silas would wait.

Until the heat of Black Annis was upon his neck. Until the notes of the bandalore filtered through the chaotic maelstrom that approached at his back. He waited until the scythe's song pitched with notes of loss and grief so intense the sky might shatter.

And then, and only then, did death's servant move. He swung around, releasing the bandalore. The collision of song and scream made the world tremble. Black Annis arched her back, her mouth impossibly wide with her death note. The bandalore sliced across her bony chest, deep enough to enable the hint of shattered bone to show.

'Again.' Pitch shouted from somewhere closer by. 'Bring her to her knees.' His voice rang with bloodlust, and Silas fed on its fervour. Black Annis straightened, her mouth running with the thick black slime, her eyes now laced with fine threads of onyx through the silver.

Silas struck again, and again she righted. This time with a chunk of her beaked nose missing, the next with a sunken, broken cheekbone.

He was making his mark. Was it possible he could truly bring her to her knees? Pitch still screeched nearby, his words indecipherable. His assistance not forthcoming.

Arm aching with the blows, head ringing with the notes of the bandalore, Silas staggered backwards, now only a step from the mouth of the cave. The bandalore's notes rose, frantic and uneven. His foot slipped on loose ground, and Silas found that it was he who fell to his knees.

Black Annis, a grotesque and bloodied monstrosity, struck her blow. She was upon him, fast as a snake. Her claws pierced through his flesh, their metal sliding into the softness beneath his ribcage.

A new agony exploded through him, his organs impaled upon such a dastardly, filthy thing. He threw back his head, but the scream would not come. He was shoved back, into Black Annis's cave. Misery and torment were thick on the air. And Silas's own joined the fray.

What a fool he was to imagine for a moment he might best such a creature. As enraged at himself as any monster that tore him asunder, Silas screamed a silent scream. Black Annis's claws sank deeper, all the way to her knuckles. She dripped her foulness on him, rancid breath making his eyes water.

Silas would die. Again.

And he did not care for it. He'd barely yet lived.

The teratism bared her teeth, oversized gums stuck with multitudes of jagged shards.

No. Silas did not care for dying at all.

He threw back his arm, the tear of muscle and ligament spreading through his entirety. The bandalore's notes drew higher, higher evermore. The weight of the wood grew in his hands, threatening to pull itself from his grasp.

Silas landed his blow, and a flash of white bloomed in the darkness. Black Annis's cry stopped dead. The claws jerked from his body, their retreat bringing fresh agony. Her wretched head fell from her neck with a dull thud upon the rocky floor. A tremendous shudder rattled stones loose from the arched ceiling, drawing his attention away from the lifeless eyes that stared up at him. Silas raised his arm, seeking to deflect the raining debris, but stopping short when he saw what it was in his grasp. A great curving scythe, the blade a shining onyx with a strange, crooked handle of pale white wood dotted with notches and stumps, as though the carver had abandoned his task halfway to finishing. Dark, sticky liquid coated parts of the blade, and a droplet swung free, descending to land right upon Black Annis's snarled, death-struck lips.

Silas pressed the tip of the scythe's blade into the earth. The weapon was all that kept him upright. His own blood ran freely, warming his legs. Eyelids heavy, he slumped against the wooden handle, only to find himself collapsing painfully forward as the scythe disappeared as quickly as it had come. The bandalore rolled from his hand, no strength in his fingers to keep it. He lay with his cheek to the ground, his ripped and ruined chest pressed to the soil, bleeding him into it. Silas blinked through clouded eyes. There at the mouth of the cave stood a fine-boned lady of middling age, the church's veil upon her head, a wooden rosary dangling at her neck. Weeping sores covered her cheeks, one so near her eye as to force it closed. Silas imagined he saw her lips move, but he was falling fast beyond conscious thought. When he blinked again she was gone. A very lost soul at last moving on.

Black Annis was no more.

His lids slowly lowered. Silas sank into numbness. As he drifted deeper into the darkness, the faint echo of a voice reached him.

'Fuck. Silas? Are you dead?'

But he could not answer Pitch's question nor make the slightest sign he'd heard it. Silas was utterly done. He faded away with Pitch's hands rough upon his shoulders and curses hot against his ear.

CHAPTER 21

S ilas came to in the grip of a furious pain. Through the white heat and ceaseless moans that escaped him, he discovered that he was no longer prone on the hard ground. Instead, he dangled over Pitch's shoulder, the slight man managing to carry his considerable load without issue. Silas was very much alive, and every inch of his body trumpeted its agony loud and clear. White specks dominated his sight, as though the snows had begun too early, but he made out enough of his surrounds to understand that they moved through the woods. He knew this for certain because Pitch seemed to be going out of his way to choose the most vigorous path possible, stumbling into depressions and pushing bodily through foliage that whipped at Silas's wounded body. Each time, Silas screamed. A sound beyond his control, his body so stimulated by pain that he barely felt a part of himself at all.

Each time the reply to his agonised cry was similar. 'By gods, if you don't shut up, I'll dump you here.'

Silas whimpered at the very thought of remaining another moment in this place. 'Put me down,' he dribbled, for his lips were not as capable as his mind.

'Believe me, I'd enjoy nothing better than to cast your great hide from my shoulders. You are bleeding all over my coat.'

Pitch quickened his pace, jumping to clear an obstacle that Silas could not see. The pressure of his shoulder against Silas's wounds was more than he could endure, and the world vanished in a sea of black.

When next Silas peered through slitted eyes, he was met with a new discomfort. Pitch had brought him to the carriage and had at last cast Silas's great hide from his shoulders. Silas lay across the seat, though of course it was not long enough to accommodate all of him. His feet rested on the floor, causing his back to add its twinges to the plethora of aches and terrible pains that gripped him. Granted, they were a small displeasure compared to the hot pincers that seemed embedded in his gut. He breathed in short gasps, for it was all he could manage with the damage Black Annis had inflicted upon him.

He shuddered, the memory of the slice of her claws rattling him with horror.

'Will he die?' A young man's voice, tight with concern. 'Such ghastly injuries...' Silas's foggy mind registered Clarence's presence.

'How the blazes would I know?' Pitch growled. 'I am no bloody doctor.'

'What did you see in there? Did you...did you see any sign of...' Clarence could go no further.

The carriage hit a rough section of road, and Silas groaned, squeezing his eyes tight. Below his belt a dampness clung to his trousers, his own blood soaking him.

'Did we see any sign of the child you lamented over?' Pitch said, careless and abrupt. Silas's pain was joined by dread. Tobias Astaroth was not an empathetic soul. 'Aside from the fact I have no idea what she looks like, I would assume it highly likely that the child is dead. I'm fairly certain you'll find that one of the skins hanging from the boughs belongs to –'

Clarence's anguish filled the cabin, a guttural cry that spoke of a heart tearing in two.

'You bastard.' Silas's words hit the air as strange grunts, utterly indecipherable.

Pitch pressed at his shoulder, his fingertips only mildly different to knifepoints. 'Stop moving. You're bloodying up the damned carriage enough as it is. By the gods, I am famished. Do you think there is any chance of tea when we return to Knighton?'

Clarence burst into a heartier round of tears, the kind that were messy and noisy and shook one's entire body. For some time there was only the clip of the horses' hooves, and the sobs flowing from Clarence. The carriage hit another brutal spot of road, and sent Silas vanishing yet again into a haze of black.

He awoke in a strange though comfortable bed, in a dark, unfamiliar room. The scent of gingerbread was thick on the air, and beneath it wafted the hint of something less enticing: the thicker rent of horse dung. But it was likely not the smells that had shifted him from his slumber, and rather the loudness of voices, raised in anger. One of which he recognised too well.

'I'm in servitude to an oaf who has not the remotest idea of how to protect himself, and yet I am to stand in blood, and shed none of it. I cannot tell you how tiresome this is already.'

'Oh do stop being so dramatic, you fop.' A feminine and firm voice.

'Piss off, Sybilla.'

'I shall not. This is my house.'

Silas braced, edging his weight so that he might roll onto his back. He moved gingerly with trepidation, but his pain had lost its jagged edge.

'Do you enjoy living in the middle of fucking nowhere?' There was the scrape of a chair upon wood and a light sprinkle of laughter. The woman's laughter.

'I rather do. Keeps me safe from the likes of you, to begin with. Very few daemons ever bother me here, especially ones with reputations as sordid as yours. Is there anyone in London you've not bedded?'

'Unlikely.'

'Don't harbour any ideas of a move to the country then.' Whoever she was, she jested comfortably with him, and with a great degree of amusement. 'Now, the gingerbread is done, with enough sugar and treacle to make anyone else but you positively ill. Why do you keep pacing by the door? Her Ladyship ordered you to wait here, and I dare say even one as reckless as you would not defy her, *Pitch*.' The emphasis was heavy and decidedly mocking. 'I have no clue why you prefer that name, it's ridiculous.'

'Says the woman named Sybilla. It sounds like an affliction.'

'One I'm sure you are most familiar with.'

'Oh, you have no idea, my sweet, frigid angel.'

As the pair continued sparring in the next room, Silas made a careful investigation of his body. He bit at his lip and lifted a hand to his chest, uncertain what he might find. Clearly, he had survived the encounter, but the memory of his fight was a raw imprint upon his mind. The sensation of Black Annis's claws pushing through skin, through his very core, would not be soon forgotten. Her foulness had infiltrated him, and even now he imagined he felt its touch upon his blood.

Silas lay staring at the ceiling. The cornice work was simple, and there was no ceiling rose or light fixture at its center. The walls about him were rough in texture, thick white paint clinging to stonework. He traced his fingers over his chest, finding the rougher texture of bandages wrapped tight around his midriff. For the first time he noted that there was not a trace of mud upon him. And something else was lacking, too. With a start he lifted the light brown blanket covering his body. He was naked, his manhood a limp slick of flesh between his thighs.

'Do you feel any pain?'

Silas jumped at the voice, clutching the blanket to him for what paltry defence it might offer. 'Who is there?'

The voice had come from the corner of the room where a large armchair hulked. Red and white chequered curtains hung down the wall to the right of the chair, and a narrow dart of light penetrated their lengths into the gloom, barely bright enough for him to make out the figure who sat there. He thought he spied the gleam of red hair.

'Hello, Silas. I am glad to see you awake.'

A familiar voice. 'Clarence?'

'Not entirely.'

Silas eyed the door. He could breathe well enough, though not entirely freely, and his joints no longer ached as though fire were in them. But feeling better and getting to his feet were different things entirely. He considered calling out to Pitch.

'I do not believe that Tobias will rush to your rescue, even if you did need it. He is not presently an avid admirer of either you or me.'

It was Clarence's voice, but it held a flat quality that Silas did not recognise. As though the young man were rather bored with speaking at all.

'Clarence, are you all right?' The loss of the child could well be responsible for his strange demeanour.

'Oh for goodness sake. I am clearly not Clarence,' non-Clarence harrumphed.

Wincing, Silas manoeuvred himself into an almost-seated position. His belly twinged at the points where Black Annis's claws had penetrated. 'Who are you?' he grunted, managing a rather uncomfortable pose with one shoulder pressed against the bedhead, a flat, solid piece of oak. The very thought of such a tree left him cold. 'Do not harm Clarence. He is a good man, much tested.'

'You've known the man less than a day, how do you know he is good? It is not prudent to assume knowledge of a person so quickly.'

Silas opened and closed his mouth not once but twice before he found an answer. 'Perhaps I do not know, but he has not been unkind to me.' Which was more than Silas could say for his supposed partner. 'And it has been a taxing time for him.'

There was a long pause in which the conversation between Pitch and the woman Sybilla rang loudly, clearly, and most unpleasantly. They had moved on to talk of a party in Oxford, where he relayed excruciating detail of what had been done to various parts of his anatomy by a visiting American businessman, with an audience watching on. Both he and Sybilla seemed highly amused by the recollection, Pitch's dainty laugh free of malice and the disconcerting edge he managed so often. Silas shook his head to clear it of the stomach-churning images conjured, and returned his attentions to his own situation. Surely a possessed Clarence would not have escaped the notice of the woman and the daemon now gorging himself on gingerbread and tasteless memories in the other room? Which meant that whoever sat in this room had been granted permission to do so.

'Might I know your name?' He worked on keeping his voice neutral, though he'd not thought it possible to feel more vulnerable than in that moment: stark of clothing, injured of body, and without a clue whose bed he lay in.

'You might.' The figure rose and moved closer.

A candle set on a stump of wood being utilised as a bedside table sputtered alight. In its gentle glow, Silas was left with no doubt that

Clarence stood before him. Granted, he appeared as awful as Silas felt. The young man's skin held the pallor of a man racked with illness, or too frequent a companionship with a bottle. His hair hung dank against his head as though he'd been caught in the rain. Perhaps he had. Considering that Silas did not know what day it was, or how long he had lain here, he certainly did not know how the weather fared. Clarence stepped towards the bed, dragging his feet a little as he moved. Bare feet, odd for a man who appeared fastidious on first meeting.

'Come no closer.' Silas pressed against the bedhead, its grooved edge finding his shoulder blade.

'I'll do as I please.'

Silas shifted his legs, testing his range of movement. But even if he were to throw off the covers and stumble out of bed, Clarence now made himself an obstacle by seating himself on the bed between Silas and the door. He stared hard, green eyes a far gentler shade than Pitch's, tracing every inch of Silas's face.

'What do you want with me?' Silas pulled the blanket higher, exposing his feet to the air, which was notably chilled. A shiver ran through him.

'You're cold.' Not a question, so Silas did not answer. A moment later, in a hearth on the far side of the room, a rosy fire sparked to life. 'Tobias was supposed to build your fire, but he chose to ignore my instruction. Is that better?'

The flames had no chance yet to deliver their warmth but Silas nodded. 'Thank you.' A sudden idea struck him with the lighting of the flames. 'Is that you, Isaac? Do you speak through Clarence?'

The answer caused a deep-set frown to pinch the young man's face. 'Don't be ridiculous. My elemental is not capable of astral projection, let alone possession.'

My elemental. The only elementals Silas knew of resided in Holly Village. And they all answered to one mistress.

He curled in on himself, ignoring the dull protest of his wounds. 'Lady Satine?' he whispered.

'Oh.' Clarence raised auburn eyebrows. 'Jane was right, you're not an idiot. Which is just as well, Silas Mercer, for I have no time for fools. And nor does this world.'

CHAPTER 22

Silas huddled naked, exhausted, and struck quite dumb. Alongside him, barely an arm's-length away, sat the mysterious Lady Satine. Well, at least the poor man she was possessing. Lady Satine's name was uttered with a modicum of awe and a dash of foreboding by most everyone he knew. All except Pitch, of course. Did the daemon fear anything at all? Silas envied him, right then and there, for he himself was more likened to a jellied desert.

The fire crackled cheerfully while Silas tried to work out what on Earth one said to such a person. In the end, he said nothing at all. Lady Satine held out Clarence's hand and opened his curled fingers. The bandalore lay on his palm, the string turned dark brown by mud. At first the wood appeared to be equally as dirtied. Silas frowned and found himself leaning in to take a closer look. A second inspection confirmed his suspicions. The boxwood now held the hue of red mahogany, as though blood had permeated its lighter nature.

'You did an adequate job yesterday,' Clarence and the lady said. 'The deterioration of that teratism was quite astounding. You were handed a formidable task, I'll grant Mr Ahari that. He would have spared you such a baptism and dealt with the creature himself, as would normally be the case, but it was a perfect opportunity to test your mettle. And we've no time for dawdling.' She thrust the bandalore at him. 'Take it. Though in truth I could not keep it from you if I so desired. The scythe is irrevocably yours, Silas.'

He pulled one hand from beneath the covers. Barely had he moved and the bandalore came to him, slipping from Clarence's palm as though Silas pulled its string. When wood and skin made contact, a shudder ran through him. His muscles eased their knots, and something akin to that first flush of heat from a downed whisky traced a path through his innards. The memory of Black Annis's blades inside him caused him to wince, but the actual bodily reminders of her assault were but shadows of their former selves. He ached, certainly, but nothing he could not endure. He had thought himself dead, again, for certain. Yet here he lay.

'Your injuries are repairing well.' Clarence, or rather Lady Satine, spoke as though she read Silas's mind. 'I suspect in another day, you will be just as you were before the encounter.'

'My wounds...how is it that they are healed? It seems that they should have been...'

'Fatal?' Clarence laughed, the lady's dismissive tone heavy upon the sound. 'You cannot regard anything about yourself as you did when you were human, Silas. Certainly the wounds were terrible, but you no longer heal as a man.' Mr Ahari had said something similar, but that time Silas had only sported light cuts, and bruised ankle and neck. His healing had not been quite so miraculous. 'You heal as an ankou, and no ordinary one at that. Now tell me, what did the local people name her? I'm sure there is some title given. The humans are nothing if not fond of naming their horrors so they might tell their tales more grandly.'

'Black Annis,' Silas fairly whispered.

Clarence pursed his lips and cocked his head. 'Not bad I suppose. Matters neither way, as she will plague them no longer.'

'She murdered children...mere babes...' He swallowed with force, the image of the skins upon the branches fluttering in his mind as they had fluttered upon the wind.

'Only a handful,' the lady said, casual as can be.

Silas gasped. 'That is a handful too many.'

'Perhaps that is true,' came the reply, no less casual. 'But there are those things we should mind, and those we should pay no mind to. In time you will come to find that age brings with it a certain, shall we say, carelessness. I did not intend for such harm to come to those children, but intentions often count for little, and I cannot be expected to address all the ills of this world at the moment they land upon us. It was fortuitous that Annis fouled in such a way really, for otherwise you may not have found your resolve. A dead child rather stirs a man to action. Which is fortunate for you and I both.'

'How can you say such a thing?' he croaked.

The fire popped in its hearth, and its heat touched Silas, but still he pulled the blanket tight to his chin. The cloth was a flimsy but comforting barrier, all that he could manage against the figure seated beside him.

'Rather readily. I have small need of pointless discourse. The task was meant to test you, and test you it did.'

Pitch's words, spoken in the midst of chaos, came back to him. *Play their bloody game, and win.*

'It was never the Order's intent that I search for a lost soul at the manor,' he rasped as though sandpaper lined his throat.

'Of course it was. No matter what else, you are first and foremost an ankou, and it is your death-given duty to remove lost souls from this Earth.' Though it was clearly Clarence standing there, Silas could no longer see the young man as he was. Even though she did not appear, the lady's presence was overwhelming. 'That is not to say that other tasks may not be set for you.'

Perhaps it was the exhaustion that flamed his temper, or the spiralling sense of loss of control. Regardless, Silas shifted himself more upright, jaw tense with his anger. 'You do not deny it then? You and Mr Ahari knew of Black Annis's existence and her foul deeds, yet did nothing. Leaving me to be sent as a lamb to slaughter, and those poor children to suffer so awfully. Pitch said you play a game with me, now I see it is true.'

'Tobias should have watched his pretty mouth. And come now, you were hardly slaughtered, were you? Just punctured a little. You do make it sound far more nefarious than it indeed was,' the lady declared with an offhandedness that only fuelled Silas's discontent.

'I had no warning, no training. And a companion that seemed content to allow me to die.'

'Pitch may have taken his instructions too literally, I will allow. But it would have taken more than a teratism, no matter how fearsome, to bring about your demise, if things were to go as I had hoped. If you had failed, we would have known the wrong choice had been made.' The lady chewed at her lip. 'You received no warning, no training, because neither were necessary. That is not how these things work. You could not learn the fortitude that was necessary. It is innate. Or it is not.'

He closed his eyes, wishing to remain for just one more moment in a dark, oblivious place. His hold on the bandalore tightened, and he recalled its most recent transformation. A crude but lethal scythe bursting into existence just as Silas felt sure he was to meet his maker. He opened his eyes.

'And so I passed your test?'

It was not quite a smile that lifted Clarence's lips. 'You saw the bandalore's transformation, did you not? You held the scythe in your grasp.' The lady paused for a laborious moment. 'Mr Ahari spoke to you of the Blight?'

Silas nodded and glanced at the door. He would rather be enduring endless, abhorrent details of Pitch's sexual conquests than linger here. He feared he was about to slip deeper into an already unrecognisable world. 'And he also told me that ankou were not capable of destroying teratisms.'

'The man does not lie.'

'So that was not a teratism I fought?' And nearly died at the hand of.

'Yes. It was.'

Silas shook his head, at a loss. 'Then how did –'

'Silas, you are an ankou, that much is true, but also far more than that.' The lady lifted Clarence to his feet and moved to the window, where she pushed open the chequered curtain to reveal not a window but a set of glass doors that opened up onto an expanse of green lawn. The honeyed touch of a sunset marked the scattering of clouds. 'You've shown fine mettle, fine indeed. I have every hope our association will see the imbalance of things set right, with no great disaster.'

'I'm sorry, but I really don't understand...' He rubbed at his raised knees through the blanket. 'The imbalance of things?'

'Yes. The Blight Mr Ahari spoke of, lies at the very heart of things. For thousands of years some small semblance has always escaped into the world, and I have dealt with it rightfully so. But there are times, rare as they may be, when the imbalance cannot be regarded with anything but concern. Action must be taken. You, and the scythe you wield, are a part of that action I take. No other ankou possesses a scythe like yours, Silas. It is quite unique, and after you proved yourself yesterday it is yours alone to handle. Henceforth you and Mr Astaroth ride not only for the Order, but for me. Together you will seek out those souls fouled beyond redemption and bring word of the Blight's direction and strength to me. You are one of my Horsemen now.'

'A horseman?' Silas said, somewhat numbly. He stood atop a great waterfall and knew with certainty he was about to be pushed forward and sent tumbling headlong into frothing, churning chaos.

'Perhaps it is more easily explained if you rise from your bed and follow me.' Clarence turned the brass key that jutted from one of the door's locks. 'Now come, it is time you meet the one who will guide you in my stead.' The door was flung wide open. The delicate twitter of small birds fluttered into the room. The lady strode Clarence outside, hands on hips, taking a breath large enough to visibly lift his shoulders. 'Such beauty. If my watch ever draws to a close, the gods shall find me here for eternity.'

Silas clamped his mouth shut, conscious it had been hanging open for some time now as he struggled to absorb what he was being told. Amongst many oddities, the lady had casually mentioned that she had kept watch over the Blight for thousands of years. Good grief, was poor Clarence currently in the grips of an immortal being? It frightened him to even imagine such a thing.

When the lady spied that Silas had not budged from his bed, Clarence frowned with her displeasure. 'Get up, get up. You cannot expect Lalassu to come to your bedside, surely?'

'No, no, of course not.' Whoever Lalassu might be. But there was a small issue that faced Silas. 'But, my lady, I'm afraid that I...' He coughed, nodding at his body. 'Have no clothing upon me.'

'You have a blanket, wrap it around you. Now come. I cannot hold this young man much longer. It puts a strain upon their feeble hearts, and he is too young for Izanami to take just yet.'

The woman in the room next door burst into a gale of laughter, as though she were having the most delightful time. A moment later Pitch accused her of cheating in their game of whist and advised that he would use his cards to remove both her eyes if it happened again. A wonderful partner, indeed.

Silas slid the bandalore beneath his pillow, a pinch of odd remorse coming with allowing it out of his grasp. *Irrevocably yours*, Lady Satine had said. Silas was not certain of that, but it was with no pleasure that he separated himself from the scythe. With slow caution, he edged out of the bed, bracing for a stirring of pain that thankfully did not come as his bare feet met the floorboards. The wood was pleasantly warm.

'Do you ride, Silas?'

'Ride? Well...I don't know. I've not had cause to do so, thus far.'

'And in your last life?'

The question brought a pang of something he could not name, bitter and unwelcome. Silas shook his head. 'I suppose I might have, though I recall nothing of the life I lived.'

'Of course. What's done is done. Well, at least you are saved the hassle of lamenting a life poorly lived, as so many are wont to do. Besides, whether you enjoyed riding or not is of small consequence now. For ride you must. Follow along, Silas. And come meet the beast that shall bear you.'

Clutching the blanket tight around his chest, and checking the lay of the fabric so as to ensure that his privates remained just that, Silas took tentative steps towards the door. Aside from the general stiffness that came with too long in bed, there was not much untoward about his movement. Even his belly, with its still-healing punctures, merely felt tight and uncomfortable, not ravaged by pain. He was healing unlike any man might. Just as the lady had said.

Silas stood in the doorway, a hand pressed to the frame, taking in the view before him. The sun blushed its last before it would succumb to the night sky , and high clouds streaked across the blueness. A low hedge marked a barrier between the cottage and the seemingly endless stretch of pasture that reached over rolling hills. Grazing amongst the hedgerows were multitudes of horses, from ponies and Shetlands to great Shire horses with coats of snow white and rich golden chestnut. Their scent was strong and not unpleasant upon the fresh air.

'Where is this place?' Silas stepped out onto a buckled layer of cobblestones. A wood was visible in the distance to the east of the cottage, and it chilled him to consider that it might be Black Annis's woods.

'Don't worry yourself. We are a long while from Leicester.' The lady spoke again as though she'd heard his thoughts. 'We are just outside of Bishop's Castle, none too far from the Welsh border. The pastures are finer here, and the finest of all things these beasts shall have. They quite deserve it after the lives I have rescued them from. Some of the greatest monster's you will meet are those of human origin, Silas. I can assure you of that.'

Silas was not so sure, but he nodded. 'How far have we travelled? I recall nothing past the...' He could not speak of it, the awful bower.

'Half a day of travel, and you've been in your bed for two sunrises. I suspect your healing will quicken as you strengthen over time. The next time you suffer such injury you might well find you only need a few hours of bed rest.'

Silas had no reply for such a statement, and stayed silent.

Lady Satine walked Clarence beneath a lopsided wooden arch that held the slumbering remnants of a rosebush. 'This is Lower Broughton Farm. Sybilla tends my land, and I am bitterly jealous of her for it. If I did not have other matters pressing upon me, I would never leave these grounds.' She sighed in the way a lover might on sight of their paramour. 'Aren't they magnificent?'

'The horses?' Silas ventured.

As though in affirmation, one of the steeds let loose a bracing neigh.

'Of course the horses. More steadfast than any man or woman I've met, and far more beautiful. Come along.'

Clarence strode through the tall grasses that stood between cottage and pasture. Silas found himself following on quickly. He swept his free hand through meadow foxtail and Yorkshire fog, whose heavy purple tips bobbed at his passing. Their names rose to mind as easily as his own. At least, that is, the name that Mr Ahari had bestowed on him. Whatever name his parents had given him was as lost to him as they were. What's done is done, the lady had said.

A piercing equine cry snapped him from his thoughts, the whinny so loud he feared the beast was almost upon him. Silas stopped short, both hands coming to fasten on the blanket. Thundering down a gentle slope were three of the most magnificent creatures he'd laid eyes upon.

Heavy with the broadness of draught horses, they tossed their heads and sent their impossibly long manes streaming. Their tails brushed the ground as they galloped. They moved three abreast, keeping perfect pace with one another, feathered hooves lifting high off the grass with each step, necks curved in thick muscular arches. Silas watched, breathless with the beauty of it: a white horse, as brilliant as fresh snow with a mane that concealed its entire broad neck; a midnight-black, whose coat rippled like the surface of a pond on a moonless night; and the third the most spectacular of all, the colour of distant storm clouds, the grey coat rippling with a strange hint of bruised green.

As the horses gathered pace, rushing ever closer to the hedge, the sun found one last burst of brightness, and a streak of straw-gold light lit up their path. Silas blinked against the sudden glare, his watering eyes blurring the horses. He raised his hand to shade his eyes. The pounding beasts were not more than a few lengths from the barrier. All but one drove their hooves into the dirt and brought themselves to a halt. The unusual pale grey did not falter. Did not slow.

He saw now its formidable height. Its withers could brush his nose, its elegant head reached far above his own. It grew ever likelier that he was to be trampled, but Silas would not move, could not move. The horse sank back onto powerful haunches and launched into the air – graceful as though it were a butterfly and not the solid, muscled bulk that it was – soaring over the hedge with its streaming mane mimicking the high windswept cloud. The animal's oddly-tinged coat shimmered with hints of the softest green, as though moss lay beneath the pale grey hairs. With silent weight the animal landed not a stride from where Silas stood and held itself still, as though a sculpture stood there.

Silas's heart marked a steady beat in his chest. He ought to have been frightened, but there was not a bead of sweat upon him. The beast's eyes were coloured as uniquely as the great body: a watery yellow, as though deeper colour had run free and only a hint remained. The pale horse's coat twitched where an insect sought to settle. Silas lifted his hands, desiring to touch that coat himself. Surely it would be like touching the very clouds.

'Do not hesitate. Lalassu will not shy from you, Silas.'

Silas jumped, having forgotten entirely that he was not alone. The Lady Satine stood Clarence at the hedge, caressing the velvety snout of the black horse. She had to stretch Clarence upon his toes to scratch the horse behind its flickering ear. Her animal was beautiful, and the most imposing of them all, but Silas would challenge any who declared that the horse by *his* side was not the most splendid, regal animal that ever existed.

'Lalassu.' The name whispered from him. He sank his hands in behind the stunning cascade of mane, the colour of shadows. The hair was fine as silk and soft against his skin. The horse nickered, blowing hot breath against Silas's shoulder, and nuzzled against him. Sudden tears pricked the back of Silas's eyes. The angst he'd carried since the moment he'd awoken to this new life dropped away, as though the horse had nudged it free. He rested his head against the powerful neck, and the animal did not protest.

'Great gods, now there's a sight to rouse a man.' Flippant laughter rang out.

Silas remained as he was, the steed's muscles rippling beneath his touch, its smell rich in his nostrils. He did not need to move an inch to know who approached.

'Oh my.' Another voice, the woman who had jested with Pitch.

This time Silas did turn. Sybilla was a sturdy woman. She marched through the rose arch, clad in britches and a patchwork blouse. Her skin was so deep brown it nudged at ebony, and contrasted starkly against her short, tight natural curls which were a startling pearl white.

Pitch followed just behind her, his shirt pulled free of its waistband, his hair tousled and unkempt. He winked, jerking his chin towards Silas. 'Why was I not invited to this party? Were you keeping yourself for the horses alone?'

A frown marred Silas's face. 'This is no party, Pitch.'

'Mr Mercer.' The woman stared at his feet as she spoke. 'You may wish to, ah...cover yourself.' She fluttered her fingers in his general direction, but it took several moments before her meaning dawned upon him. Silas glanced down and uttered a horrified cry.

'Bloody hell.' He had unknowingly released the blanket, and it now puddled at his feet.

He shook with the shame of it. The grey horse tossed its head and whinnied, pressing large, damp nostrils against his chest. Grumbling, Silas nudged it away, stooping to regather the blanket and wrap it tightly around him. He could feel the pierce of his nails into his palms as he clung to it. Why had Lady Satine said nothing of his nakedness? Heat roared into Silas's cheeks.

'What's all this then?' Pitch said.

'I have told Mr Mercer of his task,' the lady declared, her attentions still upon the magnificent black animal.

'Ah, and were you delighted to learn, Sickle, that Black Annis is but the first of the horrors you are expected to dispatch?'

It was the dispassionate and condescending way that Pitch spoke that drove Silas to nod, for he was so very tired of feeling the lesser man. 'I am ready. And Annis was not born a horror.' He'd seen it with his own eyes. That ghostly figure at the very end, standing over him as he bled. She had been a woman of god. And she had been grateful for her release. 'I do not dispatch them. I set them free.'

'Well, you tell yourself whatever you need to get you through. Self-delusion is a very effective survival instinct, I agree.'

Pitch sauntered closer, and the pale horse snorted, stamping a hoof into the soft grass. The light played against its legs, setting off flickers of the green beneath the grey. It was the gentle colour of ferns upon the forest floor.

'Where were you hiding these nags, Satty?' he said. 'I've not seen sign of these stallions since we arrived.'

'The Four are mares.' Lady Satine's indignation was evident. 'There are no stallions amongst them.'

'Cock or pussy, I truly have no issue. I assume you intend for Sickle to lope along on this sickly-coloured nag.' Pitch gave up his attempt to stroke the pale horse and moved towards Clarence. 'Shall I take that black beast for myself?'

Clarence turned at the lady's behest to level Pitch with a waspish stare . 'Nergal is mine. You will never ride her, Tobias.'

The animal, Nergal, pierced the air with its cry, lifting its front hooves from the ground in a brief rear before breaking into a maddened gallop, flicking up dinner-plate sized unshod hooves as it hurtled back up the slope from whence it had come. Soil and tufts of grass flew about in its wake. The snow-white horse followed suit, tail unfurling like a flag to snap and curl at the air. Lalassu remained at Silas's side, ears pressed forward, watching her sisters thunder out of sight.

Pitch raised his hands in mock surrender. 'Fine. I'll not touch your precious fleabag. But as you have deemed that I must follow along after Sickle like a lost lamb, I'll assume you do not intend I do so on foot.'

Clarence joined Silas at the pale horse's side, the lady muttering hotly beneath her breath, something about sending Pitch back to the River Styx. 'Your mount is over there, Tobias.'

The lady waved Clarence's hand towards a smaller paddock whose borders touched upon the woods. It contained a solitary animal, barely half the size of the heavy-set equine at Silas's side, and with its ribs on show. The dull chestnut stood with head lowered, as though it slept on its feet. The mane was clipped to a stunted ridge along its neck, and the tail was a stringy affair, as though far too much brushing had been done against it. There seemed to be a marking on its haunches, a dark line that might be a scar.

'That?' Pitch's displeasure soured his face. 'I rather think Silas should have it, for death is already resting upon that bag of bones.'

'Enough.' The lady barely raised Clarence's voice, but that single word held them all still. Even Lalassu seemed to brace. 'I'll hear no more, Tobias. Sanu is a steady mount, and she will serve you well. As you will serve me equally well. I thought that had been made quite clear.'

He glowered at her, and for a dreadful second Silas thought Pitch meant to challenge the lady. The air deadened as though a winter storm sat upon them. At last, Pitch lowered his gaze, kicking hard at the grass.

'Yes, very clear, my lady.' He set his teeth into the words.

Lady Satine turned Clarence's attention to Silas. 'As my Horseman, you must trust Lalassu. She knows where your scythe is needed. Tobias will be at your side to protect you from the living, but the dead are yours alone to fell.'

Silas ran his hand down Lalassu's solid neck, feeling every rise and fall of muscle there. The animal was strength personified, and Silas drew from it to steady his nerves. 'Yes, my lady.'

'Once you are recovered fully, Sybilla will assist you with your riding skills,' Lady Satine said. 'There is no finer horsewoman to teach you.'

'Can she bring that nag back to life?' Pitch chewed on a stalk of grass, tranquil once more. He thumbed at the dozing chestnut.

Sybilla spoke up. 'She will surprise you, Pitch. It is you who will need to prove your worth, not Sanu.'

Spitting his grass free, Pitch said, 'Then the nag will be left disappointed, for I believe I've been deemed quite worthless. Have I not, Satty?' He grinned, that arresting smile that Silas had seen disarm so many. But Clarence's cool stare did not waver.

'My judgement is yet to be passed. I cannot speak for others.' The lady turned to Silas, Clarence's freckled face unnervingly pale. 'Rest well. There is much work ahead of you, I fear.'

'Might I ask,' Silas said, 'the Blight...what causes it to act so unusually?'

The lady took her time with her answer, running Clarence's hand the long length of Lalassu's neck. 'I do not know. And that is what bothers me most. I do not raise a Horseman lightly, I assure you, but needs must. Now, I must return this man to those who would miss him. Follow the Pale Horse and do not sway from the course she sets you. Serve well in my name.' Clarence's gaze once again found Pitch. 'Both of you. I have neither time nor patience for effrontery.'

Pitch smirked, rolling a new stalk of grass between his lips. 'Of course, my lady.'

Silas rubbed absently at Lalassu's cheek. For all intents and purpose his legs should be twitching to break into a run, vanish himself over the rolling hills and far away from all this talk of Horsemen and monsters. He had no desire to run. Alongside the gleaming pale beauty, Silas felt he'd never been in more true a place.

'Be well, gentlemen. We shall meet again.' The lady took Clarence away, striding him towards the house where Sybilla waited. They spoke quietly as they stepped inside.

Silas stood alone with the daemon and the Pale Horse. Lalassu's alabaster muzzle nudged at his hands. Silas leaned into the animal's rock-steady side, enjoying the warmth as the evening cooled. He really must find some clothing, but he was not yet ready to leave.

'Lady Satine, she is quite formidable,' he said at last.

'Oh, you have no idea.' Silas jumped as Pitch appeared suddenly at his side. Lalassu threw her head in irritation, light-footed upon the grass.

'Steady on, fleabag. I've no intent on harm.'

Silas stroked the horse's soft neck. 'Who...or should I say...what, is the lady, truly?'

Pitch sidled in close, titling his head to gaze up at Silas. 'Your mistress, and mine. That is all you need bother your pretty head with.' His eyes shone luminous green, gems set in a face of perfect construct. He was so very difficult to look away from. There was an undeniable mesmerising nature about him, a graceful femininity coupled with an underplay of hardness and barely stifled temper. He traced a fingertip along the edge of the blanket around Silas's chest, his nail finding some of the dark hairs exposed there. Silas bit into his cheek, perturbed at how close the man stood, and his own unwillingness to step away.

'Are you terribly afraid, Sickle?' The richness of gingerbread moved with his breath.

Lalassu shifted, sidestepping to leave Silas without his steadying wall.

'No.' Silas scowled at the flicker in his voice. Pitch was far too close, his Cupid's bow lips too pink, too near. The daemon was toying with him, working his foul magic so as to cause Silas's groin to tighten and his pulse to trip. Playing him as steadily as he'd done the young man on the train. But it was as though one part of Silas's mind watched on uncaring, while the other blustered with protest, and both sides were equally matched.

'You do not fear being run through again?' Pitch's fingers marched southward, over the last of Silas's ribs, passing over the tender marks left by Black Annis and sending shivers down Silas's back.

'Quite sure, indeed.' Of course he was no such thing. He dreaded sleeping, for the nightmares it would bring. But he'd not say as much to this man. He could not pull his gaze from Pitch's face, the pristine rises and falls of it. 'You saw what I am capable of. And I know full well what you are capable of.'

'Caution, Sickle. You know nothing yet.'

Pitch's finger ran down over his stomach, bringing with it unwelcome stirrings. Blood thundered in Silas's head. The Pale Horse nickered, dancing upon the ground. Pitch lifted on his toes, bringing himself to within an inch of Silas's face. They breathed into one another. And Pitch's hand slipped lower. Passing over the hard press of Silas's hip, and drifting inwards and down, caressing a pathway to where a delicious, yet agonising, hardness swelled.

Silas groaned, pressing his hips forward, mortified and yet tantalised all at once. His skin was aflame, and the blanket stretched tight over the column of rising flesh between his legs. Pitch's grin was a sly, slippery thing. He sent his hand lower, grabbing hold of blanket and hardened cock, dragging a throaty groan from Silas.

'Enough!' Silas shoved the daemon hard away, his breath shuddering from him.

'Well done, my Sickle,' Pitch said, his own cheeks flushed. 'You kept your wits about you, despite all I offered. Perhaps you shall make it through this game yet. Because rest assured, we play one.'

'Whose game?' Silas said, unsteady from their encounter, the tempo of his heart still rapid.

'Those greater than you or I, my good man. And they will break you as readily as they made you. Believe me. They have a taste for torturous things.' Pitch touched his fingers to Silas's cheek. A shadow flitted across his face. And in that instant he appeared terribly well-worn, as though he'd not known sleep for an age. The daemon shook himself and stepped away. 'Fuck, I'm hungry. Let's indulge ourselves, soak in good wine and forget these bloody horses until the morrow. What do you say?'

Silas allowed himself a small smile. 'I would say it is the most reasonable invitation you've made since we met.' Thankfully, his body had ceased to betray him. All was as it should be now between his legs. But the encounter was not so readily expelled from his mind.

'Excellent. Shall we go then?'

'I'd like a moment. Alone.' To fully gather those wits Pitch thought him so capable of keeping.

Pitch nodded, offering no protest. He turned on black heels and moved in his sidling way towards the cottage.

Lalassu made her way back to Silas's side and watched the departing man every bit as closely as Silas did. Horse and Horseman stood in the darkening evening. The lights in the house threw a golden haze onto the cobbles surrounding it. The distant murmur of voices reached him, but Silas remained, again contemplating Pitch's talk of games played. If they were indeed pawns in some strange game, what purpose did they truly serve? And who were the other players?

The drift of material caught his eye, the flow of the curtains in his room lifting out through the still-open doorway. Raising his hand, Silas thought upon the bandalore. Imagined it upon his outstretched hand. The soft baying of cattle came from a distant paddock, the hoot of an owl from where it watched, perched upon a bough, and the tinkle of piano keys caressed the descending night. Through the busy air the bandalore heeded him. Sliding from its hiding place beneath his pillow, whisking through the air to settle upon his palm.

Silas regarded it in the encroaching darkness. He could not know what would face him as Lady Satine's Horseman, he barely even understood what it meant to bear such a title, but the bandalore, the scythe, had rescued him already from monsters and daemons, both. He delivered one last pat upon Lalassu's solid shoulder.

'I will see you tomorrow, my friend. And we shall let this ride take us where it will.'

He turned to find Pitch watching him from the doorway. Waiting on him silently. The daemon held two wine glasses, both filled to the very brim with dark liquid. Silas was grateful for the distance between them, for it concealed the blush he knew to be upon his cheeks. How ghastly that indiscreet moment with Pitch had been. The daemon was shameless.

His desire was there beneath the surface. I simply removed his inhibition. That is what Pitch had said of the attendant on the train.

Silas tightened his hold upon the blanket. Well he was no gullible youth, and certainly not desirous of devilish pleasures.

He resolved never to allow Tobias Astaroth to manipulate him again.

'I'm about to drink all this wine without you, Mr Mercer,' Pitch called. 'Sybilla plays well enough, but she is dreadfully tiresome company. Have you not been alone long enough?'

Silas considered him a while before he answered. 'I believe I have, Mr Astaroth. I'll be with you momentarily, just as soon as I dress.'

'Oh, how dull of you. If you must be such a prude then do be quick about it, I cannot vouch for the safety of your wine for long.' He twirled about, light on his toes, and made his way back inside.

Lalassu nudged at Silas's arm, a whole-hearted shove that pressed him towards the cottage. He laughed in surprise, but nodded.

'All right then, I shall leave you be.' It grew too cold outside for such simple attire, anyway.

Leaving the steed to graze in peace, Silas Mercer, spiritualist, ankou, Horseman, and dead man no more, found his way back to where a foul-mouthed daemon, with the lips of an angel, sang riotously off-key.

Exclusive Excerpt

The Verderer - Pitch & Sickle Book Two

Silas clung to Lalassu's reins with the fervour of a man grasping a lifeboat in a savage ocean. His shoulders ached, as did his stomach, and his thighs positively screamed for relief.

'Head up, Silas.' The shout stirred him from his misery. 'Raise yourself in the stirrups, lean forward, eyes fixed ahead of you. I have a good feeling about this run.'

Sybilla rode alongside him on a stunning dapple-grey gelding, without benefit of saddle or bridle. Silas had not yet worked out how she communicated with her steed. She moved neither legs nor arms in any obvious way, totally at ease upon her galloping mount.

Quite unlike himself.

Silas pressed into his stirrups, his eyes set on the obstacle ahead: a gorse hedge that Sybilla insisted was quite low, but to Silas's eye might well have been the tallest peak in the British Isles. He grit his teeth, and the flutter of panic rose anew. Dear god, how long would this torture continue? Lalassu thundered beneath him, her massive bulk sinking her hooves into the grass, the gorse looming impossibly large. He threw himself forward, pressing his hands into the warmth of Lalassu's thick mane. The horse gathered herself, muscles bunching, launching herself at the jump. A frightened squeak escaped from Silas as they rose drastically upwards.

'Lift your arse!'

But the cry came too late for Silas to heed. Lalassu's back legs lifted from the ground, sending her powerful haunches into the air. The saddle met Silas's backside with a solid thump, and at once he was airborne too.

He cried out, a pitiful sound even to his own ears, and soared over Lalassu's near side, clearing the jump a fraction ahead of the horse herself. Arms flailing at the fast-approaching ground, Silas braced for the impact. It was as solid and unpleasant as it had been the last time, and the time before that, knocking the air from his lungs. He was conscious of Lalassu's hooves close to his head, and he rolled himself into a bruised and mortified ball. Lady Satine may have named Silas one of her Horsemen, but the title did not come with instant horse mastery. Dear god, he was dreadful. His frustration grew with each attempt, and not only with regards to his lack of riding skill. He had no clue what being one of Lady Satine's Horseman entailed, nor when the service would begin in earnest. The waiting, the uncertainty was making him irritable beyond words.

Laughter, delicate and dreadful, filled the air.

'Oh shut up, Pitch!' Silas pushed himself to seated and punched at the hapless ground. 'Do you not have something better to do than laugh at my expense?'

For ten long days the daemon had snickered at Sybilla's attempts to imbue Silas with the basics of horsemanship.

'Well, I have *someone* better to do, of course.'

Pitch stood over him, coming as he did so often out of nowhere. When the ride began he'd been near to the farmhouse, watching from where he lounged upon the back of a straw-laden cart; and yet here he was, in the blink of an eye right at Silas's side. Far too close as usual, and discomfortingly fetching in snug-fitting moleskin trousers, a pair of heeled shoes utterly impractical for walking in a field, and a loose-fitting smock, which gaped to reveal his brazen bare chest beneath.

'But I do truly relish the daily amusement you provide, dear Sickle,' he continued. 'Have you any idea how delightful it is to see that wonderfully oversized body fly through the air?'

The late morning sunshine was too kind upon his emerald eyes. It continually astonished Silas that such a cruel tongue could rest within such a beautiful face.

'Leave me be, Pitch. I'm in no mood for you this morning.' He refused the slender hand offered to assist him to his feet, but took note of the bruises upon Pitch's knuckles. Grey-green against his pale skin. 'Be on your way.'

Silas dusted himself off, adjusting his trousers, which had slid low upon his hips.

'Unless of course, Tobias, you'd prefer to be soundly beaten once again in some swordplay?' Sybilla sat astride her horse, her light brown riding skirt structured like a pair of baggy trousers so that she could straddle her mount and forgo side-saddle niceties. Her dapple grey and Lalassu grazed upon the vibrant green grass of the paddock. 'It makes you far more interesting to look at.' She touched at her chin. 'Flawless skin is ever so dull. I rather think my nicks add some character.'

Pitch's smile was caustic. 'Do not flatter yourself. Your skills with the sword are reasonable, but you'll only inflict injury if I'm in the mood for such things. You cannot lay claim to these marks, my dear.'

With a clearer head, Silas saw that there were indeed some cuts at Pitch's chin and several more lower on his neck. But if these injuries were not made by her able blade during one of their endless tarries, then how?

'Then might I cause some injury I can name my own?' Sybilla scratched at the short, tight curls of her pearl white hair. 'How about it then? Silas is almost done for today, I fear. Take up a sword, Tobias, I am quite looking forward to seeing my point at your throat once more.'

The woman appeared fearless in many matters, not least of all when it came to goading Pitch. A pleasant turn of events that Silas welcomed, for it took the daemon's attentions off him.

'Oh my sweet Sybilla,' Pitch said. 'I see quite clearly what all this appetite for roughness truly means. It is *my* point you wish to have at your throat, stuck deep into your mouth, if I am not wrong.'

Sybilla's laugh nearly rocked her off her horse. 'Gods,' she sputtered. 'I don't know if I should be laughing or throwing up.' Her night-black cheeks glistened with wept tears. 'I imagine I'd do both if I had your cock anywhere near my lips.'

Silas choked on unexpected laughter and hurried over to Lalassu, where he might find a hiding place behind her to allow his smile free, safe from Pitch's temper.

But the daemon's smug expression did not falter. He too laughed, though not as heartily as Sybilla had done. 'Sunset then?' he said. 'Blades at the ready?'

'Of course.' Sybilla wiped at her mirthful tears. 'We shall work up an appetite for supper.'

The pair fought daily, going at one another as though enemies at war. Training only, Sybilla insisted, but Silas tried not to think on what enemies required such fierceness. Each was a remarkable master of the blade. Pitch and Sybilla pirouetted and swung at one another like ballerinas in battle, so light of foot and graceful of motion that Silas at times forgot about the sharp blades they held, mesmerised by the sway of Pitch's hips, the stretch of his elegant shoulders as he parried a blow. Sybilla too moved as though upon a dancefloor. That she was a gifted swordswoman was to state it too plainly. The blade was an extension of her, her quick step astonishing to behold. She was a soldier, Silas did not doubt it, but in what army could a woman do battle? And what war did she wage?

Sybilla's blade was a rather old-fashioned rapier, but stunning nonetheless, with an intricate hilt that reminded him rather of an elaborate crown shielding her hand. Each time he watched her manoeuvre it so deftly through the air, he was reminded how little he knew of Sybilla. Or the Lady Satine for that matter. His mysterious mistress was hardly one for fireside chats. She'd not appeared again since using Clarence as her mouth-piece, and Sybilla and Pitch had brushed off his queries.

'Very well then. Our date is set.' Pitch's smock was too large for him and had slipped down over one bare shoulder. 'Now, I shall leave you to continue bruising our dear ankou.' He nodded at Silas. 'Feel free to break your neck so that we might end this ridiculous union sooner.'

Silas busied himself with unnecessary adjustments on Lalassu's girth and did not reply. He heard no hint of Pitch's retreat, but when he raised his head a few moments later, the man was already far across the paddock, headed towards the farmhouse.

Sybilla sighed. 'I wonder if you do need a guardian, Silas, or was the Lady Satine simply desperate to rid herself of a daemon?'

Silas watched Pitch leap over the wooden fence at the paddock's edge. 'I dare say it is probably a touch of both.'

Sybilla laughed shortly and her smile bared stark-white teeth. 'You are rather amusing when you find it in you.'

'I can't say I've found all that much to jest about of late.' He ran his hand along Lalassu's pale coat, the brush of his fingers stirring that strange hue of green hidden in the strands. 'This waiting, it's leaving me in knots. I do not know where I will be led to next, or what I'm to face. I am in the dark and it's keeping me awake at night.'

He had not intended to disclose so much to Sybilla, but without Jane to speak with and air his concerns, Silas was going mad with trepidation. And he certainly would not rely on Tobias Astaroth to ease his mind.

'Well then, how about you mount and we attempt the jump one last time before we head into Bishop's Castle and get some ale into you?' Sybilla said with notable kindness. 'Tobias has certainly not kept himself secluded here, as you have done. In fact I'm quite certain he's probably bedded half the town by now, and eaten them out of cakes and sweets. The company might do you good, Silas. Keep you away from your thoughts for a while. What do you say?'

Until that moment he had declined every attempt made by both Pitch and Sybilla to have him step foot beyond the borders of Lower Broughton Farm. He'd been recuperating to begin with, the wounds from Black Annis healing fast physically but not so within his mind. The vision of the desecrated bodies of the children haunted both his dreams and his waking hours. His reticence to leave the place grew with each day he lingered, strolling the paddocks, toiling with the feeding of the horses and cleaning of the stables, and enduring the seemingly endless training, in both horsemanship and fighting. He'd not been allowed a sword, merely a crude imitation of the already rudimentary scythe with which to be battered about as Sybilla played the role of an attacking teratism. When not taking punishing lessons Silas was left to his own blissful devices, which was not as comforting as he might have liked, for he was constantly on edge. Waiting for the summons to ride that he knew would come.

But now, with the sun's uncharacteristic November warmth upon him, and thoughts of fresh ale on his mind, he nodded. 'Yes, you're right. It is perhaps time for an outing.'

He grasped hold of the reins and readied his aching thighs for the mount, hoping that Bishop's Castle was as dull and commonplace as Pitch bemoaned. Normality was a delightful prospect. He may be going half-mad not knowing when the call to set out on the Lady Satine's mysterious quest would come, but that did not mean he craved another day of horse falls and sword nicks.

'Right then, one more try.' Sybilla urged her mount into a trot. 'Then we shall have that delightful arse out of the saddle and onto a barstool.'

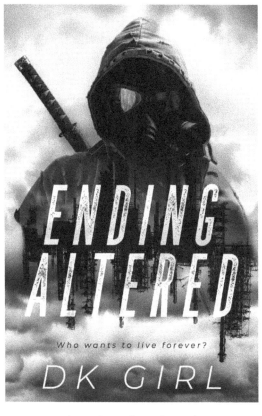

'The author truly created a world that is unpredictable, intense and hauntingly human. It is an action packed short story that fosters a lot of curious thoughts of a futuristic and desperate society.'
Goodreds Review, 2021

About the Author

Danielle K Girl is an Aussie who lives in stunning Tasmania with her three furkids, cats Luffy, Sweetie (@sweetiebyname) and Ren.
Her idea of heaven is a farm full of rescue animals, with a vegie garden that sprouts peanut M&M's and chocolate wheaten biscuits.
When she's not keyboard-deep in mysterious, beguiling worlds, she is binge watching K-Dramas, listening to K-Pop or hiking through the beautiful Tasmanian wilderness.

Join the newsletter - Get a FREE D K Girl novella!
If you'd like to receive DK's monthly newsletter, and be first to know when a new book is ready, then you are in the right place.
Head to, https://daniellekgirl.com/subscribe/ and score yourself a
FREE Dystopian novella
in the deal.
Find D K Girl online:

https://daniellekgirl.com/

https://www.instagram.com/daniellekgirl/

CPSIA information can be obtained
at www.ICGtesting.com
Printed in the USA
BVHW040249080223
658118BV00004B/142

9 780645 327410